Cardoney

Also by Robert A.V. Jacobs

Children's fiction, ten years and upwards:
Daisy Weal
Daisy Weal and the Monster
Daisy Weal and Sir Charles
Daisy Weal and the Last Crenian
Dauntless
The Adventures of Daisy Weal (Omnibus edition,
containing four of the books in the series)
Grandpa's Shed
Cindy Lost and the Black Witch

Short Stories in the Daisy Weal series
(Only Available as ebooks):
Daisy Weal and the Grelflin
Daisy Weal and the Weenies
Daisy Weal and the Millions
Daisy Weal and the Face
Daisy Weal and the Secret
Daisy Weal and the Disaster
Daisy Weal and the Ghost
Daisy Weal and the Figment

Young Adult and Adult Fiction:
The Lost Starship
The Star Queen
The Yellow Dragon
The Diamond Sword of Tor
Speaker (A selection of short stories)

Robert A.V. Jacobs

Cardoney

Cardoney
Second Edition
Copyright 2012 Robert A.V. Jacobs

Pocket Edition
Published by
Robert A.V. Jacobs

Cover Background Image by freeimages.co.uk

This is an omnibus edition and contains 'The Yellow Dragon' and 'The Diamond Sword of Tor'

This book is written in 'English' English, so there may be some differences in spelling to other international forms of English.

Internet sites quoted in this book were active at the time of writing. No responsibility is taken for web sites that cease to exist or discontinue the stated articles.

This book is a work of fiction and all characters are fictitious or are portrayed fictitiously. Any resemblance to persons living or dead is purely coincidental.

ISBN 13: 978-0-244-47236-8

Whether any of my scientific statements bear any relationship to actual fact is most unlikely.

Suitable for Young Adults, and Adults

Table of Contents

A Note from the Author

'The Yellow Dragon' and 'The Diamond Sword of Tor' were a departure from my normal books, but the idea of Magic and Dragons intrigued me. I have tried where possible, to create my own world into which dragons and magic have been introduced. I hope that I have succeeded.

Perhaps my pimply youth and accidental hero may not be an absolutely unique idea, nor the way in which the Mage wields his magic, or the fact that dragons always save the day, but I hope that I have put the story together a little differently to reflect my individual style.

For your convenience, I have combined both of the titles in this one book. I hope that you enjoy this experiment almost as much as I did.

Book One:

The
Yellow Dragon

Forward

The bronze dragon's feet were tangled in the net. She tried valiantly to lift, but the net was strong, and held her near the ground. After several attempts, she gave up and settled back down. She had exhausted her flame gasses a few minutes before, in the battle with another dragon. Both had been too good and had managed to evade the other until both could flame no more. Such a conflict was unusual where no riders were involved, and she could not help but wonder what had provoked this one. She had sent thoughts to it, but it had not replied, rather its savagery had increased. In the end she had given up trying to reason with it and, instead, turned her efforts to staying alive

The other dragon had fled away to the west, with a badly scorched wing and one leg so damaged that it would certainly have difficulty in landing. As soon as she was sure that it was gone, she had settled to the ground to rest before starting to hunt for food to build up her strength again. She was tired, and failed to see the dragon slayer, until it was too late and he had entangled her feet in his net, then ran clear. She roared her rage that she could not roast him, but was forced to sit and wait for the inevitable.

Neither of them said anything, knowing that nothing said could change her fate. The dragon slayer came around to her front, and unsheathed a long, broad bladed double edged steel sword. He appeared to be a strong muscled human, capable of applying considerable power to his sword. Several times he danced away out of range of her striking head then, seeing his chance as it passed him, he leapt forward and thrust the sword with all of his power.

The sword passed through her scales as if they had not been there, and then penetrated completely up to its hilt in her chest. He thought it was enough and did not move away fast enough. Her jaws snapped back, more in reflex than intent, and with one swift and simple movement they clamped down on his head and took it from his body.

She had been ready to lay her egg for almost a day now, and had been searching for a suitable and remote place where she could do so in safety. But now, the shock and pain of the sword stroke caused her muscles to spasm, and she felt the egg slipping from her. She pressed down to assist it, but she had no strength, and it only emerged halfway. She had nothing left, not even the strength to spit the head from her mouth.

Darkness was approaching. Her child would still be born she vowed, and to do that it would need a rider. She gathered all that she was and all of the magic that she possessed, and sent it into the sword. Before darkness took her, her final thoughts sought outwards and sensed a human approaching through the woods. She touched his mind, found him to be special and reached into it with a suggestion.

Chapter One
Erun

Erun Oncant was on the run. Well not from the law or anything like that, but from his mum. He had been given a simple task to carry out, but other things had got in the way. It had been close, but he had managed to escape with his life, or more correctly his backside, intact. So his only problem now was the difficulty he always found in judging when it was safe to go back home. The last twice had been a disaster, and sitting down in comfort had been a problem for days after that. This time though, he thought he would wait a bit longer.

He was fifteen coming on sixteen, and felt that he was a bit old to be taking such punishment from his mother, but sooner her than his dad. So he put up with it, making loads of shouting noises as it took place, and then pretending that the damage inflicted was much worse than it really was.

Living in a Castle was alright, even if it was only a couple of rooms in the lowest reaches that he shared with his mum and dad. His mum was a Castle skivvy, and his dad a stable man. Both of those were pretty lowly jobs, but his parents took a pride in their work, which is all that really mattered.

The Kingdom, even though it was the smallest of all those known, was reasonably well off in that more money came into it than went out most of the time. The castle had been built in the times when it had been pretty dangerous out there. It was large, spacious, very heavily built, and to all of the Kings of Cardoney better than a palace any day. It may have looked large and foreboding from the outside, but on the inside no money had been spared to make it fit to be the home of the King.

Erun had never felt the need to lower his head before any man, except for the King of course, and the King's Mage, and the Swordmaster, oh and a couple of the Castle guards who took a delight in clouting him round the head if he didn't. But absolutely no one else, well maybe a little nod to the scholars who tutored the Kings sons, but that was only because they tutored him as well, and it did not pay to show them disrespect.

He was almost six years old when the King had summoned his mother and Father into the royal presence. He had explained to them that even if they were the lowest of his servants, he appreciated their diligence, and as a reward for their long years of complaint free service, their son would be tutored along with his own.

He is actually a pretty good King, all things considered, thought Erun, *he certainly looks after his subjects.*

The King's two sons were not bad either, though Darthbold did tend to strut a bit, and was not as studious as his brother Nordlight. Both were good to him, even spending time to help him with things that he found difficult to understand. They gave up in despair when it came to swords though, declaring for all to hear that he was pathetic and should stick to books. The laugh in their words belied the sting of the truth in them.

He sauntered through the trees, idly swinging a stick at the undergrowth as he went. He imagined that this stick was a sword, made of the shiny new metal. Double edged, he reckoned, so that he could decapitate his foe on the backstroke if he happened to miss with the first swing. He did reflect though, that even if it had ten edges it would probably make little difference, and it would be his head lying on the ground within seconds of any confrontation.

So to make any difference, it would have to be a magic one, because he had begun to accept the reports from his Swordmaster which said, quote: "Erun will be an expert swordsman when he's about ninety" unquote. This acceptance was reinforced by the numerous bruises he received in embarrassing places, from the wooden practice sword wielded by the Swordmaster. The first time, he had entangled himself in the scabbard as he tried to draw the sword, and fell flat on his face. He would never forget that one. That day there had been dozens of people in the practice hall, and the laughter didn't die down for half an hour.

Let's face it Erun, he said to himself, *you are rubbish with a blade.*

Magic had always fascinated him though, and he read everything that he could find on the subject. He spent hours watching and trying to emulate the Mage, but had given up many years ago when nothing that he did ever worked. Not only did it not work, there was no discernible reaction to anything he chanted. So to be in possession of a magic sword, would probably mean that it would stop working the moment it was in his hand. He shrugged his shoulders, and went back to swinging his stick.

The woods he was in had been cut back from the Castle so that it was further than an arrow's flight away, and thinned out towards the edges so that an invading army would have difficulty in remaining concealed. Undergrowth had not been allowed to develop in these areas, but did thicken considerably as he moved further into the denser part of the forest.

He knew he would have to start back in an hour. He could avoid his mother, but his tutors were another thing altogether. He checked the sun's height, made a mental calculation of where it should be in an hour, and pressed on through the trees. It would not be wise to go too far though or their denseness would interfere with his view.

He was about to turn back when something

touched his mind, and a thought made him look to his right. A glint in the undergrowth caught his eye, and being curious he angled his approach toward it, using his stick to clear the thicker tangle that he came up against.

He stopped dead. The glint was gone, but in its place were two massive fiery eyes and a mouth only slightly smaller than he was, full of rather large and *very* sharp teeth. He was about to start walking very quietly backwards when he noticed that the eyes, though red and balefully glaring at him, seemed to be without that spark which would have told him that they were alive.

He moved forward quietly, taking each step carefully to make sure he didn't step on any dead twigs, in an effort to reduce the noise that he was making. As he got closer he gasped as its full majesty came into view,

"**Dragon!**" he shouted involuntarily and then clapped his hand over his mouth, hoping to silence the words that had already left it.

He sighed with relief. He could see now that it was dead, so he moved forward more boldly. It was a giant creature bronze in colour, and at least thirty feet long with a wingspan that must have been a good sixty feet, tip to tip. It was elegant and beautiful, even in death.

Lying in front of it was a man's body minus head, but his hand had obviously just fallen away from the hilt of a sword that was buried, right up to that hilt, in the dragon's chest just below the breast bone. The crushed head was still in the creature's mouth, and must have been its final act before it died.

Erun could not even start to imagine, the power that it must have taken to make that sword thrust. He could see that it had split one of the dragon's scales, and despite the strength of those, it had still penetrated to its hilt.

He walked slowly around the dragon, noticing that there were no harness or saddle marks. This one was a free dragon. He had not heard of one of these for years, the last time must have been when he was eight. They were very rare and getting rarer all the time, being hunted down in the way that they were. He thought it was a shame, particularly when their only crime was to take a few sheep now and then, and they had stopped being a threat to men years ago if they were left alone.

He looked back at the body of the man, and thought that here was one dragon slayer who would not be killing any more of these magnificent beasts. He walked on past the legs, which were entangled in a large net, and the immense danger in those was clear to see, given the fifteen to twenty centimetre claws which adorned each toe.

Shuddering, and feeling intensely relieved that he had not been here during its last few minutes of life, he moved on past the crumpled wings, noting where each was bent downwards in the middle as an aid to folding, and in fact for balance when the dragon was on the ground. A thirty to forty centimetre claw was evident at the leading edge of each joint. The wings were not feathered, but more a membrane stretched over bone and muscle, making them more like the wings of a bat than a bird.

When he got to the back of the beast, he could see that it had made one final effort before it had died, and an egg had been half laid. It was large, being about the size of a sheep, and green/white in colour. It looked just like nothing other than what it was, but somehow he knew it was alive. It would have to be removed from the dragon if it was to survive, and if it took all that he had, it would surely do just that. He began to cast about for a suitable branch to use as a lever to free it, but there was nothing close by. He noticed a suitable piece of wood, which had obviously broken off when the dragon landed, or it may even have been during its struggles to free itself, on the other side of the clearing.

He was just making his mind up to go round the dragon and retrieve it, when the mighty dragon shuddered and the egg slipped fully free, almost knocking him over as it rolled to rest.

He stepped back hastily. It was still alive!

"You need not fear me. I am Corella, and I brought you here. The sword is holding my life in its hands," a voice whispered into his mind, *"Take the egg and hide it in a warm place. I am free, but my daughter must bond if she is to survive."*

"What?" he thought.

"Don't think, listen and act, my time is short."

"Ookaay," he stuttered aloud.

"Take the egg. Hold it to you and a bond will

7

form. Not quite love in the way that you understand it. It's much deeper than that. Her life will be yours and yours hers. You will be her rider."

The dragon took a shuddering breath,

"Then take the sword. It will be difficult, but I can see that you are strongly made. You will be able to do it. When you take it, you will take my life in the most literal sense of the word. What is left of me will be in that sword, and none but your hand may wield it. It will be what you want it to be."

There was another breath, another pause.

"Now do as I say human, then go to your fate, and leave me to mine."

Erun went to the egg, glancing up at the sun as he did so. There was little time left, and he would have to start back soon. He hunkered down beside it, and wrapped his arms around it as much as he was able. He had expected sparks, fireworks, and lightning in his mind, but there was nothing apart from a feeling of physical warmth from the egg.

With a considerable amount of effort he managed to lift the egg, and staggered towards a stand of closely packed trees, whose bases were obscured by tight and tangled undergrowth. He found a space large enough between roots to force the egg inside, and crawled in beside it. Raking at the humus he made a hollow, and rolled the egg into it, then dragged the humus around and over it. Satisfied that it was well concealed, and would stay warm, he made his way back to the stricken dragon.

"Now the sword human, quickly,"

He walked around to the front of the Dragon

and placed both hands on the hilt of the sword. A shock ran up his arms that was almost painful in its intensity, causing him to snatch his hands away.

"Do not be afraid, the shock will not harm you."

He took hold of the sword, again gritting his teeth against the shock, and was about to abandon the effort because of the pain, when it just suddenly stopped. He tightened his grip and heaved on the sword, but it did not move.

"Place your feet on each side of the sword, use the strength in your legs."

Holding on to the hilt he lifted his legs, pushed them against the scales of the dragon, and heaved backwards horizontally. At first there was nothing, and then suddenly the sword came free and he rocketed backwards into a pocket of thorn brush. The dragon gave a shuddering sigh, and he knew that its life was finally over. He lay quiet for a moment, knowing as he did from his childhood, that moving in thorn brush was not recommended. Even lying still, the thorns managed to find sensitive places. Finally though, he gritted his teeth and lurched to his feet, stepped clear and wiped the involuntary tears from his eyes at the pain of dozens of thorns that were still stuck in him.

He looked down at the sword in his hands. It was made of the new shiny metal, that the Mastersmith called 'steel'. As he watched, the dragon's blood rolled down the sword to its tip and then dripped, in one large single drop, on to the ground leaving a wisp of steam, before it disappeared. The blade was clean and shiny, with an inner glow that seemed to ripple backwards and forwards along its length. It was faint, and could be put down to tricks of the light, so no one would probably notice.

He began to explore his body and remove the thorns. Each was a good seven centimetres long and strongly made, so they tended not to break off unless knocked violently sideways. So he hoped that he could remove all of them with no more than a blood spot. He would have to visit a healer later for antiseptic cream to prevent infection, but otherwise no real harm was done. After about ten minutes, he was satisfied that he had removed them all, and turned his attention to the sword.

Gathering it up, he looked for and found the assassins scabbard and being mindful of the time that had passed, turned away and made his way at a brisk walking pace for the Castle. Several times he looked at the glittering sword. Questions were going to be asked, questions that he had no answers for. If only the sword had been made of wood? *That* he could explain away.

He dropped the sword on the ground in shock. It was dull and lifeless. In the light streaming through the trees, he could clearly see the grain of the wood that it was made of. It looked like the darkest of mahoganies. It was a work of art, and would make the finest of practice swords, leaving those in the Castle armoury as strictly second class.

Oh my god, he thought, *magic is at work here.*

Erun looked from the wooden sword to the ornate scabbard and back again. Then he shrugged and thrust the sword into it. Before his eyes, he saw the scabbard change until it became plain, simple and obviously homemade. A fine piece of craftsmanship that had taken a lot of work to achieve it was true, but still homemade nevertheless.

Chapter Two
The Egg

Erun made straight for the practice hall, knowing that that was where he would find the Swordmaster. He burst through the massive doors into a scene of frantic activity, where Darthbold was doing his best to disembowel his much superior opponent. The Swordmaster casually parried his latest thrust, quickly stepped sideways and struck the royal bottom a resounding whack with the flat of his blade as it went past.

"There is a dead dragon in the woods," blurted Erun.

All activity stopped and within seconds he was surrounded by the royal Princes, the Swordmaster, and several soldiers who had been honing their battle skills to advice from the master.

Erun quickly explained where he had found the beast, and that it had died from a single sword thrust from a dragon slayer who lay headless at its feet. He told them he could see where the thrust had been made, but could find no weapon other than the wooden practice sword that he now held, and which he claimed as finder.

The soldiers sniggered and told him he had been seeing things, and should stay off the mead. A dead dragon indeed they chortled. What would be next, Fairies, Goblins or even one of the legendry Elves perhaps?

The Swordmaster silenced them with a withering look,

"Go and inform your commander," he ordered, "and tell him that I suggest he takes a detachment to investigate."

The look he gave them allowed for no argument, and muttering apologies they fled.

"I am afraid, Your Highnesses, that I must call a halt to practice for today," he continued, "I need to speak with Erun alone."

As soon as they had left he took Erun by the arm, and led him one of the bench seats that lined the walls of the room.

"Was there an egg boy?" he asked, with a hint of urgency in his voice.

Erun had never told a lie to the Swordmaster, and sensing how seriously the man was viewing the situation, could not do so now.

"Yes master, there was," he said.

"Is it safe boy? Tell me, quickly now, is it safe?"

"Yes master, it is well hidden, and I have packed it in humus to keep it warm"

"And the sword boy, show me the sword. I know you have it so show it to me as it should be."

Erun looked at the old man for a few seconds, and wondered how he could possibly know of the magic in the sword. *Perhaps it's just a Swordmaster thing,* he thought, and then picked the sword up from where it lay on the seat next to him,

"Steel," he said, and then handed the glittering weapon into the waiting hand.

The Swordmaster took it carefully as if it might bite him, and then turned it over several times in his hands, his gaze critical and thorough. But when he tried to bring the weapon up into readiness for combat his arm would not move. It seemed that he was being permitted to examine it, but would never be allowed to use it.

"This is as fine a weapon as I have ever seen Erun, and under other circumstances, based upon your prowess, I would say that it is far too good for you. But there is magic at work here, and I can see that it has already attached itself to you. Whether you like it or not lad, you have been chosen. It seems that you are destined to be a dragon rider."

He handed the sword back, and as he did so a shiver ran down its length and it reverted to its wooden form. A completely bemused Erun took it from him and slipped it back into its scabbard. *I'm only a kid for God's sake and absolutely useless at everything, so what use would I be on a dragon?*

As if reading his mind, the Swordmaster smiled,

"You are one of the best that I have seen with a bow," he said.

"Maybe… but…" Erun started to say.

"No buts," interrupted the Swordmaster, "Make no mistake, it is a great responsibility, and a great honour to be chosen. Only one in a generation is found to be fit. The dragon chose you, and deep within me I find that I cannot fault that choice."

He placed a hand on Erun's shoulder.

"Go with God boy and keep this secret. The sword is yours, and with it I suspect that you may just become a master swordsman *before* you are ninety after all."

His final words were accompanied by a grin, and he squeezed Erun's shoulder before dropping his hand to his side.

"Your mother awaits, and I suggest you go to her. For myself, I will probably have some explaining to do to the King."

Knowing that he could not delay for much longer for fear of infection, Erun made his way to the healer who asked him what he wanted the cream for when he didn't have any injuries. He checked his arms in amazement, carefully running his fingers over the places where he knew he had extracted some thorns. He couldn't find any injury, not even any scars. He made a muttered apology for wasting the healer's time, took a deep breath, and headed for his parents rooms in the Palace. He was confused to say the least. It could only have been magic that had got rid of the thorn injuries, but he had not been that close to magic in his whole life, so why now? He gripped the sword tighter, afraid that it might suddenly disappear. It had to be something to do with that, or maybe it was the dragon's last act before it died. It was no good, he *had* to tell someone and he just hoped that his mother would listen and understand.

Erun had known that his mother would be preparing their midday meal by now, so he started off in that direction with some trepidation, being absolutely convinced of what would happen in the next few minutes. He was surprised and even more confused than he had been before, when she just looked up from the hearth where potatoes were roasting and said,

"Hello Erun," and returned to her preparations.

"I'm really sorry mum," he said, hoping the apology would be enough.

"I know Erun," she said, "you always are. But I can't carry on chastising you anymore. You are about full grown, and it isn't seemly. You have to learn responsibility, and know your obligations. In short, you have to grow up."

"Mum, you're right, and I'm beginning to suspect that I'm about to be forced to do just that," he said, "I need to tell you what happened."

He outlined the whole story of the day's events. He told how he had found the dragon, removed the sword from it, and hidden its egg. He finished by placing the sword in its full glory, upon the table. Her reaction shocked him to the core. It was definitely not the result that he had wanted or expected, as his mother turned to him and dropping to one knee took his hand and kissed it.

"My son will be a dragon rider," she breathed, then got back to her feet and returned to her preparations, "sit yourself down, dinner will be ready soon."

When his father returned from work his reaction was equally unexpected, and Erun decided that he was not sure whether he could bear to live in a household where parents revered their son. He was so used to their harsh but fair discipline that anything else would be far too odd for him to cope with.

After they had finished dinner he sat with them, and taking his mother's hands, explained how he felt. Through their tears they told him that they understood. His father suggested that he move in with the palace guard until the King, which he surely would, found new and better quarters for him. At least he would be around and they would be able to see him from time to time.

"Why do you think that the King will find me better quarters?" he asked.

"Because," his father told him, "you will be the first dragon rider in Cardoney in more than thirty years."

After that there was an embarrassing period where they just sat and looked at him, but Erun, having made his decision, excused himself, picked up a rug from his bed, and slipped out into the late afternoon sun.

At his enquiry, one of the guards on the Castle gate informed him that a party of twenty men had been despatched at least three hours ago to bury the carcass of the dragon.

"The ground in the woods is soft and rich which should make their work easy," the guard said, "and I doubt you could find a more fitting resting place for such a fine creature."

After a slight pause and a glance at the position of the sun, he added, "They should be back pretty soon now."

They were on their way back in fact, and Erun passed them on his way into the woods. They shouted to him and waved. He could see that amongst their number, were the same men who would rather clout his head than speak to him, and was rather shocked when they inclined their heads to him as a mark of respect. He stood looking like an idiot, with his mouth open.

Making sure that they were well out of visual range, he wriggled into the gap where the egg was hidden. It only took a couple of minutes for him to scrape all the humus away from it, and he was about to cover it with the rug, when a thought whispered to him,

"*Place the sword against the egg,*"

He had seen and heard enough in the last few

hours to make questions unnecessary, so he slipped the sword from its scabbard, relishing the song it made as he did, and placed the flat of it against the egg. There was a brilliant flash, and then the egg and sword looked no different to what they had a second before.

"My mother has explained everything to me through the sword. Stay with me, I need you to be close. I feel a bond forming."

He too could feel a bond forming with the egg, or rather the dragon inside it, and it all finally caught up with him. He knew how well everyone treated the odd dragon and rider who happened by on rare occasions. They always received the highest respect and the best of everything. Was this what was going to happen to him from now on? He was nothing, but the son of two lowly servants. Why had the dragon chosen him?

"You are not 'nothing', my mother chose you, which is why you came."

"Ok then," he said aloud, "that's what happened, but it isn't the *reason*. But I'll accept that as an explanation for the time being. But right now I have a couple of questions, and a couple of conditions."

"Fire away, my bondmate,"

"Right! Number one, you were only laid a few hours ago. How come you can think at me when you must still be all yolk and egg white?"

"Dragons are magical creatures, and because of this it is not safe to stay in one place for too long. There used to be a place where we went

where it was safe, but not anymore. So we emerge from the egg in only a matter of days. We take to the air within two months of birth provided that we can find enough food. And our rider can take his place within six months given the same conditions, my bondmate."

"OK, that takes care of the questions, now the conditions. I know that we are bonded, and I know that it is said that one cannot live without the other, which doesn't surprise me as I know how I feel about you already. But please, please none of the lovey dovey stuff. Just call me Erun. I'm only fifteen, very nearly sixteen, and I am easily embarrassed."

"That was only one question, and one condition Erun."

"Well you answered all of my questions before I asked them, and I could only think of one condition."

He turned and setting himself into a comfortable sitting position, he leaned back against the egg.

"You know that it is difficult for me because of my age, and I must get back before it gets dark and they send out a search party. I will come every day, and you can teach me everything that I need to know, but I must go now."

He found out that it was not that simple, and the wrench of leaving left him trembling as he made his way back to the Castle in the fading light. As he approached he was surprised to find the King's Mage waiting for him, but then realised that things like this were going to happen more and more often from now on.

"Your new quarters," said the Mage snappily, thrusting a key into Erun's hand, "I have been instructed to show you the way and to instruct you. As if I had nothing better to do than instruct the snivelling idiot son of servants."

For some unaccountable reason this really provoked Erun, and his hand dropped to the hilt of his sword. It seemed that the King thought enough of him to give him new quarters, so who was the Mage to get so petulant?

"Take care Mage," he said quietly, "you may be well versed in the art of magic, but my sword will still sing as it takes your head."

The Mage snapped round and really looked at Erun for the first time since he had handed him the key. For a moment he gazed at the stony gaze that met his, and then with a brief inclination of his head he turned and led the way into the Castle. The room that he led Erun to was next to the Kings own apartments, and was one of those usually reserved for visiting nobility. Erun could only stare at the opulence, and marvel at the enormous four poster bed.

"Your instruction will begin at nine in the morning," said the Mage with, in his opinion, just the right touch of false humility, and then he walked out of the room and closed the door.

"Well it might, if I feel like it you old goat," thought Erun, feeling the warm glow that comes from facing down a Mage and coming out on top.

After he had settled in, because he had nothing of his own, consisted of exploring the room, he went to see his parents. Whatever was about to happen to him he would make sure that he did not forget them, and vowed that he would visit at least once a day.

Chapter Three
Lelia

He was awoken the following morning by a maid servant who knocked, timidly entered, curtsied, placed a breakfast tray on the table beside his bed, and then fled. He could only stare open mouthed at the tray in astonishment. There was more food here than he usually had in two days. Perhaps being a dragon rider would not be such a bad thing after all, but all the same, he might just have to watch himself lest an expanding waist-line be the result.

As he got stuck into the breakfast, he began to feel weird. He knew he was still in his room in the castle, but he also had the feeling that he was in the woods next to a very large egg. Realising that it had to be as a result of the bonding, he struggled for a moment before his reality coalesced back into a single place and into his bedroom.

Fifteen minutes later, after he had wolfed as much as he could wolf, there was another knock on the door and a liveried footman came in. He gave a sweeping, and Erun believed exaggerated, bow and announced,

"His Majesty King Arunay requests the pleasure of your company in the throne room in one hour."

He gave the same exaggerated bow and backed out of the room.

So that's what the King's name is, thought Erun. *It's funny that, I only ever thought of him as 'the King'. And he sends a request to see me, rather than a summons. Things are looking up.*

It did not take him long to dress in his usual tattered clothes, which he picked at and brushed to try to make them look just a little better. Totally unsuccessful of course because whatever you do, rags will always look like rags. He hoped that the King would understand and not be too angry at his appearance, but in any case he had no other choice.

Exactly to the hour he was shown into the King's presence, and dropped on to one knee before him. The King was a jovial person. In fact very few people ever saw him without a smile on his face. He had ruled Cardoney for the last twenty years or so since his father had died, and was a benevolent monarch clearly loved by his subjects, none of whom had a bad word to say about him.

Today though, not a smile was present.

"Get up Erun. My Seamstresses here," he said, indicating two women standing quietly at the side of the room, "are at your disposal. They will make whatever you wish."

He didn't want to embarrass Erun by telling him that he looked like a scarecrow, so his reference to his seamstresses was as diplomatic as he could get. He waved his hand, and the two ladies curtsied and backed out of the room.

"I asked you here," he continued, "because there are mounting tensions between the Kingdoms. Partonin is in dispute with Amtor, and I have heard that soldiers are massing on both of their borders. Just in case you don't know, Partonin is to our north and Amtor is to the south. We stand between them."

"I don't know why I am telling you this boy, because that is not why I called you at all. I just wanted to officially congratulate you on becoming a dragon rider. Our first in thirty years, so you must realise how big this event is," he paused and grinned. It was a bleak grin, but a grin nevertheless, "I know you haven't actually ridden one yet, but don't worry that will come soon enough. Whatever you need, if it can be provided it will be."

"Your Majesty," said Erun, "This Kingdom is my home, and whatever threatens it threatens me also. Would Your Majesty continue?"

"I had hoped that you were not an ordinary boy years ago when you were six, which is why I allowed you to be tutored with my sons despite the fact that your parents are not Noble;"

He paused,

"Very well, my spies tell me that several other Kingdoms are arming themselves, and I fear that things cannot get better. Ours is only a small Kingdom and it has always been coveted by both Amtor and Partonin. My belief is that the dispute has finally come to a head over who shall possess it. We will go down fighting of course, but we cannot win, Amtor has dragons and Partonin is much larger. Most of the other kingdoms will remain aloof from such petty squabbling, but there are others..."

He let his voice trail off, then took a deep breath,

"I have sent messengers to Vanticor, which is the largest of all Kingdoms, and pledged that one of my sons will marry King Porden's daughter should they side with us. I've no idea what she looks like, she may look like a bear for all I know, but what I do know is that she has refused, point blank, any suitors that have been introduced to her. Her father is at his wits end. She is his only child, and heir to the Throne."

Erun stood politely listening.

"Oh, do sit down boy," the King snapped.

Erun moved a seat into place before the King and sat in it, waiting for the story to be concluded.

"She is on her way to us via caravan, and should be here in six to eight days. While she is here, none of the others will dare to attack us. But I fear that both Partonin and Amtor may have discovered that she is on her way and may just be tempted to chance their arm during the journey. We

26

can only wait and hope. Anyway never mind all that, you may be wondering how to feed your dragon. I have heard of your proficiency with the bow and know that you have proved your ability to hunt, but in the meantime if you want meat for your dragon, get whatever you need from the Castle kitchens."

"One other thing," he continued, "I intend to retire your parents," he held his hand up as Erun was about to protest,

"I cannot have the parents of a dragon rider as servants, so I will install them into a nice little cottage that has become available in the village, and provide for them. On reflection, even if you were not to be a dragon rider, they have served me for many years and it is no more than they deserve."

The rest of the audience was taken up with general pleasantries and idle chatter, until the King finally announced that the affairs of state called and he excused himself. Erun wandered back to his own room, his thoughts in turmoil. He was but one person, and only a boy at that. There was nothing he could do to help. He didn't even have a dragon yet, so all he could do was sit back and watch as events unfolded.

He just made it to Mage Scriven's class on time, which was just as well as he was not the flavour of the month, and couldn't expect any latitude for tardiness after Scrivens had been forced to meet him at the Castle gates. The rest of the morning was

spent being lectured on the dangers of magic, *as if anyone except an idiot is not already perfectly aware of how dangerous it is,* he thought, *but it **is** odd being in a class of one.*

It only took an hour or so before he realised that being on his own did help the learning process. It took the same hour for him to also realise that this was monumentally boring, and he began to fervently hope that some practical applications of magic might surface soon. He was unlucky and the morning continued to drag.

When he was eventually released, he did wonder who was more relieved, him or Scrivens. But he only wondered for a second, and then dismissed the thought and then all but ran for his hiding place in the woods.

He dived under the bushes and dragged the rug from the egg, and was horrified to find that it had one large crack and a multitude of spidery ones over its surface.

"*Hello Erun, it will be soon. It appears to be much quicker than normal, and most unusual. But I feel ready.*"

"What colour will you be? Will you be bronze like your mother?" he asked.

"*No, a great many things influence colour, not least of which is my own preference and the direction in which the magic pushes me. I thought gold, and there does not seem to be resistance to that. Golden dragons are rare, so we shall see.*"

Suddenly her thoughts became urgent and afraid,

"You were followed here. Take care when you leave. There is an enemy at your right."

Oh god, he thought, *I hope it's some amateur idiot or I'm a dead man.*

"Have faith in the sword Erun."

He struggled out of the underbrush, and had just regained his feet as he saw the glint from the blade as it swung at him. His own sword sang as it leapt into his hand without reaching or bidding, and flashed out to parry the downward sweep from his opponent. His hand flicked in a perfect riposte, which he had never managed to achieve in practice, sending his enemy's sword sailing into the brush. His own blade entered just below the man's military breastplate, and continued through to emerge at least a foot beyond his back. Erun let go of the sword and leapt back in horror at what he had done, or more correctly what the sword had done with virtually no help from him.

The man, who was dressed in the uniform of an Amtor guard, gasped once and dropped to his knees, and with Erun's sword still protruding from his chest he fell over to one side. Erun fell to the ground on his knees beside the man in shock, and leaned forward to catch the would be assassin's last words,

"He told me you were no good with a blade," the man muttered, and then died.

Erun had never injured, let alone killed anyone in his entire life. He felt his stomach coming up into his mouth, and turned away before being violently sick. Looking at his hands through tear filled eyes; he could see they were shaking so much that he could not focus on his fingers. He was only fifteen coming on sixteen, and if it had not been for the touch that he felt from the dragon at that moment, he could easily have broken down completely.

"It was necessary. He would have killed you. There is much evil in the world. Be calm, sit quietly for a moment, and I will help it pass."

The feeling he had was of someone stroking his mind, and gradually the horror of what he had done left him. Eventually he calmed enough to know that the body could not be left there, and he would have to carry it back. He reached for the sword and closing his eyes pulled it from the body. The action brought back the feeling of sickness, but he fought it back and hauled the body up on to his shoulder. It was heavy, but he was strong for his age and only struggled a little on the uneven ground.

The soldiers at the castle gates recognised him as soon as he emerged from the tree line carrying the dead body over his shoulder, and one was immediately despatched to find out what had happened and to give assistance if needed.

The guard relieved Erun of his burden when he saw that the boy was starting to stagger under the weight. Erun handed over the dead assassin gratefully, thanked the soldier and together they broke into a trot for the Castle.

As soon as the body was recognised as that of an Amtorian soldier, the full guard was mobilised and men were despatched to comb the closest reaches of the woods to make sure that there were no more able to carry the word back to Amtor. If an attack was imminent they stood no chance, but to a man they were determined to die trying.

The Guard Commander noticed how pale Erun was, and thrust a glass of brandy into his hand. He held his hand up to Erun's protestations that he was too young to drink it, and told him,

"I only wish someone had given me a brandy when I first killed a man. Know this young Erun, a true man never rejoices in killing, but will not hesitate when there is need."

So Erun drunk his brandy, gasping as the fiery liquid slid down his throat. He had to admit that apart from the slight wooziness, it did make him feel much better. As the warmth of the Brandy began to spread round his body, he realised that he liked it and would have to use all of his self-control to make sure he didn't become a drunk.

It was too much of a coincidence for an Amtorian assassin to have turned up at that precise moment, so someone in the Castle must have betrayed him to Amtor, and until he knew who it was, he did not know who to confide in. He considered telling the Swordmaster what he suspected because he liked the man, but then changed his mind. Like is not the same as trust, and he didn't know Squerrel well enough to be sure. So for the time being, the knowledge would have to remain between him and his dragon.

When nothing happened in the next few days, the state of heightened alert was relaxed and the

Guard returned to their normal routine, though with instructions to remain extra vigilant. The only noticeable change was in the increased number of snap inspections that they had to endure, together with far more practice call to arms. Most of the guards thought it was a small price to pay, being far less of pain than all of the extra guard duties that they had been called upon to perform at the height of the alert.

The Castle moat had been dry for many years, having been viewed as completely unnecessary in the political climate that prevailed at the time. Consequently it had been allowed to fall into disrepair and had eventually lost all of its water. With the new situation though, the King's advisors suggested that it might be a good idea to repair it as a precaution. It seemed to be the consensus of them all, so the King ordered that work start on clearing, deepening, and clay lining prior to it being refilled. The gully that was used to feed the moat led from a close-by river, but had also been neglected and consequently almost disappeared in places, so it too was placed on the repair schedule. Teams of men and women were soon hard at work, some of whom were employed by the Castle, but many others were volunteers from the local villages.

Erun had visited the egg every day, and earlier had found that he seemed to have gained two shadows in the form of two Castle swordsmen. They had appeared shortly after he had first reported finding the dragon, and had followed him out every day after that. He had to admit that he was thankful for them, and was quite disappointed when they had disappeared after he had killed the Amtorian without their help.

Later, they told him that they had seen the Amtorian, and were moving forward when Erun had killed him. They had stayed back for fear of embarrassing him when he had broken down, but had stayed alert in case the assassin had company. The fact that telling him this in a room full of people embarrassed the hell out of him, more than it would have at the scene, seemed to be lost on them.

His friend Egmar who was a little older than him, had joined the Guard a couple of months previously, and they only managed to get together on rare occasions these days. On one of those occasions Egmar had confessed, when asked, that he did not know who had ordered the escort. He did know however, of the extra fifty guard duties that had been earned by Erun's two erstwhile escorts for their failure.

When the time came for him to visit the egg once more, he decided to swing by the kitchen and pick up some meat, because for some reason he felt that the hatching would be soon. Once he arrived at the hiding place, he wriggled through the brush with his burden, and was greeted by the sight of a small dragon sat in the middle of the remains of the egg.

Tiny by dragon standards she may have been, but to Erun she was the most beautiful thing he had ever seen. She was bright yellow... a blindingly brilliant, bright yellow.

"What happened?" he asked, "I thought you wanted to be gold."

"*I did,*" she thought, "*I have searched my mother's memories and there has **never** been a yellow dragon... **never**. There have been legends of one in the far past, but no one knows if they are true. Looks like I am the first unless the legends are true. Be a bit difficult to hide though.*"

"Have you a name yet?" he asked, pushing his burden of meat towards her.

She leapt on the meat and began to tear chunks off and swallow them. She was obviously so hungry, that what had been a considerable burden to him, was only a small amount for her and no more than a snack.

"*Not bad,*" she thought, "*I could do with some more of that. My name is Corella, my Erun.*"

"But that was your mother's name," he said in surprise.

"*Yes, I know. The name passes on to the next offspring born when a dragon dies.*"

"Ok then, Corella it is. It seems to me Corella, that your birth was unnatural. It was much too fast. It has only been seven days since you were laid. That's just impossible. Even a chicken couldn't hatch that fast"

"*Chicken! Now that would be nice,*" she replied, running her tongue round some needle sharp teeth, "*Of course it's impossible, but I think it is the last small amount of magic that my mother had. It could not be anything else."*

"Ok then, it's obvious we need to feed you, so I'll go back to the Castle and get you some more meat. What do you think? Will three or four times a day be enough?"

Three days later, excitement was rife. Today was the day that Princess Lelia of Vanticor was due to arrive. Her caravan had been spotted some hours out, and the King's fears of her being kidnapped on the way were alleviated by the enormous number of Vanticoran Guard that accompanied her. Not even the hot heads in Amtor, or Partonin, would risk the wrath of Vanticor or the losses that they would surely endure by attacking them.

The King had managed to field questions from Amtor with regard to their missing guardsman, and had offered to put search parties into the surrounding countryside to help find him. Erun knew that they were fully aware of his fate through their spy in the Castle, but Amtor could say nothing for fear of exposing their role in the affair.

Meanwhile, Erun was ferrying meat out to the dragon so fast that it was threatening to deplete the Castle supplies. Corella had grown to more than twice her original size, which according to her was about fifty percent faster than normal. At this rate of development she would be speaking in a matter of weeks, and would be ready to start flying at the same time. She told him that he could expect to be flying with her in three to four months maximum.

As he was terrified of heights, and had never even been able to look over the Castle battlements without going weak at the knees, the thought left him witless, and it took Corella a good half hour to calm him down.

"*It will be OK Erun,*" she said, "*I will take you a little at a time, and you can get a saddle made with a safety harness.*"

"It's alright for you," he said, his voice trembling, "you were born with wings, and flying is going to come naturally. I'm a human being, and I am supposed to be on the ground."

"*No my Erun.*" she thought, "*You are a dragon rider, and supposed to be up there with me.*"

Even from here he could hear the noise of excitement from the Castle, and knew that the Princess must be nearing the gates. He stepped forward and kissed Corella on the nose, to which she lifted her head and thought, "*More, more.*"

"One is enough for now," he laughed, "I must get back. I want to see the caravan when it arrives."

When he cleared the woods and was walking back towards the Castle, he could see the mêlée at the gates and knew that the Vanticoran party had at last arrived. He broke into a trot hoping that he would be able get to the gates, and get a glimpse of the Princess before she was welcomed by the King and shown to her quarters.

He arrived just in time to see the rear end of the vanguard enter the gates, and the Princess's carriage draw level with him. It had slowed down to a virtual crawl to allow the huge number of people ahead of it organise themselves inside the Castle. She turned and looked at him. She could not have been more than fifteen or sixteen. It was a beautiful face surrounded by a halo of hair the colour of spun gold. Large and very frightened blue eyes stared at him through the open window. And then the carriage entered through the gates, and she was gone.

Chapter Four
Death of a Prince

Over the next couple of weeks, Erun gratefully received several sets of new clothes from the King's Seamstresses, and could at last confine the rags he owned to the rubbish heap. When asked what he wanted, he had to confess that he had no idea, never having had to decide for himself before. In the end he said that he would leave it to them, and wear anything they made,

"Provided," he added with a grin, "that it is not a dress."

The clothes finally offered were well made, fit for a young gentleman, and he accepted them immediately with his thanks. Wearing them with pride, he began to feel more at home in the central parts of the Castle, and could stride openly to his room rather than slinking there like a thief in the night.

He couldn't resist going to see his parents in his new finery. It was only a kilometre or so to the village and the little cottage that they had been installed in, so at a brisk walk he arrived there after only twenty minutes. He could see that they were pleased for him, especially when his mother rushed to him and wrapped him in her arms. He saw tears in her eyes and wondered, but felt it best not to ask.

He spent the next couple of hours there and found that they were comfortably provided for by the Castle, and had been told that if they wished to supplement this income by finding work locally, there would be no objections. There was a small garden attached to the cottage which his mother had found was easily within her capability to plant and look after, but his father had already become restless and had found a job with the local stables. It did not pay much, and was nowhere near as hard as he was used to. But with this and the provision from the Castle, they at last found time to enjoy life and also to save a little money.

His time with them seemed to pass all too quickly, but as he needed desperately to be with Corella he bade his farewells and started on the walk back.

As the days passed, he continued to ferry food out to Corella supplementing it when he could with game that he shot with his bow. He may not have been very good with a sword, but he excelled with the bow, and invariably won all of the competitions that were held, that is until the Bowmaster had come to him and pleaded.

"Erun," he had said, "the archery competitions are hard pressed to find any competitors when you enter them. Everyone knows you will win and it discourages them. We all know how good you are. Consider not standing, I beg of you."

As the competition was only really practise for him, he agreed to withdraw and instead entered all of the ones for fencing, and deliberately lost every one. Some with foils and epees he didn't have to try to lose, but when he was able to use the dragon sword, he had to take care not to appear too good. As a result, no one minded him taking part in those at all.

He always stayed with Corella as long as he could, and never tired of her company. He only felt really alive and at home while he was with her, and was always reluctant to drag himself away. *It would be easy*, he thought, *to get completely lost in the bond*, but he knew that no useful purpose would be served by it. So he always took a deep breath and dragged himself away far sooner than he really needed to. On this day though, the deep breath felt easier, because he was looking forward to spending an hour in the company of the Swordmaster, and the King's two sons. He had heard through the grapevine that some rivalry had developed, and it seemed that Princess Lelia was the cause.

Both boys had finally clapped eyes on

Princess Lelia, and in that instant were smitten, each demanding that she should marry him alone, while at the same time pointing out the shortcomings of his brother. When it eventually descended into physical violence, the King lost his temper and demanded that they settle their differences like gentlemen with swords. As he did not want to lose either of them, he stipulated that it should be wooden swords in the practice room under the eye of the Swordmaster.

There was no way that he could possibly know that even there disaster could strike, particularly with the level of violence that the two were now exhibiting whenever they met. The Swordmaster had to part them several times even before the contest had even started, but finally order was restored long enough for it to begin.

Both boys were equally matched and their sword conversation* carried on with no one gaining advantage for over an hour. Finally though, exhaustion brought it to an end, and Swordmaster Squerrel demanded they cease like gentlemen.

"(http://www.synec-doc.be/escrime/dico/engl.htm)
Sword Conversation is defined in fencing terms as:
The back-and-forth play of the blades in a fencing match, composed of phrases (phrases d'armes) punctuated by gaps of no blade action.

The boys faced, brought their wooden swords up to the traditional salute, and then walked past each other. As they did Darthbold raised his hand to acknowledge his brother, and Nordlight suddenly turned and drove his wooden sword into Darthbold's armpit. It was a move designed to cause hurt, and perhaps give Nordlight some advantage in future contests, but certainly no more than that.

Perhaps it was fate or just simply a weakness in the protective garment that Darthbold wore, but whatever it was, the thrust had considerable power and the point of the wooden sword, though quite blunt, penetrated deep into the chest cavity and he was dead before he hit the floor.

Nordlight stared in horror at what he had done, then dropped to his knees beside his brother and screamed out his torment. The garment should have been strong enough to protect Darthbold, so it was called a regrettable and tragic accident, with no one held accountable. But no matter how many times this was said, Nordlight could not forgive himself. It was he who had killed his brother. It was a senseless act, and to him at least, unforgivable.

The Kingdom went into Mourning, with the King inconsolable at the loss of his first born. It should never have happened, given that Princess Lelia had declared earlier that she would rather die than marry either of them. A point she had emphasised, by holding a blade to her own throat as she uttered the words.

The King had bowed his head in defeat as he had left her room, wondering how he would be able to tell his two sons. It was through his inaction, which he would have to live with, that he finally ended up with only one to pass her decision to.

Erun sensibly distanced himself from everything except for rearing his dragon. She had begun to say a few words, not very clearly and with an appalling lisp, but at least she had begun to talk. She had also taken to feeling her wings, by using the strength in her legs to leap into the air, then spreading her wings to glide to the ground. It was never very far, just ten or twenty metres, but at least it was helping to build up some much needed muscle.

It was only six weeks after she was hatched that she first took to the air for real. Erun arrived into their clearing to find that she was not there. He called out to her with his mind and received no answer, but then the air above him darkened and she swept in, claws extended forward and wings beating backwards as she braked to land. It looked good, was executed almost perfectly but she ended up nose first in some dense undergrowth, pointed tail waving skywards in a most undignified crash landing.

"Well," said Erun, "that will teach you not to answer me when I call."

"That wath the fourteenth," said Corella,

extricating herself, "Not ath bad ath the otherth though."

"You're not supposed to be able to fly at all yet. The Swordmaster seems to know all about dragons, and he told me. He said dragons are at least three months old, and in some cases older, before they first take to the air. So what is going on here?"

"Magic, and the fact that I am very advanthed for my age," she said.

"I believe the magic bit, but the rest is questionable."

"And you are not a nithe perthon," she retorted, "lovely, but not nithe."

"Well your lisp doesn't seem to be getting any better," he said, "but as you *are* a dragon, can't you hiss? I'm sure it will help you with your essess."

"Thatth what I am trying to do," she said, "but it cometh out… hithhhh."

Erun gave up and sat down next to her, leaning against her neck. If she had been a cat she would have purred, but not being one of those she just softly 'hithhed', and leaned back against him.

He told her about the visiting Princess, the death of Darthbold, and as much of the politics surrounding the Kingdoms as he could remember or understand. She listened with interest and when he had finished, she began to interrogate him about the Princess.

"Hey hang on," he said, "why are you so interested in her?"

"Jealothy," she said, "there wath too mutth warmth in your wordth."

He grinned, "Well she is a bit nice... ouch."

The 'ouch' was in response to her tail coming around, and whacking him on the head.

"I know," she said, "that thometimeth you will need a human woman, but rub it in and I will whack you again."

He turned and stretched his arms around her neck. She was still small enough for his fingers to meet on the other side, but at her current rate of growth it would be only a matter of days before they didn't any longer. He buried his head into the softer and smaller scales on the side of her neck, and then said,

"I have to go now, my love. For my sins, I have lessons with Mage Scrivens this afternoon."

"You thouldn't thin then, and bethideth which, you thaid no lovey dovey thtuff, tho watch it. Anyway, I have thome hunting to practithe. I actually caught a rabbit yethterday."

He jumped to his feet, patted her snout, gave an airy wave and trotted away towards the Castle. Every time he left it was a wrench, seemingly into his very soul, and was only made bearable by their telepathic link. He knew he would not be away for long, so he gritted his teeth and hurried on. When he got to the gates, he realised that it was his friend on guard again, and shouted to him,

"Hey Egmar, are you on duty *again*?"

"'fraid so," said Egmar, as Erun reached him, "I really need to learn to keep my big mouth shut."

"What was it this time?"

"Well it's the Princess. She flatly refuses to

marry Nordlight or anyone else that the King introduces her to. And what is worse, she refuses to go back to Vanticor. She said she's only ever seen one man that she might be interested in. But she won't say where or when. My mistake was in saying that she could always have me, within hearing distance of the sergeant. Ten extra guards, do you think that's fair?"

"Oh, absolutely," said Erun, and danced out of range of his pike, "I would have given you twenty."

Erun realised that he was a little early for the Mage, so he decided to get in some sword practice in the hall. He pushed open the massive doors to find that there were only a couple of soldiers engaged under the watchful eye of the Swordmaster, and realised that there was no one else to partner with. The Swordmaster was remonstrating with the two combatants, as they parried and thrust with absolutely no enthusiasm at all.

"Keep your arm up goddam it. At least pretend you know what you're doing," he shouted.

Then he saw Erun,

"Hi Erun," he said, "this pair are a waste of space if you are needing some practice? I need a bit of exercise though, so you can join with me if you like."

"My pleasure Swordmaster," he said, and drew his blade from its scabbard, "Wood!" he added and watched totally fascinated as always, as it rippled into its wooden form. Then he walked to the rack where the protective over garments were hanging and selected one. Making sure that all of the buckles were tightly fastened, but not so much that they would impede his movement, he turned towards Squerrel and raised his sword in salute.

About half an hour later, with the score standing at six to nothing in Erun's favour, the Swordmaster saluted him and said,

"All you have been taught over the years was not lost, but sat dormant until brought out by the sword. There are none that I know, who could stand against you now. You truly are a dragon rider, and as fine a swordsman as I have ever met."

So why did he have the feeling that he had won by design, rather than by his own skill? It had been so easy. He felt that he had made a couple of mistakes that the Swordmaster had not taken advantage of, but put that down to distraction by the others in the room. He shook it off knowing that it was a stupid thought, as he had never seen the Swordmaster perform at anything other than his best. It had to be the magic in the sword as Squerrel had said earlier.

He was late arriving for lessons with the Mage, who was less than happy to be teaching him anyway, and who felt slighted by his tardiness. As he walked through the door the Mage showed his displeasure by flicking a fireball at him. Without thinking he held up his hand, and it stopped no more than a foot away. He snapped his fingers and it shot back towards the Mage, who only just managed to duck in time. The fireball burst on impact with the wall behind Scrivens, and showered him in sparks.

Erun had absolutely no idea how he had managed it, and right at that moment he didn't care. He just sniggered, which upset the Mage even more.

Frantically beating out the smouldering remnants that clung in his hair and on his clothes, he screamed,

"Get out, and don't come back,"

Erun shrugged his shoulders, turned back into the hallway, and knocked the Princess flat on her back. He quickly leapt forward, his hand outstretched.

"I beg pardon your highness. It was careless of me," he took her hand, and helped her to her feet.

A shock ran up his arm at the touch of her hand, much the same as he had received from the sword, and he found himself snatching his hand away. But her grip didn't relax and her fingers closed even more firmly around his.

"No harm done," her soft voice said, finally releasing his hand, "I should have taken care not to walk too close to open doors."

"I am glad I have not offended you," he said, "I think offending the Mage was enough for me today."

She looked at him closely,

"You are the dragon rider that I have heard of, aren't you?"

"Well I do have a dragon," he said, "but I've not ridden it yet. It's a bit too young."

An idea suddenly came to him,

"Perhaps your highness would like to meet her?"

"Can I?" she said excitedly, and then sobered quickly, "but is it far? Will I need to bring my guard?"

"Today if you will permit it, I will be your Guard and guarantee your safety."

"Then, Dragon Rider, what are we waiting for?"

He led her out of the Castle past a green-eyed jealous monster called Egmar, and into the woods. She was hardly dressed for the occasion, having high shoes whose heels stuck into the ground, and a long flowing gown that caught against everything. She didn't care though and soon removed the shoes, casting them aside, and continued without them. Several pieces had already been ripped from her dress, but she did not seem concerned about that either.

They arrived into the clearing, and Corella came from her hiding place. She saw Lelia, her teeth bared and a savage "hisssss" came from her throat.

"She's *yellow*," exclaimed Lelia, "I've heard legends of a yellow dragon, but no one really believes it. I didn't even think one could exist."

"And who is this?" said Corella menacingly.

"Hey Corella you have lost your lisp," observed Erun.

Then remembering what Corella had asked, he introduced the Princess Lelia,

"This is the Princess Lelia from Vanticor, I'm afraid I ran into her and knocked her over in the Castle, so I thought seeing you might be some recompense."

"Your Majesty," said the dragon, dipping its head.

Lelia walked around Corella, who by now was quite a bit larger than a horse with wings to match, and examined every part of her.

"Corella," she said, "you are truly magnificent and I must say, on reflection, that I love the colour."

"Thank you Princess," said Corella, "the colour is beginning to grow on me as well."

She sniggered, if the snuffling grunting noise that she made was a snigger, "growing on me!... Quite good if I say so myself."

"Right Corella, we didn't tell anyone we were coming to see you, so I had better get the Princess back before they come looking for us," said Erun.

Lelia was still losing bits from her dress, and revealing quite a bit of skin as they made their way back. Erun didn't mind in the least, and couldn't stop himself from admiring everything that became visible. In between staring at the gaps in the dress, Erun was keeping an eye open for the place that she had left her shoes. Spotting them lying on the ground he made to go and get them, but Lelia stopped him.

"Don't bother," she said, "I never liked them anyway, and they will make a good find for someone less fortunate. And anyway I much prefer you staring at me."

He looked away, his face flaming, as he re-joined her. They entered through the Castle gates to be met by an irate King. He looked at Lelia's shoeless feet poking out from the bottom of a dress practically ripped to rags, and demanded an explanation.

"Explain yourself girl. This is no way for a Princess to appear before her public."

Lelia curtsied before him,

"It was the undergrowth in the woods, Your Majesty," she explained, "I was eager to see the dragon and neglected to change to more suitable attire."

"And your shoes?" he demanded.

"Lost in a bog," she lied, "the dragon rider was at hand and saved me."

Erun's eyebrows went up involuntarily as he heard this, but he said nothing. *One does not question the honesty of a Princess,* he thought.

She excused herself, thanked Erun and hurried off to her room. The King gazed at him for a while, and then murmured softly before walking away,

"There are lots of bogs in Vanticor, but here in Cardoney, I don't recall one ever being reported."

I suppose it's alright for a King to question one though, he thought.

Chapter Five
Solon of Pintor

OVer the next few weeks, Cardoney's spies were continually bringing news of an increase in tension between Partonin and Amtor. Suspecting that it would soon degenerate into open conflict, they urged the King to bring the Kingdom to readiness. Eventually they reported that their worst fears had been realised, and conflict had indeed happened, with an expeditionary force from Amtor probing Partonin defences by travelling through the wild unpopulated areas to the West. Partonin had managed to repel this incursion, but it had only been beaten back at some considerable cost to both sides.

After this unsuccessful foray, when the rag tag remains of less than half their army returned, it became obvious to Amtor's Generals that further incursions through that area would be unwise. For any hope of success an all-out attack with overwhelming force would be required, but unfortunately Cardoney stood between them and would have to be dealt with first. Most of those that returned were injured to one degree or another, and Amtor paused to lick its wounds and prepare its plans.

From the intelligence that he had received, the possibility of an invasion by Amtor was becoming obvious to King Arunay, but he also knew from the same sources that it wouldn't be in the short term. Of course hostilities between the two countries were unlikely to cease, but any attacks would be probes rather than major incursions. Realising that any probes would in all probability be through Cardoney, he acted on advice and brought his forces, such as they were, to full alert. Men of all ages, even the young and the old, began flocking in from all parts of the Kingdom in answer to the call. Anyone who could wield a sword, use a bow, or even a pike was eager to serve, and indeed there were even those who had never ever used a weapon of any kind during their lives.

None had any illusions about their chances of survival, but all still came and offered their lives for their Kingdom which, after all, was also their home. Even Erun, patriotic as he was, joined the call but was turned away.

"Your place is with your dragon," he was told, "before this is over we may have need of you both."

So Erun concentrated on Corella with frequent help from Lelia, who turned up dressed in the tight fitting tunic and leggings of a page boy. Her figure was seriously accentuated by the new clothing, and it was not helpful to Erun's concentration at all, especially when she brushed against him, which she frequently did. It happened so often, that he began to suspect that it was deliberate, or at least he fervently hoped that it was. It did allow her to move more quickly through the woods though, and she turned out to be hard working and helpful.

Corella had reached at least three quarters of her expected size, and was urging Erun to get a saddle made so that they could make their first flight together. She would often take to the skies, soaring to great heights and ranging over many miles, but would always try to keep the sun behind her to project a darker image.

When he came into the clearing she would sweep in for a landing to be near him, and would not take to the skies again until he left. She tolerated Lelia's presence and was always civil to her. *Not friendly, but at least she is civil*, he thought.

"*It's the least I could be to my bondmate's lover,*" she said to his mind.

"*What?*" he gasped in shock, "*She is not my lover. How could she be, given the differences in our positions?*"

"*You are a dragon rider. Well you would be if you would hurry up and get on with it, and the equal of any man."*

"Alright you win. I will go to the Saddlemaker. Let him measure you, and we'll get a temporary saddle made that will last until you reach full size."

Erun had no money, in fact he never had. Sometimes he wished that he could have some in his hand just to see what if felt like, but he was pretty sure that he would not be able to spend it, only just keep feeling it. But even to have some just for that purpose would be nice.

His visit to the Saddlemaker would therefore have to be cap in hand. He was pretty sure that a promise to work for the man for a month would be enough to get him a saddle. That is if he could find the man in one of his less difficult moods. Earden definitely was not the easiest of men to deal with.

"Hello Erun," Saddlemaker Earden said jovially, as he saw him approaching, "come to have a saddle made for that dragon of yours. About time, I expected you here days ago."

"I have no money," said Erun, "I can..."

"Already taken care of," interrupted Earden, "the King has paid for two, one for training and one for when she is full grown."

He noticed the confusion in Erun's face, and added,

"Don't worry yourself boy, you are about to find out that no one wants your money," he grinned, "even if you actually had any."

"Thank you Saddlemaker," said Erun, "I didn't know. The King never said anything. If it's OK with you, I will bring her to the Castle gates tomorrow so that you can measure her. I'm not good with heights, so my training saddle will need safety straps."

"My pleasure Erun, I will see you tomorrow."

Erun was just about to leave when the Saddlemaker laid a hand on his arm,

"By the way, I have heard from other dragon riders that it is very cold up there, so I would suggest a warm coat and gloves at least."

"Thanks, I'll do that," Erun grinned, and could not resist adding as he left,

"I will do my best to stop her from eating you," and ducked as the Saddlemaker threw a very large saddle buckle at him.

Perhaps it's the thought of more creative work, rather than the continual small repairs that he has to do, that has lifted his mood, thought Erun.

In truth, it wasn't the more creative work that appealed to the Saddlemaker. It was just the simple fact of being engaged to make a saddle for a dragon. As soon as news of this spread around the countryside, he would have more work than he could cope with, even enough maybe to engage an assistant, or take on an apprentice. The possibilities were endless and he chuckled in anticipation.

Corella had turned out to be a quick learner, and very soon had become an accomplished hunter. So it was only now and then that Erun brought her fresh meat from the kitchen as a treat. He had told her to concentrate on wild animals, and leave the many sheep in the fields surrounding the Castle strictly alone. As he explained, shepherds get really miffed when large flying things start taking their sheep without permission, and are likely to start hunting the offender themselves.

But on this day when she swooped in to land as he arrived at the clearing, he told her that she needed to be at the Castle gates to be measured for a saddle. She was so excited that he had to keep ducking to avoid poorly controlled wings and tail which seemed to be flying about everywhere. She was hopping from one foot to the other waving her fore claws and chattering,

"Can we go now, can we, can we?"

"No we can't. I will have to go first, and then you can fly in when I am at the gate. By the way you lost your lisp pretty smartly, where did that go?"

"I was so jealous when you brought Lelia the first time, that I hissed properly, and that seemed to have sorted the problem out,"

"That's a pity because I found 'hithhh' to be quite attractive. Anyway I'll give you a call when I reach the gates."

As he walked towards the Castle gates past the rows of men ferrying buckets of earth and stones from the moat, he reflected that she was visibly larger than when he had seen her yesterday. At this rate, she would be full grown in only a month to six weeks. He hadn't asked, but from one or two burnt patches he had seen in the forest, he wouldn't mind betting that she had already started spitting the odd fireball here and there.

He tripped on a shoe tie and bent down to fasten it, and an arrow passed through the place where his chest had been a moment before, and impacted into the shoulder of one of the moat workmen. The man screamed and fell backwards into the moat, closely followed by Erun looking for cover. Virtually everyone had their heads below the lip of the moat, with only the most daring of them taking a quick peek to try to determine where the arrow had come from.

It had to have been closer than the trees, but no one could be seen. The alarm was immediately raised and the Castle Guard bowmen deployed at the double, arrows nocked*, and eyes searching for the would-be assassin. After a few minutes when no one could be seen the bowmen quivered their arrows realising that whoever it was, they had made good their escape.

*(http://www.howtomakearrows.com/how-to-make-an-arrow/how-to-make-arrows-nocking-the-arrow)

And

(http://www.examiner.com/article/nocking-an-arrow-and-shooting-the-bow)

Erun clambered up out of the moat, reaching down to help some others bring up the injured man, and watched as they carried him off towards the Castle and medical help. He brushed as much of the loose dirt from his clothes as he could, and sent out a call to Corella as he followed them to the gates. The sky actually seemed to brighten as Corella swept in. She was not just yellow; she actually seemed to *glow* as she made a perfect landing in front of the bridge to the Castle.

Long ago the drawbridge had fallen into disrepair, and the King had never bothered to replace it, thinking that a drawbridge over an empty moat was a waste of time. Instead a temporary bridge over the moat gully had been built, and over the years had somehow become permanent. Now though, as it was intended that the moat should be refilled, workmen were hard at work removing the remains of the old drawbridge, while carpenters were laying out the timbers for a new one. Other workman had started to dismantle the bridge, leaving a temporary narrow walkway, which would be removed at the last minute.

Corella's landing startled them, and most ran for cover before they noticed that Erun had walked up to her and looped an arm around her dipped neck. Then they all ran forward, but stopped at a safe distance at her warning roar which left a tiny wisp of smoke rising from the corner of her mouth. The Saddlemaker pushed his way through the crowd and came forward.

"Wow," he said, "she is *really* yellow, never seen a yellow one before. Will she let me touch her?"

"Only to measure me for the saddle Saddlemaker, do more than that at your peril," she said, before Erun had a chance to reply.

"Oh by the way Erun, I made this for you," said the Saddlemaker, handing Erun an exquisite leather quiver, "It'll look more fitting than that tatty old bag you normally carry your arrows in."

It was a seriously fine piece of craftsmanship, which the Saddlemaker must have spent hours on. Erun could only take it in trembling hands, relish the feel of the polished leather, and mutter,

"Thanks, but I can't pay you for this."

The Saddlemaker waved this aside, and started his measurements of Corella. It only took him a few minutes to complete them, making a few notes on a small piece of parchment as he did so.

"It will be about three days," he said, "bring her back then, and I will fit it and make any final adjustments."

"Another is coming," interrupted Corella.

"Another what?" asked Erun.

"Another dragon," she said, "it is coming from the far south. It should be here very soon, I sense it's almost here."

The sky darkened above them, and looking up they could see this enormous wingspan descending towards them. It looked to be at least fifty percent larger than Corella, and was a glistening emerald green in colour. This time all of the onlookers did run for cover, mostly into the safety of the Castle walls, but some just rolled down the moat sides and hid under what was left of the bridge.

With a couple of massive beats of its wings it settled to the ground about fifty metres away from Corella and dipped to allow its rider to slide off the front of its wing past its neck. He strode purposely towards Erun, while both dragons turned to face each other, low rumblings in the throat of each of them.

"Calm yourself Corella," said Erun, as the man approached.

"I am Solon of Pintor," he said, "I greet a fellow rider."

Thinking that, that was quite a nice way of introducing oneself, Erun replied,

"I am Erun of Cardoney. I welcome you."

"Not bad young Erun especially since you have not ridden yet. I see that it is true and there is a *yellow* dragon. I did not believe the rumours of such a beast so I had to come and see for myself, and to bring you a warning."

"What is your warning Solon of Pintor?" asked Erun, and thought *steel.*

The ripple up the scabbard as the sword took on its true form, was not lost on Solon as he continued,

"Amtor has formed alliances with three Kingdoms further to the south, my own being one of them. It is not something that my conscience would allow me and a lot of my brothers to accept so we have left our allegiance, and will have no part of this. I come to warn you that they have heard of the yellow dragon, and of the legends surrounding it.

They are afraid, and know that the boy who rides it must be the easier target. They *will* try for your life Erun, knowing that it is the only way to stop your dragon. Amtor's ambitions have moved on from coveting Cardoney, and they are also looking to subdue both Vanticor and Partonin. I do not believe that this can be the voice of Queen Aspasia because she has always been a gentle lady and has never been so ambitious. No, there are other voices at work here."

"There have already been two attempts," said Erun, "One fell to my sword, and the other missed by chance."

"Not by chance," said Solon, "Nothing is ever by chance with a rider, some sense must have warned you. But enough now, you need guidance and with your permission I offer myself in that role. Should your dragon wish, then my Bethny will teach her."

"I accept with thanks Solon, but first there is protocol. I must take you to the King."

Chapter Six
Dragon Rider

It had been several days since Lelia had last come out to see Corella. Erun knew the King had not been happy with her being in the woods alone with him because of the two attempts on his life, so he had taken to seeking her out in the palace to keep her updated on the dragon's progress.

He had taken Solon to the King, who had welcomed him like a long lost brother, and installed him in the finest rooms the Castle had to offer. The King knew that having him in the Kingdom, as well as Erun, would cause any invading army to pause for thought. No army, no matter how large, would take on two dragons lightly.

Erun found Lelia practising embroidery under

the watchful eyes of two Seamstresses, not because she had to, but because she liked it and was quite skilful. He brought her up to date with Solon's arrival, and explained that the next few days would be taken up with his, and Corella's training. He promised to make sure that she was kept up to date, blushed furiously when she thanked him and kissed him on the cheek, and hurried out of the Castle.

He was surprised to see that Corella and Bethny were already off the ground, and seemed to be engaged in formation flying. Occasionally Bethny would roar if Corella's turns were not quite fast enough, or she drifted too far away. But on the whole, both seemed to be enjoying the experience, so he turned his attention to Solon.

Solon had a very large two handed double edged practice sword in his hand, and without any preamble lunged at Erun, whose wooden sword leapt miraculously into his hand and parried the mighty downward strike of Solon's blade. For a while after that it became very much a conversation of swords, backward and forward, with no one gaining the upper hand. Erun found that he was tiring much faster than Solon, so he stepped back, brought his sword up in salute and dropped to a sitting position on the floor.

Solon stepped forward and laid his sword against Erun's neck, and pronounced him dead.

"In battle, your opponent will not have sympathy that you are tired, and will have the advantage however he can. If you tire easily, then you must finish him quickly. Use magic if you have to, but finish him."

"How can I use magic," asked Erun, "when I have no idea how?"

"So then, the story of a young student who turned a fireball against a Mage, is a lie?"

"No, that's true enough, but things just seem to happen to me," said Erun, "and I don't know why. I fell in some thornbrush, had a couple of dozen thorn holes disappear and I don't even know how that happened."

"So that is where the thrust of our teaching must be. You are more than adequate with the sword, and I have heard that your prowess with the bow is quite legendary. So, just a daily practice to keep your skills up will be sufficient for that."

"You have been busy, in my brief absence," observed Erun

"It is well known that guardsmen have loose lips and talk a lot," Solon replied, and then continued,

"You must learn to be in charge of your magic and not let it take charge of you. Everyone has magic within them, but most are never able to wield it except for a very few who become Mages, and of course the dragon riders. It is the bond with their dragon that gives life to this force."

He came over and sat down beside Erun.

"I believe, from the gossip, that power was given to your magic when you took hold of the sword as it was embedded in Corella's mother, and while you possess that sword it is the path through which your magic gains its life. Maybe we will never be able to give you full conscious control, but even a little would be to your advantage. Now to work, and see if we can teach you the skills you will need to survive."

He jumped to his feet and hauled Erun up beside him.

"Our first task is to teach you to divert a dragon's fire."

Erun was a willing pupil and quite clever for his age. However, the whole thing was a waste of time since every time he tried to do anything nothing happened, so there was nothing for him to control. Solon eventually gave up, completely puzzled as to why Erun could have been picked to be a dragon rider when he was incapable of performing even the simplest of magic. Instead he just concentrated on telling him what magic could do, and what it could not. The only interruption to his lessons came when the Saddlemaker turned up with his practice saddle for Corella.

She could hardly sit still while it was being fitted, and the special leg straps explained to Erun. While the Saddlemaker and Erun were engrossed, Solon moved up to stand beside Corella's head and started to whisper some instructions to her. She listened in silence, and then sniggered and thought "*Agreed*"

"These loop up from under your legs and buckle to the centre of the saddle. Theoretically the dragon can turn upside down and you will not fall off. That is if you have fastened them correctly and tight enough," the Saddlemaker said, bringing his instruction to an end.

Corella lifted off to test the feel of the saddle, made a few circuits of the field and then came gliding it to land about thirty feet away. Erun started to hurry towards her, eager for his first flight, when she coughed. A massive plume of flame burst from her open mouth to dissipate harmlessly against the shield that had appeared around him.

"**Jeesus, you could have fried me,**" he yelled, "**Are you trying to kill me or something?**"

"But she didn't though did she?" observed Solon.

"Well, if it wasn't for you," said Erun, assuming that it had been Solon who had shielded him, "I would be a cinder."

"True, I was prepared to protect you," admitted Solon, "but in the event I did nothing. It was you. You did it yourself."

"Me? But I didn't do anything," Erun protested.

"Not knowingly," explained Solon, "It was your subconscious at work. I suspected that it would be the case, so I asked Corella, promising to protect you if you did not do it yourself. It seems that if your life is in danger then your magic works."

"Well don't do it again, you frightened the life out of me," said Erun, though he was glaring at Corella as he did.

His first flight was without incident, with Corella gaining height slowly and carefully flying straight and level. She was whispering into his mind in an effort to calm his terror, because terrified he most certainly was. Despite the straps his legs were clamped against the saddle in a vice like grip, and he was lying forward with his arms wrapped around her neck as far as they would go.

To his mind, it did not come to an end quickly enough, and as soon as he had finished being sick into the bushes, he said as much.

"In that case, remount your dragon and go again," said Solon, "but this time keep your eyes open."

The second time was only marginally better than the first, and the remainder of his breakfast ended up in the bushes.

"You have to believe, *really* believe, that your dragon would never allow you to fall. Her life is your life, and she will protect you with it," explained Solon.

"Strange as it may seem." said Erun, wiping his mouth with a handful of grass, "I never even thought about falling. It's just the actual flying that I have trouble coping with, and the cold. The Saddlemaker was right, it's freezing. I'll have to see Lelia and ask her if she can get the Seamstresses to make me a decent warm tunic."

When Solon thought Erun had recovered enough, he prodded him with his foot and bid him to get back on board his dragon,

"Enough lying about, this time we are going to try something new. Sit upright in the saddle, open *both* eyes and hold on to the reins. You have been grabbing her neck so hard, that I fear your dragon may have trouble breathing. Remember though, the reins have no purpose other than to occupy your hands. You decide between you with your minds where you want to go. Make sure you tell her to keep fairly low, I don't want to unload an ice block when you land."

"Not *both* eyes," groaned Erun, in mock anguish, "are you sure I can't keep at least one shut?"

But having exhausted what little resistance he still had, he dutifully climbed back on to Corella, and basked in the glow of her pleasure as he did so. This time he gathered what little backbone he had, and locked himself upright in his saddle and forced both eyes open. Now that he could see everything that was around him, his fear dropped away and he began to actually enjoy it. At his request, she kept him low enough to keep him reasonably warm and started to do banks, turns and dives after warning him that she was about to. Gradually he found that everything started to be automatic with Corella responding instantly to whatever passed through his mind. It was exhilarating. For the life of him, he couldn't see what he had previously been afraid of.

At his thought she returned to the ground, with him sitting high and proud in her saddle. There were resounding cheers and some prolonged applause from the crowds that were lining the Castle walls, and gathered outside of the gates. He smiled as he realised that they had been there all along, and he had never noticed. Waving to them all, he knew that he was now truly a dragon rider.

"That was good," said Solon, "how did the

answer come to you?"

"I kept both eyes open," explained Erun, grinning from ear to ear.

"Well apart from Bethny teaching Corella some of the sneakier tricks in flying, I think we are about done, I admit, you have been one of the easier riders that I have ever needed to train, and certainly the quickest, except for the magic that is." and then he added, "You need to fly as much as you can until you and the dragon do it as one. I will stay for a while and help you with that, but then I think Pintor needs me."

"The 'as one' business seems to already work," Erun replied smugly.

Even though he had not been flying particularly high, the slipstream as they moved through the air was still pretty cold, so getting some warm clothes was something he needed to do sooner rather than later.

"Thanks for the help. I'm not sure I would have ever got there without it. But I do think some proper clothes are now a priority," he told Solon, "I can't believe how cold it is up there. I'll see you later when I've sorted it out."

Taking his leave of Solon, he made his way back into the castle and on to Lelia's quarters where he was told by a maid that she was once again with the Seamstresses. The thought crossed his mind that she seemed to spend an awful lot of time there, but went to find her anyway.

As soon as Lelia saw Erun she jumped up and ran to him. Enveloping him in a bear hug, she pressed her lips firmly to his cheek and then snuggled into his neck. After a couple of minutes he thought that he had been hugged for longer than was really decent, and explained that he needed some gloves and a warm tunic. She pulled back from him, and grinning delightedly she took a beautifully tailored, heavily padded jacket from one of the seamstresses. It was then that he realised why she spent so much time here, as she presented it to him and pointed out the rearing yellow dragon embroidered on the back.

"I'm sorry, but I didn't think of the gloves Erun." she said, "I'll get started today and they should be ready by the day after tomorrow."

The next few days were taken up with as much flying and sword play as he could manage, with him proudly displaying his dragon jacket at every opportunity. Then he would drag himself exhausted back to his room, and fall into a deep dreamless sleep. Every morning was the same, he awoke feeling almost as tired as when he went to bed, and it took at least an hour of activity before his body would admit that it was awake.

News came via Bethny that the combined armies of the south had moved against Vanticor with no warning. Vanticor's single dragon and rider had succumbed to two rogues from the opposing army. It had not gone quietly but had taken one with it and severely injured the second. Vanticor had been unprepared, but it's much smaller army fought valiantly and managed to hold the invading force until reinforcements from other parts of the Kingdom had arrived. Then the tide had turned and the attack had been repulsed.

The invading armies had underestimated Vanticor, but Solon did not think that that was the end of the matter, or that they would do so again. He was pretty sure that they would withdraw, regroup and come back with a larger force.

"How did she know?" asked Erun.

"Know what?" asked Solon.

"About the attack on Vanticor."

"Oh that, well every dragon knows where every other dragon is. They don't know what they are thinking or anything like that, just sense where they are. But what they can do is receive thoughts directed at them specifically by another. Your Corella is just realising that she can do this. The news was directed at Bethny by the dragon of one of the riders of Pintor. When you visit the dragon hold or some of the Weyrs, you'll get a better idea.

"Dragon hold? What dragon hold? And what's a Weyr?" asked Erun.

"There is only one dragon hold, and it's far to the south, past even the most southerly Kingdom. Not used anywhere near as much as it used to be. Hundreds of years ago it used to be the meeting place for all dragons and riders, and it was there that most eggs were laid. It's still used by some, though not very many, even though it was virtually destroyed during the great dragon wars some five hundred years ago. Weyrs are usually set up by small groups of free dragons, but what with dragon slayers and such there aren't too many of those either."

"If we have time before you leave, you must tell me more of this, but for now we must convey this news to the King and Lelia," said Erun, and together they started trotting toward the castle,

"*Practice with Bethny my love,*" he projected towards Corella as he and Solon ran, "*I will see you later.*"

"*None of the lovey stuff,*" she replied, though there was a song of pleasure in her thought, "*I will go all maudlin.*"

"My concern, is that there were two rogues," said Solon, as they walked through the corridors towards the Kings personal chambers, "I fear that there will be many more. It has been custom with us for generations, that dragons and riders will not support aggression. We will only act in defence of our Kingdoms. It is this fact alone that has maintained the peace for so long. Being rogue does not sit easily with a dragon, but the bond with their rider is so intense that they cannot ignore it. It is strange, that they should be so. To my mind, I think the riders are being influenced or controlled in some way. I'm pretty sure they don't know what they are doing."

"So in fact then, it's the riders who are really the rogues and not the dragons?"

"Yes. dragons are dragons, and free ones will eat anyone who doesn't leave them alone, without worrying which side they are on. It's not that they are rogues, it's just their nature. It's the bond with the rider that, you could say, civilises them. Though having met some of them, sometimes it's the bond with the dragon that civilises the rider."

No rider is ever refused by a King, so they were ushered into his presence almost immediately they arrived, and had soon brought him up-to-date with the situation in Vanticor. He expressed relief that there was no summons from King Pordon to forcibly return Lelia, accepting that she was indeed, for the moment, safer where she was. Privately he was sure that Pordon must be relieved that she was away from any danger.

For Arunay though, his own kingdom's security was foremost on his mind. He had to put his neighbour's difficulties behind him and prepare for the difficulties of his own that looked certain to be just around the corner. So, he went on to ask if they had finished with the area in front of the Castle, because he would like to make it into a training ground for the ragtag army that he had managed to form. A significant percentage of the Kingdom's population had signed up, but none of them were soldiers and they needed to be made into some very soon. Luckily the Vanticor Guard that had arrived with Lelia had been given orders to remain in Cardoney, and assist with its defence. In a training role, they were becoming invaluable.

Enough weapons was the main problem, though most of the throng flocking to the call had brought what they had with them. The blacksmith was working around the clock with several of the stronger volunteers being co-opted to assist. Enough time was the problem, and all anyone could do was pray.

Losing the training ground itself was not a problem for Erun and Solon. They could train anywhere, so they readily agreed to find an alternative place for themselves, and to help in the training of the new recruits wherever they could.

Chapter Seven
Together

Soon, there was so much activity taking place outside of the Castle walls that it was not safe to walk there for fear of being wacked by a practice sword, or even speared by a real one. An area of one hundred paces to a side was set aside for archery training, with care being taken that the sharp end of the arrows pointed away from the main training field. One hundred paces was not a particularly long flight for an arrow, but it did serve to teach accuracy. Longer distance practice would begin once most of the training had been completed and a larger space made available. The Bowmaster asked Erun to assist in the archery training because he was actually one of the best that they had, and his advice would be invaluable. He readily agreed to take a couple of hours a day out of his own training with Corella, to provide help where he was needed.

The professional Officers and Sergeants of the Guard were actually quite good, and soon some semblance of order started to emerge. Gradually trainee swordsmen began to survive without bruises from the wooden swords for longer and longer periods, and archers began to actually hit some targets.

There was an air of controlled panic about the Castle, as everyone began to accept that training, which normally took months, would have to be completed in a matter of weeks. That is of course if the enemy, whoever he might turn out to be, actually gave them that much time. So training commenced at first light, and carried on until it was almost too dark to see.

About the fifth day into training, disaster was narrowly averted when Corella coughed, and only just missed frying Erun and Solon as they stood chatting. It was Erun who saved them. A whisper of thought from Corella brought an instant reaction from him. His magic reached out, and diverted the plume of flame as it blazed towards them. They were scorched, but diverting the fire saved them from being charred to a crisp. Those soldiers who were within sight were literally doubled over in mirth, and training came to a stop for at least half an hour.

"So," said Solon, reaching into a pocket with trembling hands, to retrieve a handkerchief to mop the sudden beads of perspiration from his brow, "for the second time your magic seems to have saved us. It is lucky for us that it is more instinctive than controlled, for I could not have reacted in time."

Corella was aghast and couldn't stop saying sorry, so at Solon's suggestion, Bethny agreed to take Corella off to some remote spot to practice some control.

"It's sort of like a cough," she explained to everyone, "that mixes the gasses, causing them to ignite on contact with the air. Individually they are non-flammable, but mixed? Well that's another story entirely."

"It's just as well," she added with a chuckle as she took off with Corella, "that we dragons are not susceptible to coughs and colds."

From the ground, Solon joined the chuckle, and added,

"You need to watch out in a dusty atmosphere though," he said, "because sneezes have the same effect. There is a tale about a dragon and rider who were being introduced to the whole royal family in a Kingdom, when a dust devil passed the dragon's nose and she sneezed leaving the Kingdom without a King or even succession. I'm not sure whether it is true, but it makes a good tale, don't you think?"

Bethny and Corella were away for almost a week, which was only made bearable for their riders by the bond between them, and the fact that they threw themselves into training with forced enthusiasm. The hurt becomes almost physical for them both, if they are apart for two long, and this is the reason that every single rider or dragon gives up on life if anything should happen to the other.

Dragons and riders kept in constant contact, keeping each other informed on the situation in the Kingdoms. The two dragons were prepared to instantly abandon training and return if called, or they themselves sensed any danger. But the fates seemed to be with Cardoney for the moment, and time stretched on and vital training continued.

Erun was shocked when they returned and he saw that Corella was now the same size as Bethny. He had expected accelerated growth, but nothing as fast as this was turning out to be. As they swept in, the brilliance of Corella's colour glared against the sun, making the sunlight seem dim in comparison, and left Bethny's iridescent green looking dull and lifeless.

"Hello Erun," she said hopping over to him, and shoving with her head, "did you miss me?"

"Yes I did," he replied, clambering to his feet from where the head butt had put him, "look at you, you are massive. I do think we need the Saddlemaker again."

"We were near the border with Amtor, so I borrowed a few of their sheep. Delicious I must say, particularly after you have burnt off all of the wool. It seems the more I eat the faster I grow."

A couple of burly workers stationed at the

side of the moat informed him that the castle entrance was now closed while the bridge was dismantled. They could enter over the newly installed drawbridge when it was test lowered later. Tomorrow, they said, if everything went to plan, the sluice gate would be opened and the river allowed to flow into the moat. It would probably take the entire day for it to fill, but already there were signs of relief that it had been completed in time.

To while away the couple of hours before the drawbridge was lowered, he sat down next to Corella, with Solon and Bethny nearby. He leaned against her, let his eyes shut and dozed off. After about an hour Solon came over and poked him in the ribs with a toe, and then dropped down beside him,

"When we can get into the Castle," he said, "I will have to take my leave of the King and head back south. It seems that my friends have knowledge of the voices that seem to be influencing the Queen of Amtor, and are planning to move against them. They are cautious though, and need my guidance. Even at Bethny's best speed, it will still take the best part of two days to get there. I am sorry I could not stay longer."

"I will come with you," said Erun.

"No, my friend you are needed here."

They watched as the final timbers of the old bridge were cleared away, and the new drawbridge began to creakily descend. It settled down on to the bank of the moat, and they stepped up to be the first across.

"Still needs some work," said a work

supervisor, "we have to build a ledge against the moat for it to descend on. It will soon break down the edge if left like this."

He started to make sketches on a piece of parchment, using a measuring stick to double check his calculations as he did so. Erun and Solon waited until he had finished, and then crossed the bridge and entered the Castle. It was the work of only a few minutes for Solon to make his apologies to the King, thank him for his hospitality, and bid him farewell. Then he gathered his belongings from his rooms, and together they returned to their dragons.

He clasped Erun's arm, and then mounted his dragon,

"I know, my friend, that you have questions. Suffice to say that in this we are departing from tradition and acting aggressively rather than in defence. It has to be done though, because we believe that in the long run, we will be defending against the long night, lest it fall and consume us all."

He raised his hand in salute. Bethny leapt from the ground, and with several mighty beats of her wings, climbed skywards. Erun watched as they became smaller, and were eventually just a tiny speck that disappeared away to the south.

"Right Corella, I think I will really miss them. But I must be off to the Saddlemaker."

"I will miss them too," she said, "but there is no need to go, because he seems to be coming to us."

Erun   looked   round   to   see   that   the

Saddlemaker was indeed on his way, staggering under the weight of a mighty saddle that was on his back. He knew that Earden was probably one of the best Saddlemakers in any of the Kingdoms, and surmised that he had based his measurements upon his view of Corella's projected growth.

Let's hope he's as good as I think he is, and it actually fits, he thought.

It did.

"I have included the leg straps," he said, "there is no telling when a sudden change of direction may be needed, and it wouldn't do to have you fall off before you've hardly started."

Erun did not reply because he was too busy admiring the superior workmanship of the saddle. The stitching was exquisite as was the leather tooling, and the whole thing had been polished to a deep mahogany shine. It was literally a work of art, and by far the best one that he had ever seen.

"Wow!" was all he could say.

"Wow is enough thanks for me," said Earden, as he walked away grinning like an idiot.

While Erun was positioning the Saddle and making sure that the straps were firm, but not too tight, he felt that he was being watched. He stopped and looked around, only to find that Lelia was standing nearby and watching him. She had on the tight leggings and tunic that she invariably wore now when she was outside of the Castle, and it was enough to take his breath away. As with him, she had now passed her sixteenth birthday, and was filling out her clothes much more than she had done before.

Corella hissed quietly, but made no hostile moves as she picked up his thoughts. She just thought, "*Naughty,*" as they turned to fantasies and visions of Lelia without the tunic at all.

"She has got to be quite big now," said Lelia, "Is she fully grown?"

"Well, I'm beginning to hope so," he replied, blushing a little in embarrassment as he remembered his thought.

"Are you going flying now?" she asked.

"For about an hour or so," he said, "we usually do that every day. Then I have to get in some archery practice to keep my hand in."

"May I watch?"

"Of course Your Highness," he said.

She came over to him and reached up to kiss his cheek, but it was unexpected and he did not turn his head quickly enough, and her lips brushed his. It was as if a bomb had exploded in his head, and it was not until he and Corella were gliding along at about a thousand feet that some sanity eventually returned to his brain.

Three days had passed since Solon had departed for the south and Erun and Corella were practicing some intricate manoeuvres a few thousand feet up, when she suddenly twisted a wing and dropped like a stone. When it began to look as if it might surely be fatal, she gave a few rapid beats and settled on to the ground.

"I am sorry Erun," she said, "the news shocked me."

"What news?" he asked, wiping a few beads of perspiration from his forehead.

"Solon and Bethny are gone. The news came from another who is fleeing to the south. They thought that their combined force, and magic would be enough. They moved against their enemy, and it was not. Solon and two others fell before they could do anything. The sole survivor could only flee."

"Do we know what they were facing?"

"It seems to have been one man, a Mage of imaginable power. The like of which has never been seen before."

"I have to inform the King and Lelia," he said, "so let's get back to the Castle."

A little later, having told the King, he made his way towards Lelia's room to give her the news. Her door was slightly ajar and without thinking he pushed it open, and stepped inside. She was there, naked to the waist where she had taken off her tunic, and was in the process of rolling down her tights. She heard the sound and grabbing for the tunic, held it in front of herself as she looked round.

She looked at Erun for a few seconds, and said nothing. Then coming to a decision she didn't move, but dropped the tunic to the floor, stepped out of the tights, and stood naked before him. The blush of pink in her face was slowly working itself down over the rest of her body, but her head was held high and she did not falter. Hesitantly she raised a hand to him. He gazed, in rapture at the vision before him for what seemed like an age then he turned, closed the door and twisted the massive key in the lock. When he turned back, he had not been dreaming, she was still there, and this time both of her arms were open and waiting.

Chapter Eight
Alliance

About three hours later, they both emerged fully dressed from her room. Erun had a silly grin permanently etched on his face, and Lelia's eyes were wide open in surprise. Both kept looking at the other as if they could not believe what had happened, so for a while the excitement in the Castle just drifted over their heads.

As they stood outside of her door, lost deep in each other's eyes, a maid came scurrying up,

"Your highness," she said to Lelia, "a messenger from Partonin has arrived. He is at this moment with the King. The King has sent me to find Erun."

"I'll have to go then," said Erun, and leaned

down to touch Lelia's lips with his, but it turned out to much more than a touch. The maid's mouth dropped open in shock, but she said nothing and hurried away.

Erun was shown into the King's presence. Two Earls that he recognised were stood flanking a third man who he rightly assumed must be the messenger from Partonin. The messenger turned his gaze towards Erun and with a curl of his lip said,

"Has this youth a purpose here, Your Majesty?"

"This youth, as you call him, is the rider of the yellow dragon. Take care, messenger that you are able to return to Partonin," replied the King.

"I beg your pardon Your Majesty," said the messenger hastily, and he turned and made a slight bow to Erun, "and yours young rider. I spoke in haste."

"My King has sent me to propose an alliance," he continued, "in the face of the increasing threats from the south. While our Kingdom is by far the larger of our two, we have no dragon, so with yours we may join on equal terms."

"Has your King then renounced his wishes to annex us?" asked the King.

"Your Majesty," said the messenger, feigning surprise, "my King has never had such wishes."

"Erun," asked the King, smiling at him, "would Corella be disposed to roast this knave until he learns to speak the truth?"

"Indeed she would, Your Majesty," replied Erun, playing along, "though I fear he may not be able to speak at all after such a roasting."

The messenger suddenly looked terrified.

"I spoke in jest Your Majesty," he said hastily, "my King realises that the thought of annexation would be a mistake."

"I'm glad to hear it," said the King. "I accept the proposal, and these two gentlemen who now stand with you will accompany you back to Partonin to finalise the details. You are dismissed."

The messenger bowed deeply and together with the two Earls backed out of the chamber.

"I am starting to believe that this may be a good thing. For a number of years, I have thought Partonin the better of the two that border us to the north and south. I also believe that King Bardon's talk of annexation was just posturing to Amtor."

"You are probably right Your Majesty," said Erun, "but I am afraid I know little of these things."

"Of course you don't Erun, but no doubt you will learn," but then he added, "but what am I to do with Nordlight."

Erun realised that since the tragedy with Darthbold, Nordlight had not been seen around the Castle at all.

"He confines himself to his rooms and will not come out or allow anyone in except to bring him food, and he eats precious little of that." explained King Arunay. "I hold little hope, but you are near his age, perhaps..." he let his voice trail off.

"I will try Your Majesty, but we were never close."

"Do what you can Erun," he said.

After the king had dismissed him Erun went straight to Nordlight's rooms, to find a maid with a tray of food, banging furiously on his door. He came up to her and she stepped away, head bowed and said in a trembling voice.

"He has always allowed me in with his food Master Erun, but I can get no answer and I may not enter unless bid. I beg pardon, but I was frightened for him and I was about to go in anyway."

Erun pushed open the door to be greeted by the sight of Nordlight standing on a chair and trying to fix the other end of a rope that was around his neck to the iron chandelier in the ceiling. Erun hurled himself forward, kicking away the chair before he could tie the knot and they both crashed to a heap on the floor.

"**Get help girl**," he yelled at the maid, who dropped the tray and ran from the room, skirts flying and screaming for help at the top of her voice.

Nordlight struggled to get away, but Erun held him fast.

"No, you cannot do this Nordlight. Think of your father," Erun hissed into his ear, "You are all he has. Think of him, and less of yourself."

All of the fight suddenly left Nordlight and he collapsed, sobbing hysterically against Erun's shoulder."

"I cannot live with this," he sobbed, "what am I to do?"

"You are a Prince of the realm," said Erun savagely, "you can behave like one. Find something to occupy your mind. For a start, you could train with me and help with Corella."

The maid had returned with several people in tow, and Erun caught her eye and raised a finger bidding her silence.

"All is well here," he said to the others, using his body to conceal the rope, "just a small accident, but the worst is averted. Thank you for coming."

When everyone had left, except for the maid who was cleaning up the remnants of the tray she had dropped, he settled on one knee beside her, and placed a hand on her shoulder,

"Don't speak of this to anyone, except in the story that I have told. Nothing will be gained by it."

"I will not, my lord, you have my promise."

'My lord', he thought, *things are really looking up.*

Nordlight rose considerably in Erun's estimation when he went to his father. He knelt and hung his head in shame as he explained what had happened,

"I could not live with what I have done," he said, his voice hoarse with emotion, "I was about to take my own life, and would have succeeded had it not been for Erun. He showed me that it would not be a solution worthy of a prince. I beg my father's forgiveness."

"There is naught to forgive boy," replied the King, "I had contemplated such a course for myself, but the responsibilities of my position forbade it. What are we to do with you my son."

"By your leave Your Majesty, perhaps Erun could move into Darthbold's old apartments to be close and keep an eye on me," Nordlight suggested, "Erun has suggested, and I have agreed, that I train with him and help him with Corella."

They both knew that it was not the work for a Prince, but under the circumstances it might just be the ideal solution.

"I agree," said the King, "but see that you listen to Erun, that boy has a man's head on his shoulders."

The engineer in charge of the moat project announced that there would be a delay of a day or two before the sluice gates were opened to fill the moat, as it was necessary to drive a number of piles into the bottom to support the reinforcing where the drawbridge would be landing. Several men were holding each pile into place, and a huge tripod had been erected over each one. A massive solid cylinder of iron was being winched up, by a team of about fifty, and dropped repeatedly onto the top of the wooden pile.

The piles were large wooden tree trunks, which had been worked to a point at one end and their edges smoothed as much as was possible. A metal cap had been fitted to the top of each, to prevent damage to the wood from the huge metal driver. With each strike of the driver, each pile was sinking into the ground about seven or eight centimetres. It was not very far, but at least they were going in. The rest of the day was taken up by the grunts of the men who were raising the weights, and several deafening 'clangs' as the same weights were dropped.

Each strike took about ten to fifteen minutes to accomplish, and it was estimated that to drive the piles the three metres or so that was required, would take twelve to fifteen hours. There were three teams of men to each tripod, and they rotated after each drop. It was hard work, so the rotation was essential to provide sufficient rest. Braziers were being brought out to provide some light, and some warmth, for the resting teams because it was intended that work should continue after dark.

With the level of noise this process produced, no one was likely to get any sleep this night so cauldrons of soup were being prepared by the wives, girlfriends, and mothers of the workers to provide some sustenance as the work progressed. The spectators were delightedly yelling 'heave' as each iron driver was hoisted up.

Before work could start it had been recognised that the points to the piles should be fire hardened, and Erun's suggestion, that this might be just the job for Corella, was accepted with delight. She accomplished a job which would have take men several hours, in only a few minutes. A delicate 'cough' over each one, a wash of flame and the job was done.

Pile driving had commenced at first light, and was nearing completion when midnight approached. Three of the six piles were fully in place to the supervising engineer's satisfaction, and the teams from these split up and joined with the men from the other three. Carpenters had started to bring out timbers to complete the staging, determined that the whole thing would be complete by morning. It had proved to be a small problem, as the drawbridge could not be lowered fully yet, but this was solved by firing an arrow from a window and setting up a pulley system to get the materials out of the Castle, and to the other side of the moat.

As the sun rose the last nail was driven, and the order given to raise the sluice gate. The gate creaked upward in its track and the water began to pour in. The moat, for the first time in over forty years, began to fill. A massive cheer went up from the spectators and the exhausted, but entirely satisfied workmen, when the water level began to rise.

'This dragon is filthy." announced Nordlight, wrinkling his nose, "The amount of dirt on her would dim the sun, let alone that magnificent yellow that she is supposed to be."

"I feel fine," protested Corella, uncertain at what was to come next.

"Well you don't look it. I intend to take you to the lake, and see if I can really make you shine."

"Huh!" exclaimed Corella, having never been bathed before, "What do you think Erun? Am I not beautiful or what?"

"Of course you are," said Erun, "and filthy,"

he added.

"I will seriously roast anyone who takes me near water," she declared.

"Don't care," said Nordlight, grabbing the claw on one wing and tugging, "you would be doing me a favour. Save me hanging myself. So come along like a good little dragon."

Corella shrugged both wings, whispered, "*help*," and meekly allowed herself to be dragged off towards the lake.

"I'll be here when you return," said Erun, and eagerly took the opportunity to lay down for a snooze, knowing that visions of a certain unclothed princess would occupy most of his sleeping time. It wasn't surprising really as the same vision occupied most of his waking time as well.

He felt like he had hardly dropped off when the clanging alarm wrenched him back to reality, but he must have been asleep for at least an hour judging by the height of the sun.

"Steel*"* he said as he scrambled to his feet, and then projected a thought to Corella.

"*I am on my way,*" she thought. Hardly had the thought been completed before there was a flash of yellow, and she zoomed in for a landing with Nordlight clinging to her dripping wet bare back for all he was worth.

Be prepared, thought Erun towards Corella, *we can find out what is happening later.*

"Wow," said Nordlight as he rolled off of Corella, "now I know why riders ride."

"Don't get used to it," she said, "this was an

emergency."

"Quickly," said Erun, "help me fix her saddle, and then you go and find out what is happening."

It was much faster with the two of them, and the saddle was soon in place. Nordlight gave one final check and then ran off towards the Castle. Erun could see that the new army was forming up in front of the Castle, and Archers were moving into place behind them and along the walls. The deployment looked surprisingly efficient given the short amount of training that the new soldiers had been given.

A couple of minutes later Nordlight came trotting back, hastily buckling on a sword.

"A large force has been seen crossing over our southern border," he explained breathlessly.

"How long have we got?" asked Erun, "Who brought the word?"

"The word was brought by Eloise, a young girl of about eleven still in her nightdress, and aboard a bareback and bridle-less shire horse. Her father has a smallholding near the border," explained Nordlight.

Erun, was acutely aware that even a full grown man would have been hard pressed to stay afloat on one of those at the gallop, and hopefully the youngster was being treated like royalty having managed to do this for more than fifty miles. They were meant for pulling, not galloping, but on the lumbering and almost exhausted horse, she had managed to stay ahead of the invading force, thus giving the Castle enough time to prepare.

It was an epic journey for one so young, and Erun knew beyond doubt that this would go down as one of the greatest of things that had ever happened in this Kingdom.

"The exhausted horse has been taken away to be cared for and Eloise has been taken to Lelia to find her some clothes, and to let her rest," Nordlight finished.

"But how long have we got?" persisted Erun.

"Oh sorry… We have about three, maybe four hours," said Nordlight, "from the reported numbers, we will be outnumbered about three to one. Messengers have been despatched to Partonin and Vanticor, but it will take them longer than that to get here. We can expect no relief for at least twelve hours, and it will be much longer from Vanticor."

He continued,

"I heard from inside the Castle, that both the Swordmaster and the Mage are not within. Apparently the Mage is attending a family gathering for a few weeks, and the Swordmaster has personal business south of Amtor. Let us hope he passed through Amtor safely."

Both of them have pressing business when we have need of them, do you not find that odd Erun? he asked himself.

"I was about to observe the same," thought Corella.

"Corella and I will fly to intercept them and see if we can reduce their numbers a little, or at least delay them as much as we can. If they are sensible and far spaced, we might not have as much luck as we would like, but we will try. You go and let the King knowwhere we've gone."

He climbed over Corella's wing and into the saddle and as a precaution buckled the leg straps, something that he had not done for a while. Corella leapt skywards, the brilliant flash of her wings flaring so bright that Nordlight had to shield his eyes. She turned, moving faster than Erun had believed that she could, and headed south.

He looked down at the woodlands rolling rapidly past them, and marvelled at how different the trees looked from up here. After about half an hour, the woods gave way to grassland and he finally caught a glimpse of ant like creatures, together with the glint of reflected sunlight on armour and weapons. Here was his quarry. Not as sensible as he had feared. He could see clumps of men looking up in horror, and hastily grabbing arrows for their bows as Corella swept down towards their ranks.

He bid her to concentrate on the archers, and she coughed. A massive plume of fire almost thirty feet across roared out and slashed across two companies of archers, leaving little more than ash in its wake. She was going so fast, that she overshot the ground movement and dipping a wing, whipped around in a one hundred and eighty degree turn, coming at them from the rear.

These archers though, were no slouches. Erun and Corella were so low that they could see the looks of terror on faces looking up at them as they flashed by overheard, but arrows were still nocked to bows and the better of them managed to unleash a volley before they were reduced to ash.

Arrows such as these stood no chance of penetrating her scales, and those that did hit her just bounced away. One though penetrated her wing, fortunately not through muscle or anything vital but through the softer membrane. She gave a grunt of surprise, but otherwise said nothing, but turned to renew her attack.

"No," thought Erun, *"see they are dispersing, our element of surprise is gone. It will be a case of too much energy for little reward. Let's return to the Castle. But it might delay them a little if you can get some of that grass to burn."*

"Good idea," returned Corella, and streaking across the front of the army, she ignited a wide swathe of grass before banking away to the north and gaining altitude, *"to attack the Castle they have to come back together, then they will learn the folly of making holes in my wings."*

Erun was puzzled by the fact that he had not felt sick at all as the archers had been roasted, then realised that it was because it had been done by Corella, and not by him. Thinking back, he had seen many dead people, and it had never affected him until that is, he had done it himself.

She swept in to land outside the Castle next to a waiting Nordlight. The portcullis had been lowered, and the drawbridge was now raised. Nordlight immediately saw the arrow sticking through her wing, and jumped to administer aid. He removed it by breaking off the feathered end, and then pulled it straight out to reduce further injury. It was apparent then that the injury was slight compared to the size of the dragon, and would quickly heal. In fact it did just that, as he stood watching.

"God, I wish I could do that," he said, "might have saved me a whole heap of discomfort over the years."

The Captain of the Guard, having seen Erun land, came over to find out what had been learned, and Erun briefed him on the size and makeup of the enemy force.

"It is larger than even we feared," he concluded. " we accounted for a large portion of their archers, but there are still more left than we have soldiers.

The tension started to grow as the defenders waited, but young or old they stood their ground, eyes fixed on the distant trees, and weapons firmly gripped in their hands. There was much fear evident in their faces but much more determination, and each knew that whatever the outcome of this day, those that survived it would be proud to have been here.

Then they heard them crashing through the undergrowth in the woods, and getting ever closer. Erun unsheathed his sword, remounted Corella and turned her head towards the trees. She leapt into the air and with rapid beats of her wings moved towards the forest's edge. Building up speed, she roared her defiance and swept down to run parallel with the trees as the first of the enemy broke through. More than two hundred perished, in the mighty bursts of flame that marked her passing, but then there was no more flame to use, and the rest of the army burst forth unchecked.

Corella landed, Erun dismounted, and with both hands held his sword high towards the enemy. He was about to do something stupid, like scream, "Come and get me", when he was shocked at the sight of Corella's colour lifting from her body, and curling towards his sword. For a brief moment he had a vision of a deathly white dragon, and then a flare brighter than anything he had ever seen, flashed out from his sword. It was so bright that he involuntarily closed his eyes against the glare, even though it was directed away from him. Such was its intensity that it must have instantly blinded all who faced it, as its wave front spread across the battle field.

It was over in an instant, with those who could flee, fleeing, and those who could not, dropping their weapons and pleading for mercy from an enemy who they could no longer see.

Erun sheathed his sword and was relieved that his vision of a deathly white dragon, had only been a vision, and she was her usual brilliant yellow once again.

"Well I must say that was different," observed Nordlight.

Chapter Nine
Dame Eloise

The Kingdom of Cardoney found that it had more than one thousand prisoners on that day, all of whom were blind. What was more important to this fledgling army though, was the fact that the weapons of all one thousand were there to be gathered up. There was nothing to be done with one thousand blind men at arms, so an escorting force of a hundred or so of the oldest soldiers that could be found, were assigned to march them back to Amtor. It was a deliberate insult to the southern Kingdom, and King Arunay hoped, a salutary lesson.

In public King Arunay thanked all of his people for their support, and wished that he could honour them all, but as he could not, he decided that

101

a symbol was needed. He offered a knighthood to Erun, who apologised, and turned it down on the grounds that such an honour had no place in a rider's life.

"If I may be so bold though Your Majesty, I have a suggestion," he said.

King Arunay was tickled pink and readily agreed, and so it was that a small eleven year old young girl called Eloise Plater became the youngest ever Dame of the Kingdom of Cardoney for services to the Kingdom. Having ridden fifty miles on the back of a lumbering shire horse in her nightgown, frozen to the marrow, she was somewhat relieved to arrive back home in her own carriage and dressed in the finery that Lelia had provided. The day that she made the historic ride was declared a holiday in perpetuity, and would be called Eloise's day.

"What actually happened out there?" asked Nordlight.

"Happened out where?" asked Erun.

"Out there on the battle field, the yellow flare thingy with the sword,"

"No idea," he said, "I was about to utter the immortal words 'come and get me', and it just happened."

Nordlight drew his sword,

"Perhaps they are magic words," he said, holding the sword aloft.

"Come and get me," he yelled.

"Sorry Your Highness, but I am a bit busy," said a passing swordsman, who then ducked as Nordlight picked up a rock and threw it at him.

"You try," he said to Erun.

"Not likely," said Erun, "you saw what happened the last time."

"And I don't want to be white again, even for a second," declared Corella, shuddering all over.

"Ah," observed Erun, "so it wasn't a vision after all. You really did go white."

"No it wasn't, and yes I did." replied Corella, "It felt really weird, so don't do it again."

Despite the fact that the Kingdoms finest healers had said that the blindness in the prisoners' eyes had been permanent, because of the damage that the flash had inflicted, news had come in from Amtor to say that the sight of every single one had been restored. It could only have been done by a Mage, and a very powerful one at that, nothing other than magic could put sight back where none existed

As coincidence would have it, both the Swordmaster and the Mage returned that day. The Swordmaster was not looking his usual ebullient self, but by contrast the Mage was looking happy. It was somehow as if they had swapped personalities. That was not the case of course, it was just that things had not gone as well for the Swordmaster as he had hoped, but for the Mage it was the opposite.

"Nordlight," asked Erun, "out of interest, who returned first, the Mage or the Swordmaster?"

"I'm not sure," replied Nordlight, "but I believe it was the Swordmaster."

"That puzzles me." said Erun, "Another one. Who went away first?"

"Oh that was definitely Squerrel, because I saw him go. Why do you ask?"

"I don't know. It seemed like a question that needed an answer, but the answer only deepens the puzzle."

"Do you suspect something?" asked Nordlight.

"What is there to suspect? But something just does not sit right with me."

"What about their last times away from the Castle, should I enquire softly?"

"I don't know what that will achieve," said Erun, "but I'm inquisitive so, yes. Do it anyway."

Corella had found that the massive blasts that she had used as she passed in front of the trees during the battle had depleted her gas reservoirs completely It had taken at least half an hour before she had enough for a half decent cough, and a full hour before they were back to normal levels. She passed on the information to Erun who had been surprised because, for some reason, he had assumed that the gasses were more magical than physical, and would not run out.

So, between them they decided that it would be wise to avoid such depletion and perhaps short bursts would be more effective in the future, rather than a 'putting all their eggs in one basket' blast. Some, if only a little, recharging could take place between the short bursts, serving to prolong their usefulness. Whichever way, it still used up large amounts of energy, and after the battle she was famished and had taken leave of him to hunt 'before I start eating people' she had said.

Erun decided that he needed to look in upon Lelia early today, so he left Nordlight with Corella, who grunted her disapproval, and entered the Castle. He made his way towards her room, striding purposely down the corridors, and when turning a corner he very nearly flattened the maid who had been delivering Nordlight's food.

"My pardon my lord," she gasped, "I was clumsy."

He looked closely at her. She was a very pretty little thing, with long auburn hair and a really passably decent figure.

"Your name girl?" he grunted.

"Marta, my liege," she said.

"Well Marta, less of the 'My lords' and 'My Lieges', I am a commoner, as you are, who just happens to be a dragon rider. Call me Erun."

"Thank you Erun, may I enquire of Nordlight. Is he recovered?" she asked.

Something in her voice gave pause to Erun, and he looked carefully at her face.

"Marta," he observed gently "Marta, It must hurt greatly to be so in love with a man that you cannot have."

She said nothing, but a single tear coursed its way down her cheek,

"I have loved him since I was twelve when I first saw him. I know our positions make it impossible for us to be together. But should he ask I would lay with him without hesitation..." her voice trailed away.

Erun touched her shoulder, and not knowing what else to say, "You serve him well Marta," was all that he could manage.

He hurried away until he reached Lelia's room and then revelled in the softness of her touch and the comfort of her arms.

Sometime later, he rejoined Corella and Nordlight outside the Castle, and without preamble said,

"Nordlight, do you know of Marta?"

"Oh wow yes, most definitely," he replied, "she is the maid who brings my food. For obvious reasons, I couldn't say anything, but I have been in love with that girl since I was twelve. Every time I see her I want to just grab her. I insisted that it was her who brought my food. At least I got to see her every day."

"She said as much, and more, to me about you," said Erun.

"I had hoped," said Nordlight, his face brightening considerably, "but she gave me no sign. While Darthbold much desired Lelia, I only professed so for the Kingdom. Truly I was relieved when rejected,"

There was sadness in his voice as he uttered his brother's name.

"From me for what it's worth, whatever her background, she is a find that should not easily be cast aside," said Erun, and then cryptically, "Vanticor have need of accomplished swordsmen."

"I must go," said Nordlight, suddenly coming to a decision, "I have a scribe to see."

It was an hour later that Nordlight craved audience with the King, and presented him with a parchment. The King took it, but did not unroll it to read, just got up and wrapped his son in his arms.

"It does this heart good to see how much better you are my son. Erun seems to be the influence that I had hoped."

"It was more Corella," replied Nordlight, "though Erun played his part, but father please read the parchment."

The King unrolled the parchment and read,

> *I, Nordlight, son of Arunay of Cardoney do relinquish all title to the throne of Cardoney for myself and all my heirs and successors. I do this in the full knowledge of what I do and acknowledge that there is no coercion in my decision.*
>
> *It has, for a while, been evident to me that I am not a person fit for such an office, and I intend to leave the Kingdom with my new bride at the first opportunity.*
>
> *Nordlight of Cardoney*

The King sighed, re-rolled the parchment and said,

"I would be lying if I said I was shocked or surprised. I do have one question though. What new bride would that be then? No wait, would it be little Marta? You have made cow eyes at each other since you were twelve."

"If she will have me, my liege," he said, addressing his father as a subject rather than a son.

"Your decision is a great disappointment to me in terms of succession to this throne, but it has given me greater regard for you as a son than I have ever had. You will not leave here to struggle in life. Will you do me the honour of marrying here, with all of the ceremony that I can give you, and accept the position of ambassador to Vanticor?"

"It is more than I deserve Your Majesty, but I accept with grateful thanks."

"Good, now go find your girl."

Nordlight hurried from the Kings Chamber, and headed for his room. When he arrived there, he grabbed hold of a richly embroidered bell pull, and began to tug on it frantically. Within seconds he heard the patter of her running feet, and her hasty knock on his door.

"**Enter**," he yelled.

The door opened, and she was standing before him, breathless and flushed. At that moment, there was no one more beautiful in the Kingdom, than the love of his life that stood before him now.

"Your highness," she said, dipping in a curtsey.

"Will you be alright," he asked slowly, "being married to the idiot son of a King?"

For a moment she stood there, as his words gradually sank in, and then her screamed, "Yes," echoed through the Castle corridors, and she flung herself into his arms.

In his chamber, the King smiled as the screamed 'yes' echoed and re-echoed throughout the Castle. *I don't think an announcement will need to be made,* he thought.

Chapter Ten
The New Ambassador

No one had any illusions that Amtor's incursion would be the last, nor were there any illusions that Erun's and Corella's flare would be successful a second time. The King knew that he could not prevent parts of his Kingdom from being taken, but as long as the Castle remained in his hands, no victory could be had.

The main upside to the previous battle was the acquisition of enough arms and armour to equip a thousand men, with the prisoners being stripped of their weapons before they were marched back to Amtor. All of the weapons were to a high standard, and accepted gratefully by soldiers who had been inadequately equipped before.

There would be some breathing space though before Amtor was in a position to move against Cardoney again. And this time they were sure there would be dragons. King Arunay used this breathing space to construct defences around the Castle. Teams of men were sharpening thousands of stakes, and planting them at forty five degree angles into the ground. Narrow paths, wide enough for only one man at a time, were left through them to allow free movement of people on foot. But no more carriages were allowed. Everything that was needed was being ferried in by hand.

That is except for one carriage, which was positioned outside of the defences to ferry a new Ambassador and his wife to Vanticor. The wedding had been magnificent. No expense had been spared and dignitaries from Vanticor and Partonin had attended. Vanticor had accepted Nordlight as Cardoney's new ambassador, and also accepted reluctantly, that Princess Lelia was staying where she was.

King Porden was shocked and so was King Arunay, when she told them that the only man in her life was Erun, and she would not leave him. When asked when this had happened, she replied that it had been as the coach had arrived at the Castle and she had spotted him watching her from the crowd.

"Does he return your feelings?" asked Porden.

"Oh yes father, he most certainly does," replied a bright pink Princess.

At this point, both Kings felt it unwise to

pursue the matter fearing where that could lead, and instead agreed to her prolonged stay in Cardoney. King Porden later confided in Arunay that he was delighted that at last she had found someone, and that someone was a dragon rider. It was custom amongst royalty of all the Kingdoms that they encouraged their children to form attachments at a young age, so that they could be sure about their feelings before considering marriage when they were old enough.

After the wedding and just before the end of the riotous party that ensued, Nordlight and Marta slipped away to start their new life together in Vanticor. Before he left though, Nordlight sought out Erun,

"I made some enquiries," he said, "The last six times, Squerrel and the Mage have left the Castle at nearly the same time, and for the same period. Always," he added, "Squerrel has left and returned first. What does it mean?"

"I don't know," replied Erun, "but you have to admit it's odd."

Marta said,

"Thank you Erun, I will remember you always for what you have given me" and kissed him on the cheek. Then they said their goodbyes and made their way through the stakes to the waiting carriage. Erun watched until the carriage and escort had disappeared through the trees, and then came to a decision and turned to mount Corella.

"*Let's go flying,*" he thought.

"Stay back and out of sight," thought Erun to Corella, *"we are fast enough if we need to be."*

"I can see much further than you," replied Corella, *"so don't worry if you lose sight of the carriage. I will not."*

Erun removed the bow from his back, and laid it beside his saddle. A small quick release buckle, which had been thoughtfully provided by the Saddle maker, held it in place. He had only recently taken to carrying it at all times when he was away from the Castle, and would explain to all that asked, that it was:

"I carry it as a precaution, because these are dangerous times,"

Strangely everyone else started to follow suit. Either carrying a bow, a sword, or in some cases an axe.

He was here because he had seen Squerrel leave the Castle earlier that day, and shortly thereafter the Mage left as well. He did not know why, but something within him was disturbed. Something was going to happen. It could not be another attempt to invade, because Amtor was not ready yet. The Castle was well prepared and guarded, so no incursion was likely until the enemy had sufficient strength. He couldn't think of any other possibilities, so that only left Nordlight and his new bride.

"There is movement ahead of the carriage," thought Corella.

"Move closer," thought Erun, but she had caught his thought as it was forming, and was already moving forward.

On the ground, they only discovered that something was wrong when the lead officer dropped from his horse with an arrow through his throat. Then they were surrounded, and the Guard held helpless. Nordlight unsheathed his sword and leapt from the carriage, but a voice stayed his hand.

"Sheath your sword Nordlight or the woman dies."

He said no more as Erun's arrow entered through his left ear, and protruded at least eight inches out of his right. Nordlight decapitated the nearest one to him, and removed the arm of the next that moved towards him. Corella dropped like a stone towards them, and her roar of rage left most of the enemy in fear of their lives. She grasped two in her claws, and all five claws on each foot went through them killing them instantly. With a couple of beats she was up to two hundred feet before she dropped them on their fellows, frantically shaking her feet to get the bodies off of her claws. It was enough of a distraction for the carriage guards, who struck down the men nearest to them. Then it was over and only the crashing sounds of retreat could be heard.

Corella landed just clear of the carriage. Erun alighted and walked forward. As soon as he saw the victim of his arrow, he turned and was sick.

"Thank you for following, my friend," said Nordlight, then noticing the vomiting, became concerned and asked, "Are you ill?"

"No, I just can't get used to taking a life. It will pass in a moment, I hope." replied Erun then went on, "I followed because something did not sit easy with me."

"It was set to look like bandits," said Nordlight, "but they were not. The man you pierced with your arrow addressed me by name."

"No matter," said Erun, "Corella and I will stay aloft near you until you reach the borders of Vanticor."

The rest of the journey to Vanticor was completed without incident, and the Cardoney Guard handed over to the Vanticoran honour Guard at the border. Food had been prepared by the border guard, and the Cardoney men stepped down from their horses for a well deserved rest and some refreshment. Then fully sustained and rested they said goodbye to their neighbours, and headed back on the long journey for home.

Erun mounted Corella and waved to the men who were still in shock from seeing this mighty yellow horror descend from the sky, and then having it sit there looking at them. Corella had amused herself by putting on her most savage face, periodically stretching out her massive wings, and coughing small fireballs now and then just to keep them uneasy.

"You are supposed to be nice to friends,"

thought Erun, "*not amuse yourself by frightening them to death.*"

"*I was being nice to them,*" she replied, "*I didn't eat a single one.*"

"*You are a wicked lady, let's go,*"

Corella dropped down on to her belly and then gathering her legs under her, thrust downward and launched herself skyward clear of the trees before spreading her wings and turning towards Cardoney.

Erun decided long before they reached home, that this little incident was not something that the King needed to hear about, well not right at this moment he didn't. Fortunately, it had ended well, and besides which the King had enough worries without having another burden added. Nordlight was safe and that was all that mattered.

He landed outside of the castle, removed Corella's saddle, and watched for a moment as she took off and disappeared to the south, probably to hunt some Amtorian sheep. Egmar spotted him as he approached and eagerly told him that it was now general knowledge that Queen Aspasia of Amtor was a prisoner in her own palace.

"It's pretty certain that she didn't order the attacks on Vanticor and Cardoney," he added.

"Where did this news come from?" asked Erun, "we haven't managed to get anyone inside Amtor yet."

"A couple of Amtorian guards handed themselves over to our border patrol."

Apparently the two Amtorian soldiers had

been late for parade, feared punishment, and had crept forward hoping to sneak into line when they witnessed the enthrallment of the rest of the men. They had not waited around to see the Mage responsible, but had fled and headed for the border. They had eventually been missed, and had to hide from search parties, so progress had been slow. It had taken many days before they spotted some Cardoney guardsmen, handed themselves over, and were immediately brought to the Castle.

When Erun confirmed with Egmar exactly how long ago this had happened, he realised that it coincided with the Swordmaster's and the Mage's absence from the Castle. He was beginning to suspect that the Mage was a traitor and responsible for everything that was happening, but he could not see how the Swordmaster fitted in. He had to admit to himself though, that he had couldn't believe that the Mage was actually powerful enough to be the orchestrator of their current troubles. True he could have been concealing his true capability, but somehow Erun doubted it. Perhaps there was another explanation for his absences? What concerned him more though was the Swordmaster. Why was he leaving at the same time as the Mage? Were they up to something together? Or was it just a bizarre coincidence?

What he needed was a soldier who had actually been turned. Well he couldn't expect one to come to him, so he would have to go and find one of his own.

"Corella," he thought, *"how do you fancy a*

bit of night flying?"

"I thought you would never ask," she replied.

"This time though, when you pick one up don't stick your claws through him like you did with those two at the ambush. Remember how hard it was to shake them off. This one, I want alive."

"Right my liege, whatever you say, but I am not guaranteeing anything. I am roasting a nice sheep at the moment, so I should be back in about an hour."

"I need to pop off on a little errand in about an hour when Corella gets back," he told Egmar, "so I had better let you get back on duty."

"Oh err… yeh... I'm late. See you later," Egmar said as he broke into a run for the guard house.

Erun could have gone into the castle to partake of any delights that Lelia had to offer, but he was afraid that he might get lost in her charms and miss Corella's return. He was not sure he would be able to cope with his dragon's disapproval, so he sat down on the grass to await her arrival.

Almost to the hour it seemed, there was a brilliant flash in the sky and Corella swooped in to land about twenty metres away. He hefted the saddle up and staggered over to her, and at the same time found his regard for the Saddlemaker, who had brought it out from the castle with apparent ease, increasing with every stride. When he eventually reached her, he threw the saddle over her back with his last gasp, and collapsed against her side to catch his breath before strapping it in place.

"I think some body building classes might be in order," she thought.

"I thought you loved me the way I am. Am I not nice?" he replied in kind.

"Of course you are, weak and pathetic but nice."

He thumped her in the neck scales, but being extremely well armoured she didn't feel a thing.

"Well I didn't feel that, so is that not proof enough," she said, rubbing it in.

"Oh shut up and get your head down here."

She dipped her head and he climbed up the leading edge of her wing, swung himself into the saddle and strapped his legs down. Never having been night flying before, he was taking no chances. As he settled himself into the saddle, the feeling of complete love and devotion passed between the two of them and their minds became virtually one. It seemed to be much more pronounced in the dark, and as he couldn't see anything it was actually quite comforting.

Then they were aloft and heading south.

Suddenly he found that he could see through Corella's eyes, and having been blind as a bat up until now it was a really weird experience. She saw in the Infrared at night. Not that Erun knew that it was infrared; all he knew was that they both could now see everything below them that was warm. It was surreal watching all of the bright coloured blobs moving in all directions below them, and he was fascinated when he saw four larger lights two by two with six smaller ones behind, and realised that he was looking at a carriage.

When Corella really got moving she could fly at over fifty miles an hour, so it was only forty minutes or so before the border came into view. Not the actual border of course, but a long row of heat signatures from the guards made its position clear. Erun reflected that the border had always been an open border, and these guards were something new.

"Shall we just go and pinch one, or do you want to land first."

"Drop down out of sight, I need to answer the call of nature first." he replied.

Corella swooped down behind a small hillock about two hundred metres from the line, and Erun quickly jumped off to relieve himself. He had been bursting to go for ages, and thought he would never stop.

"I wouldn't have thought your body was big enough to hold all that." thought Corella, maintaining mind to mind contact so as not to disturb the guards.

"Think yourself lucky that you got down as quickly as you did," thought Erun, as he remounted.

None of the guards could see anything in the clear night sky apart from stars, so a dark shadow swooping down over them was quite a shock, especially since one of their number disappeared as the shadow passed by. Corella had grabbed him by his armour rather than his body, so apart from a couple of nasty gashes he was at least still alive. In his panic at suddenly being hoisted aloft, he had dropped his pike, and his screams echoed through the night as he was carried away. Eventually Erun couldn't stand the noise any longer and leaned as far over as he could, and shouted down at the figure hanging from Corella's claws,

"I would shut up if I were you. You wouldn't believe how much it annoys her, and you wouldn't want her to drop you."

The man became silent immediately, and stayed that way with his arms wrapped around Corella's leg in a vice like grip as they headed through the night towards the Castle.

Corella dropped the man when she was almost on the ground, giving a quick flip to loosen his grip, and then with a single flap moved herself clear of him before settling down on the ground herself. It would not do to squash him before they even got to talk to him. He immediately tried to make a run for it, but found himself surrounded by Castle Guards before he could even cover twenty metres. Realising how fruitless his efforts were, he stopped running and reaching into his tunic drew out a quite vicious looking long bladed knife. The guards, who were armed with pikes and swords, just stood back out of range and grinned at him.

Suddenly he reversed the knife and drove it into his own body, killing himself instantly. For a second or two he just stood there, but then he fell forward onto his face. Instinct drew Erun's attention away from the body and his gaze was drawn to the castle. He was somehow not surprised when he saw the Swordmaster standing at the gate, and the Mage leaning out of one of the windows. Both noticed him

121

looking at them and returned his glance briefly. Then the Mage withdrew, and the Swordmaster turned and walked back into the Castle.

Snatching soldiers from Amtor was obviously not the answer, as he was now certain that each would take his own life before he could be interrogated. It was an incredible level of enthrallment that Erun hadn't even thought was possible. With every incident that happened, he was becoming more and more certain that another plan would have to be created, which would probably have to involve his own magic, and that of Corella

Chapter Eleven
Allies

Erun decided that the only way he was going to get anywhere near the answer to the questions flying around in his head was to get close to the people he suspected. So it was that he arrived at the Mage's class head bowed respectfully, and the most contrite look that he could find fixed firmly on his face. To his surprise the Mage just looked at him, and said,

"Come in Erun, I'm glad you decided to come back."

There were four other boys of roughly his own age in the room, and all of them who he recognised as apprentices to the Mage, looked at him with curiosity as he entered. Nodding in acknowledgement, he went to an empty bench, and reaching under it pulled out the stool that he found there and sat down.

Four hours later the Mage brought the session to an end for the day, having spent the time teaching methods of defence against the magic of others. To a man, the pupils were relieved, because he had been getting grumpier and grumpier each time Erun had managed to penetrate his defence demonstration. The problem was that Erun still could not fathom out what he was doing. It just happened. The main thrust of the lesson had been the use of reflection and deflection against projected energy, but none of these methods seemed to work against Erun. His energy projections got through every time, that is until the Mage had finally managed to erect a defence shield that was reasonably effective, but even that seemed to be getting visibly weaker all the time.

As all of the apprentices filed out, he waited for them all to leave and then beckoned to Erun,

"Don't mind me Erun, I was born grumpy. It's in my nature and I can do nothing about it. I mean no harm and those that know me understand that... "

"Yes Mage," interrupted Erun.

"Don't interrupt boy," snapped the Mage, bringing life to his words, "I'm only just getting started."

"Yes sir," said Erun.

The Mage glared at him, and then continued,

"A great power lies within you which, up

until now, has been blocked, but the sword and your link with Corella has finally allowed it to flourish. I have never seen its like, or never known of any man, rider or otherwise, who could wield magic and not know what they were doing. In you it seems akin to breathing. You don't think about it, it just happens. Had I known, you would have been my apprentice long ago."

He paused and then held up his hand as Erun opened his mouth,

"Swelled heads do not sit well with me, but I have to tell you this. This Kingdom will have great need of you and very soon if I am not mistaken. It's beginning to look as if you and your dragon could be the hope to divert this catastrophe, because my pitiful power is simply not enough."

Again Erun opened his mouth to speak, but a glare from the Mage made him shut it again,

"Powerful forces are at work here. I have been doing what I can to mitigate their effects, and that is little enough believe me. Their ambition is to enslave us all. The southern Kingdoms have already succumbed, and I fear Vanticor to be next. It is only you and your dragon that have saved us thus far. A yellow dragon has never been encountered before and the thought is, why now and why here? What does it portend? As long as they have indecision and are afraid to act then we have some breathing space, and I intend to use it by making you the best that you can be."

Erun was stunned. How could he have misjudged this man so completely? Perhaps it had been the public persona projected by the Mage that had wrongly influenced his judgement. It must have been, because the man before him now was a different matter entirely.

He reached and took the Mages arm, who returned the clasp,

"I have wronged you sir," said Erun, "I had imagined that you were behind these things, but I see now that you were not. I came to your class to expose and condemn you. For that I apologise."

For the first time in Erun's life, he saw the Mage smile,

"We are allies against this darkness Erun, and together we will not fail. I will approach the King and suspend my apprentices for a few weeks, which I believe is all we have. Then I intend to concentrate on seeing if I can, somehow, move your magic up to the conscious decision making level. Go now though and eat, or your belly will consume itself."

At this time the best place to eat would be the hall adjoining the guard quarters. They had food available for longer than the main kitchens, because of the need to cater for changes to the Guard. They had never objected to him eating with them and were always friendly. Even his erstwhile head clouters would sit and chat with him amiably.

When he entered the hall, several shouted to him as he lined up to receive a large bowl of mutton stew and potatoes. He noticed that he had a choice of the new metal spoons that the Mastersmith was fashioning or the more traditional wooden ones. He selected a wooden one because the handle fitted more easily into his hand, and sat down at the nearest table.

"How is the stomach Erun," said a voice, and he looked up to see the Guard Commander moving into the seat opposite him, and placing his own bowl on the table.

"Fine thanks. The brandy did the trick, so I have taken to carrying a flask against future need."

"Wise decision boy," he replied, and then attacked his mutton stew with considerable enthusiasm.

The Guard Commander was a Captain and from the tales of the men, a fair and just one too while at the same time being quite a disciplinarian. His name was Captain Joshua D'Arnot, being of foreign descent from somewhere across the eastern ocean apparently.

He was a jovial man, but a glint could appear in his eye when some miscreant guardsman fell short of the high standards that he expected, and the poor man would be left quivering at the roasting he received. Always at the end of the roasting a word of comfort and encouragement would be given, and the guardsman would stand straight and proud again.

Erun liked the man and had always found him to be helpful, so having finished his stew and washed it down with a flagon of the weak beer that the men were permitted with their meals during duty periods, he bid him farewell courteously and hurried outside.

He had been away from Corella too long and the strain was beginning to tell, so he reached out to her and asked her to come and get him. Almost immediately, it seemed, there was a rush of air and she settled down beside him.

"*I have missed you Erun. Climb aboard,*" whispered her thoughts sweetly.

"*What, without a saddle? You have to be joking, I will fall off.*"

"*My Erun, will you never be my knight in shining armour?*" she asked.

"Huh," he replied aloud "If I was in shining armour I would be too heavy, and you'd never get off the ground. Nope I think I will remain a coward."

"I see that it is not the Mage then?" she said, as the closeness let their thoughts mingle.

"No it seems not. But I don't see how the Swordmaster could be involved. He has never been seen to wield magic."

He knew she was going to do it before she leapt from the ground and flew away. It was a bit disconcerting to always know what the other was about to do. He had just been about to ask her to go and fetch the saddle, when she had picked up the thought as it formed in his mind. He knew she had, so had never actually asked, just watched as she went to fetch it.

Within a couple of minutes she came swooping in, with the saddle hanging from its straps that were firmly held in her mouth. Two quick flaps of her massive wings, and she settled down a few metres away to prevent any injury to him. It was only the work of a few minutes to strap on the saddle, and then he swung himself into it and she launched into flight.

She turned towards the South at his thought, and headed towards Amtor. They encountered a free dragon on the way which took one look at her yellow brilliance, and roared it's defiance before fleeing away as fast as it could.

"Nice," said Erun, "I like that. It makes life much easier than conflict all the time."

Her thoughts smiled at him,

"My colour is starting to have some advantages." Her thoughts smiled at him, but then… *"On the road ahead a carriage has been stopped by what looks like, heavily armed men."*

"Those are not Cardoney soldiers. There can be no lawful reason for that here, so let them feel our presence," he replied.

Corella banked around and rocketed forward. Erun nocked an arrow to his bow and held it ready as she descended to land amongst them, scattering them away from the coach. He noticed that the man nearest to the coach was obviously their leader, so he drew back the bowstring and pointed the arrow towards him

"**Hold**," he shouted, "**what is happening here?**"

"Nothing to do with you boy," said the man condescendingly "so take your painted dragon and be away before you learn the price of interference."

"*Can I roast him,*" asked Corella.

"The price of my interference will lay heavily on you and your men if you do not withdraw. This is no painted dragon, but the yellow dragon of Cardoney and I am Erun its rider."

The man bent down to retrieve his sword from where it had fallen when he has been startled by Corella's arrival, and then cursed in pain as Erun's arrow pinned his hand to the ground. He looked up and Erun already had another arrow nocked and pointing at him.

"That was by design, not by chance," said Erun coldly. "The next can just as easily pin your throat, as indeed it will if one of your men makes another move."

The rest of the man's followers had been inching forward with weapons drawn, but came to a sudden stop and froze into position at his words.

"Whatever purpose you have here is not lawful," Erun continued, "so go while you still can. You may keep the arrow lest you forget this lesson."

"We will meet again," spat the man, gritting his teeth against the pain in his hand, "and you will not survive that meeting."

"Go," said Erun calmly, "or you will not survive this one."

For a few moments, looks were exchanged and briefly the man seemed to be about to do something foolish, but then he shrugged, signalled to his men with his good hand, and moved away from the carriage. Within thirty seconds they were all gone, disappearing away through the trees.

"Keep an eye on them and make sure they have truly withdrawn," he thought, *"let me know if any try to return."*

Dismounting from the dragon's back, he walked towards the carriage, noting that two footmen and the driver were all dead. Perhaps he should have killed the bandits because that was obviously what they were, but he still could not bring himself to take a life lightly. Arriving at the carriage he peered through the window to be startled by the biggest pair of green eyes that he had ever seen, in an extraordinarily beautiful face, peering back at him.

"I am Erun, dragon rider of Cardoney," he said, "I apologise for your reception in our Kingdom my lady. Unfortunately your driver and footmen have succumbed, so as I see you are alone I will drive you on to the Castle. My dragon will watch from aloft."

"My name is Serena of Amtor," she whispered in a voice that sent shivers up his spine, "My father placed me aboard this coach and bid me flee before the soldiers came. He said that they would be sure to violate me, as all humanity was gone from them. I thank you for your assistance."

"I'm not sure you can handle two," the whispered thought said into his mind, *"I think Lelia would kill you. Anyway take care, as I am not happy with what is happening here. Something is disturbing the magic."*

Chapter Twelve
Serena of Amtor

The sight of Erun returning, and driving a carriage, caused a considerable stir amongst the Guard at the Castle, and he was soon surrounded by the clamour of voices wanting to know what had happened. He caught a glimpse of Lelia at a window, and waved at her as she leaned out to get a better view. Her face though turned to stone as he opened the carriage door, and handed down the impossible vision that was Serena of Amtor. He would have to smooth things out with her later, but for now he had to get Serena to the King.

The King listened quietly as Erun related what had happened, and then immediately granted Serena sanctuary, arranged one of the better rooms for her, and assigned maids to see to her needs. When the King was finally satisfied, he dismissed Erun who then left the throne room and went to patch things up with Lelia. As he and Lelia lay together behind securely fastened doors in her room with their naked bodies locked together, he began to think that maybe he needed to make her jealous more often.

Sometime later they reluctantly parted, he kissed her passionately before he left, and then wandered down the Castle corridors towards the main courtyard. He was passing one open door, when a voice called out,

"Do you have a moment Erun?"

He looked around in confusion until he realised that the voice had come from the room that he was just passing. He stopped and entered the partly open door, only to see Serena's head looking over the top of a screen.

"I wonder if I can have your opinion Erun," she asked.

"Of course My Lady, in what matter?"

"I just wondered what you think," she said, and stepped totally naked from behind the screen.

His breath caught in his throat at the vision that had emerged. He had never seen a woman with such a magnificent body. He loved Lelia dearly and thought that her body was the best in the world, but this one was truly incredible and he felt an unbidden stirring in himself, despite the activity that he had only recently undertaken.

But Lelia flooded into his mind and he

stepped backwards.

"Your dress my lady, is exquisite," he said diplomatically, and then turned to walk out of the door closing it softly behind him.

He leaned against the wall outside and his breath came raggedly. It was not the vision that he had seen, but more something that he was sure he was not supposed to see. As he had turned away to leave he had seen her flicker, and for the briefest of moments a portly seriously old hag of a woman had stood in her place.

He took a deep breath. There were several people that needed to know about this, the first of which had to be Lelia. So it was to her that he went straight away, spent ten minutes explaining to her what had happened, and then another fifteen exploring options with her on the bed. So it was virtually half an hour before he sallied (well staggered) forth again, and headed for the Mage.

He found the Mage sitting at a bench reading an enormous leather-bound book, and hurriedly explained what he had seen.

"Can people change their appearance like that," he asked the very old woman who sat in front of him, and not waiting for an answer he added, "I see they can."

The Mage turned back into himself.

"It's probably one of the hardest things to do, but you say she showed herself to you naked?"

"Yes,"

"She is trying to use the wiles of a siren to enchant you. So it has to be you that she is here for.

And you were not tempted?"

"Had it not been for Lelia filling my mind, then I surely would have been."

The Mage's lack of surprise or response to that, confirmed Erun's suspicion that everyone in the Castle knew about him and Lelia.

"Your feelings for Lelia are truly opportune, for without them I fear you would now be dead. There are two ways that this could happen," explained the Mage. "She could be controlling her appearance or someone else could be. Though, it is unlikely that she would have flickered had she been the controller."

He paused in thought,

"It is possible though. Your unexpected refusal may have surprised her enough for a lapse in concentration."

He paused again,

"I have felt disturbances in the magic, which is why I have been travelling to try to get near the source. I can never quite get to it, but I can project some interference. It has never been much, but it is all I can do. I felt it in the Castle, but could not pin it down. This magic is directed at you. You will have to deal with it. My belief is that in the end, you will have to kill her."

"So then I need to turn my attention to the Swordmaster. All of this has to be his doing. He must have magic that we know nothing of."

"No, Erun no," he snapped, "take that from your mind. He has nothing to do with this. I have sent him ahead to afford me some physical protection. He is party to the knowledge of what is happening. It was he who ordered the guards to shadow you before you killed the Amtorian. He has also made a few small mistakes in his swordplay, to instil some confidence in you. All of this with my knowledge."

"Then who can it be?"

"Neither I nor Squerrel know, but know this, we will both be supporting you as much as our pitiful abilities will allow."

Erun walked briskly along the corridors towards the King's throne room. He had been told that His Majesty was in conference with Serena of Amtor, and had been for thirty minutes or so. His resolve was steadfast. He knew that she could not be left alone with the King for too long, though the King was never truly alone with his personal Guard always being present. But from the immense power of the magic that had been witnessed thus far, he did not think these would be a problem for her.

"Steel," he whispered as he approached the door.

The Guard on the door raised their swords in salute to him, and turned to open the doors. He walked into the room to see that the King and Serena were closely huddled in conversation.

"What is it boy," asked the King testily.

Erun said nothing. He just smoothed all of the expression from his face and strode forward as

Serena stepped backwards from the King. She smiled at him then the look of shock as his sword sang from its scabbard, and then no look at all as her head left her body and rolled away from the King.

The Kings Guard were on him in an instant, disarming him and knocking him to the floor. He was held fast as the King roared his rage and came to his feet.

"Look at her face, look at her face," Erun gasped through the pressure on his chest from two guardsmen. From the corner of his eye he could see Corella's face at a window, and knew that even the Castle walls would not have been a barrier to her if harm were to befall him.

"It's alright Corella," he thought.

The King looked down at the face that had rolled to a stop. It was a wizened, old, haggard, and toothless face. He turned towards the body, and could see where the fat of the witch had ripped the tight dress that Serena of Amtor had been wearing. Altogether it was not a pretty sight.

"Release him," he said. "How did you know Erun?"

Erun scrambled to his feet as the guardsmen withdrew back to their posts. He felt sick, but at least he did not have the indignity of vomiting in the Throne room. The last guard dipped his head, and offered Erun's sword back to him, hilt first.

"I saw briefly when she offered herself to me, and I refused Your Majesty," he explained, "I needed though to confirm it with the Mage. It had to be me. I was the only one who could kill her, because I was the last one she would suspect."

"Once again we are indebted to you. Hand me your sword, step forward and kneel before me. There will be no protests this time," he said, silencing Erun's opening mouth.

A little later Sir Erun, Dragon Rider of Cardoney, left the Throne room, and made his way in a daze to Lelia. As always she jumped into his arms.

"What brings you here at this hour my love," she asked, "You are normally with Corella."

"You are looking at a knight of the realm," he said grandly, "there is no longer a barrier between us. Though all already know, at least we need not make any pretence of secrecy anymore."

After they had finished celebrating as only two lovers can, Sir Erun kissed Lelia for the sixteenth final time, and then dragged himself away. As he left the Castle he called Corella to him.

"I have a confession to make," she said as she landed, "so let us fly off to somewhere quiet so that I can tell you."

A little later she glided in to land on a grassy slope near to the edge of the forest, and the Vanticor road. Erun slipped off of her back and then sat beside her as she made herself comfortable. For a long time she was silent. Then eventually she sighed and said,

"It's in relation to the Dragon Realm."

"What's that?" he asked.

"It's the one thing that no dragon has ever told its rider. It's the only secret that we have from you. It was ingrained in us thousands of years ago that this is something no one other than dragons must know. It's part of our racial memory."

"What's that then, some sort of dreamscape thing?" he interrupted.

"No definitely not, this is a very real and physical thing. But don't keep interrupting. No dragon ever enters the realm with a rider on her back. Though according to legend it did happen once, and it was the fabled yellow dragon that did it. A dragon that did this today would be hunted down by the others, and killed. But they have let me know that because they think that I am the yellow dragon of old reborn, no such sanction will be taken against me. So that is why I am telling you now."

"Go on," he said, sensing the seriousness in her tone.

"There is great fear amongst the dragons. They are finding that too many of their riders are moving away from the path, and into acts of evil. They fear that it will mean the end of us all. The only dragons that can be trusted are the free ones."

"The Dragon Realm?" he prompted.

"This place is one reality. There are others. The dragon realm lies between realities. A dragon may enter the dragon realm at will, and re-emerge in another part of this reality instantly. It is not a fine art, and accuracy of transit is somewhat lacking. But it tends to be within three or four kilometres of the intended emergence. Good thing for travelling very long distances, and a good place to stop and rest away from danger."

She paused to gather her thoughts,

"It can be dangerous. In the past quite a few dragons have managed to emerge in a mountain, or with a tree through their middle. But I have found that for some reason I can picture where I am going to emerge, and do it with incredible accuracy to a couple of metres of where I intend. I do not think it is arrogance to suspect that fate knows what is happening here, and we have been brought together to prevent it."

"I really hope you aren't right, I would hate to have the fate of the world resting on my shoulders. With my level of competence we don't stand a chance."

"As usual my Erun you underestimate yourself and the effect of the bond between us."

"Maybe, but if I have to stake my life on it, I may have to find somewhere to hide."

They rested against each other for a while enjoying the company, even dozing a little. But then Corella began to rise to her feet.

"Come," she said, "I want to take you to the Dragon Hold."

"But that's days away," he protested.

"Not by the Dragon Realm it's not," she replied.

It was not like anything that he had ever experienced. In fact it was not like anything at all. He felt nothing. One moment he was in the air flying over forest, and the next he was still in the air and still flying over forest, but not the same one. Then they emerged and before them was the Dragon Hold. It was a great complex of caves in a semi-circle of craggy cliff faces. Only about three or four dragons were present in a place where, hundreds of years ago Erun imagined, thousands must have gathered.

Corella flew straight for the largest of the caves and settled down in the entrance.

"This was the hatchery," she explained, "at that time almost every dragon that was ever hatched, was hatched here. Now we are lucky if there are two or three a year."

Erun dismounted and went into the hatchery. It was an enormous cave. Sand was thick on the floor, and two solitary eggs lay in the centre. A warning hiss alerted him to the two dragons, one bronze and one green that were resting off to one side, and he made sure not to approach the eggs too closely.

Corella followed him into the cave and the other two dragons, obviously startled by her appearance, rose in defence. Then they saw her brilliant colour amplified by the sunlight streaming through the cave entrance, and brought their heads down in deference before returning to their resting positions.

Erun and Corella moved back out of the cave, and as he gazed around he could see the signs of disuse and neglect everywhere. There were even a couple of caves where the entrances had collapsed into nothing more than a pile of rocks. Numerous scorch marks were everywhere on the rock face, belying the enormous battles that had been fought here in the past. Scattered here and there were the skeletal remains of the dragons that had perished during that conflict. Few had been here in hundreds of years, and those that had, had touched nothing, because if they had then these remains would surely have crumbled into dust. But for all of that it was a magnificent place, and certainly a fitting gathering place for dragons.

"This must have been magnificent," he said, and then with unaccustomed determination "One day when all of this is over, we will have to come back to this place and make it live again. Meanwhile my Corella let us go home."

It seemed like only seconds after they left the realm, that they descended to land in front of the Castle to find the Mage and the Swordmaster waiting for them at the gates.

"It has begun *Sir* Erun," said the Swordmaster, allowing a little sarcasm, and amusement, to enter his voice, "A massive army has moved against Vanticor. It was so large that all of the outposts were overrun in a matter of minutes, and the garrisons at Perquet and Trelon which are just inside the border, succumbed in only a few hours. The latest news we have is that the force is moving rapidly towards the capital and the palace. I fear it may even be over by now."

"It seems that unusually there were no dragons with the invaders, and I am not quite sure why," added the Mage.

"I know," said Erun, "using dragons would have alerted Corella and any other friendly dragons. They obviously wanted this pre-emptive strike to be a secret until it was all over."

"Good point," acknowledged the Mage, "the last messenger told us that another would be despatched every six hours as long as they were able. The next should be due in about four hours."

"Then we can do nothing but wait," concluded Erun, "I must go to Lelia, she must be worried sick for her father. Corella, stay near the gate and keep watch. We cannot be too careful."

Erun found Lelia pacing up and down in her room, face deathly white and hands clenched into solid knots. As soon as she saw him she came to him and he held her close, assuring her that he had heard the news, and was hoping for the best.

Four hours later their worst fears were realised, when the news was brought that King Porden had fallen beside his soldiers in defence of the Kingdom that he loved. It was all over and Vanticor was occupied by the combined armies of the southern states. Princess Lelia was a Princess no more, but a Queen in exile. She sobbed uncontrollably for hours in Erun's arms, but he held her and sat with her long into the night until it stopped, and she drifted into sleep.

He summoned her maids, and bid them stay by her bedside until morning,

"Mind that you remember that it is a Queen that you care for now," he instructed.

Later when he rejoined the Mage and Swordmaster he asked of news of Nordlight,

"A prisoner in the dungeon of the prison compound, separated from his wife, and probably beside himself with worry. We know where he is, but we are waiting to find out where they are holding her. His execution is scheduled for the day after tomorrow."

"They could have killed him straight away," said Erun, "so they must be waiting for me to rescue him. It will be a trap of course, but who am I to deny them a little pleasure."

"You can't really mean to attempt a rescue," said Squerrel.

Erun grinned,

"Corella, you remember those two free dragons at the hold, could you persuade them to go on a little trip with us do you think, and any others that you might find on the way?"

"With pleasure," she said and launched into the sky only to vanish a second later.

"Well I never knew they could do that," commented the Mage.

Chapter Thirteen
Free Dragons

About half an hour later, Corella returned with two bronze and two green dragons who made sure that they landed far enough away from the humans to prevent panic, but inside the stake defences. Corella dropped down beside Erun.

"I found five," she said, "one has gone on to Vanticor to land amongst them, frighten the life out of them a little bit and see what she can learn. The others know what is at stake and ask only that someone care for their eggs should the unexpected happen."

"You can assure them that it will be done." said Erun, and climbing into Corella's saddle he added, "Well, there is no time like the present."

As they lifted off, the four others came up to take station a little behind and to both sides. As they were about to enter the realm, Corella explained that the others would stay with her and use her as a guide to emergence. Then Vanticor, the capital city named after the country, was below them and they were joined by a fifth and silver dragon. Linked with Corella, as he was, he found that all of their thoughts came to him.

"*Well that was fun,*" thought the silver dragon, "*can some of those humans run? You should have seen it. I got one, and shook out of him where Marta was being held. He didn't taste nice, so I am afraid that I left bits of him behind.*"

After a brief discussion, it was decided that Corella would stay back, and the other five would land in various parts of the city. There they should cause as much disruption and noise as possible, taking care to protect the local population. Corella would then pass through the realm to emerge as close as she could to the prison compound. It had been discovered that Marta was also in the Compound, but in a cell far removed from Nordlight. It didn't matter to Erun. They were in the same compound, and he would find them.

The five dragons peeled away and streaked downwards, roaring, bellowing, and coughing great gouts of fire as they went. Pandemonium ensued, with soldiers from other parts of the city rushing to the aid of their fellows. Corella waited until things began to get really interesting then shifted through the realm to appear in front to the massive oak gates of the compound.

Erun slid from her back and his sword flashed from his scabbard into his hand. It always happened that way, and never ceased to amaze him. Corella didn't wasted time on threats or requests, she just lifted from the ground rammed her massive claws into the gates and ripping them from their hinges, flung them aside. Several unarmed Vanticoran guards, acknowledged him with a smile, and stepped to one side. One came up and offered to guide him to Nordlight and Marta.

An Amtorian soldier was reduced to ash by Corella as he made to interfere, which served as warning to the rest who laid down their arms. Erun told them to gather into a group and sit down on the floor under the gaze of the Vanticorian guards who eagerly picked up the discarded weapons.

Nordlight was in a sorry state when Erun found him, obviously having been tortured, and needing Erun's help to get him outside to Corella. Erun indicated to the Vanticoran Guard that he should lead him to Marta. She was unharmed and delighted to see him, and grabbed him in a bear hug, from which it took a while to extricate himself before he led her outside into the arms of Nordlight.

Both of the bronze dragons had settled down outside the gates, volunteering to carry the two ex-captives to safety. It was only the work of a few minutes for a couple of Vanticoran guards to find some rope, and to tie them both firmly onto the dragons. Erun told the guards to head off to the border while they could, and they would surely be made welcome in Cardoney.

Remounting Corella, he saw that surprise was beginning to fade and archers were beginning to appear along the tops of most of the buildings surrounding them. The situation was becoming dangerous. He knew it was all over, when at some unknown signal a volley of arrows was unleashed towards them. There was nowhere to run and he braced himself for the inevitable. The arrows streaked towards them, only to impact on the shield that had appeared out of nowhere around all three dragons. Always the opportunist, he shouted,

"**Time to go.**" and the three dragons launched into the air, each one surrounded in a perfectly transparent bubble of protective energy.

"*Well done, Erun. Nicely timed,*" thought Corella as she led the trio away as fast as they could go. This would be several hours of flight, as she was mindful of the rules governing dragons carrying humans through the Realm, and knew that this time the bronze dragons would not have followed her.

"*What was nicely timed?*" he asked

"*Why the shield of course,*" she replied.

"*What do you mean? I didn't do that.*"

"*Yes you did,*" she thought, "*I sensed the energy flow from you.*"

He didn't reply. What was there to say? He believed her when she said it was him, but still he had no idea how he was doing it. The only explanation was that it was occurring at subconscious level. If it was needed, it happened. That was all there was to it, and having accepted that, he stopped worrying.

Almost five hours later the Castle came into sight, and they were pleased to see that both green dragons and the silver one were already there. There was limited space between the stakes and the moat, so the two green dragons lifted to join Corella in circling, as the two bronze dragons, carrying Nordlight and Marta landed. The Castle Guard quickly assessed the situation and ran forward to release them from the Vanticoran bindings. As soon as they had been helped down and moved away from the dragons' wings, they were hustled into the Castle. The two bronze dragons lifted off, to join their green colleagues.

Erun felt rather than heard their farewells as they turned majestically in the air, and headed away towards the south. Corella waited until they were safely on their way and then alighted just in front of the drawbridge.

When Erun got to his rooms, which were still Darthbold's old apartments, he found a small chest beside his bed with the words 'Thank you" in the King's hand. His hands were trembling as he opened it, then he gasped and swore as he dropped the lid on his fingers. It was full of gold and silver coins. It was not a large chest, and it may not have been a fortune to a nobleman, but to Erun it was all the wealth in the world. He reached into the chest, taking a double handful, and for the first time in his life, knew what holding money felt like.

He was admiring each silver and gold coin, turning them over and over in his hand and relishing the feel, when he heard the sound of increased activity outside in the corridor. The sound of running feet and voices raised was getting closer and he was turning towards the door, when several hands started pounding on it, and the door was unceremoniously pushed open.

"Beg pardon Sir Erun," gasped a maid, "Partonin is being attacked."

He reached for his sword, only to find that it was already buckled in place around his waist. How it had got there from the back of the chair, where he had placed it moments before, was a mystery that he had no intention of fathoming, instead he hurried past the maid and out into the corridor. The problem of finding the Swordmaster and the Mage in a place as large as the Castle was solved when they came hurrying round a corner towards him.

"You have heard?" asked the Mage.

"Only of the attack on Partonin," he replied.

"A very large force was spotted moving rapidly through the country to the west. It was moving fast and by the time we received the news it was already too late to warn Partonin. The next message we received confirmed that the enemy had entered the capitol Parton, and the King has been slain. The reports say that they had sixteen dragons with them."

"So, now we are surrounded," observed Erun.

"There is worse," added the Swordmaster,

"Queen Aspasia of Amtor, could no longer bear what was happening to her Kingdom, and has taken her own life."

"I fear that we are next," said Mage Scrivens, "and even your yellow dragon cannot stand against sixteen. I think it is only fear of her that has saved us thus far."

"How could one man have been allowed to come so far?" asked Erun.

"If it is indeed one man," commented Squerrel, "then his power beggars belief."

"I for one would not wish to stand alone against him," said Scrivens.

"We need to go on full alert," said Squerrel, "I will advise the King of the real threat that we now face," and he turned away hurrying off down the corridor towards the King's chambers.

"You need to prepare yourself and Corella," said Mage Scrivens, "There is no hope of dragon riders coming to our aid, they seem all to have gone rogue. I see no hope, no hope at all," he finished as he walked away, his shoulders slumped. Suddenly he looked very old, and completely lost.

Erun's call brought Corella swooping in with her saddle hanging from her mouth.

"I shared your thoughts," she thought, *"but we will not be as easy as they presume."*

"I have a task for you my lovely Corella," he thought.

"My lovely Corella? We are not dead yet my Erun."

Quickly he outlined what he had in mind, and she listened silently until he had finished.

"I can do that. Though with what success, I am not sure. Don't get into trouble while I am away."

Then there was that sudden flare of light in the sky and she was gone.

Erun waved over a couple of soldiers who were moving into position at the drawbridge, and asked them to take the saddle for him and put it inside the Castle for safekeeping. They agreed, and struggling between them they lifted it and carried it away. The Saddle maker, having carried it by himself, was obviously stronger made than he looked.

He was about to go and find Lelia, to bring her up to date, when she came out of the Castle buckling on a sword.

"Can you use that," he asked.

"Enough to split the gizzard of a sceptical knight," she said.

"I believe you, I believe you," he said in mock alarm as she came and kissed him.

"Where is Corella?" she asked.

"Oh she'll be back soon. She's just popped off on an errand for me."

Soldiers were streaming out of the Castle, some on horseback and some on foot, heading off in different directions to carry the alarm to the rest of the Kingdom. It would be a few days, if they were allowed them, for the whole Kingdom to come to arms, but at least the word was going out.

For the last few days dribs and drabs of men from Vanticor, who had managed to get away before the total enthrallment of the entire country, had arrived to pledge their allegiance to Cardoney. Freshly armed they were moving, with determination, into defensive positions alongside their Cardoney allies. The time that Cardoney had been given thus far, had served well in allowing her army to finish its training, and at least look professional. Whether it actually was, only time would tell.

The closest villages were being evacuated, and the occupants moved into the Castle for safety. Among them as they streamed past Erun and Lelia were his parents, who stopped to greet him with considerable enthusiasm. His mother, as mothers do, looked at Lelia with raised eyebrows then suddenly reached for her, hugged her, and whispered in her ear,

"Welcome to the family Your Majesty,"

Several dozen men with fast horses were being despatched to all the borders of the Kingdom, with orders to report back at the first sign of any hostile movement. It was all being done efficiently, but with an air of despondency. Everyone knew that soon they would be called upon to kill neighbours who had no control over what they were doing. In their minds it was tantamount to murder, but it would have to be done. There was no choice.

Erun worried that Corella had not yet

returned. He could sense that she was ok, but like his magic, he didn't really believe it. Lelia could see that he was worried, but knew that no words would help right now so she just linked her arm in his and pulled him closer.

Chapter Fourteen
The Wizard

The breathing space stretched from days into a week, then ten days and still no word from the spies that had been sent out. It was becoming more difficult all the time to keep the army on full readiness as boredom set in, and the soldiers became less alert. To boost morale, the King for the first time in a decade, strapped on his sword and joined his men in the field. He was not particularly young anymore, but he had considerable prowess with a sword, as many soldiers found out to their embarrassment.

Eleven days passed, and suddenly there was a flash against the sun and the huge wingspan of Corella appeared. She glided in towards the Castle drawbridge and the waiting Erun, and flapped her massive wings a couple of times to brake for landing.

"Success?" he asked.

"Yes," she said, "I'm sorry for being away so long, but it took longer than I thought."

"No worries," said Erun, "I knew you were ok."

"I think your spies may have been compromised, because I saw movement on the border with Vanticor. To be sure, I used the realm to check the borders with Partonin and Amtor. There is movement there also."

Erun stopped two nearby soldiers who were practicing with pikes, and despatched them off to raise the alarm and to fetch Corella's saddle. They dropped their pikes and raced away.

"I do have a surprise for you though," said Corella, and there was laughter in her voice, "look up."

Erun looked upwards to see the silver glint of a dragon descending towards them. She was slightly smaller than Corella, and the silver sheen of her body looked like burnished steel in the sunlight as she dropped down to land beside them.

"This is Glenra, she is a free dragon. She knows that our very existence is at stake here, and has volunteered to be ridden. She is frightened, but she has stomach for a fight and will serve her rider well."

"Who will ride her?" he asked.

"Why, Lelia of course, who else?"

Lelia, who had been standing to one side examining Glenra, almost fell over in shock.

"Me," she gasped, "Me ride a dragon?"

"Yes," said Corella, "The same bond that is between me and Erun will not form, because bonding takes place at a very early age and Glenra is too old. Your minds will not be as one either. But directed thoughts will get through and she will do your bidding. I thought my old training saddle might work."

The two soldiers had arrived puffing and out of breath, carrying Corella's saddle with them, but Erun gave them no respite, and despatched them to the Saddlemaker to see if he still had the old training saddle.

Archers were now forming along the walls and soldiers were moving into ranks facing the stake defences and the woods. Men were placed ready to drop the portcullis and raise the Drawbridge at the last possible moment. The Captain being the highest rank in the guard had been promoted to General, in full command of the army. He moved out with the soldiers and began barking orders to his officer subordinates. The King moved to stand by him.

A few moments later the two soldiers returned with the training saddle, and a number of pads to use if the saddle was ill fitting. They dropped them in front of Erun, raised their hands in salute, and hurried off to join their friend in line. It was odd but opportune that only two pads were needed to make the saddle comfortable on Glenra's back, and she lowered her head so that Lelia could climb up. Lelia steadied herself in the saddle and fastened the leg straps.

"Gently at first," she thought.

"If we have time," came back the smiling thought.

Sure that Lelia was firmly seated, Erun turned to fixing Corella's saddle for himself. He took extra care this time. Direction changes were going to be sudden and violent and he didn't want to be embarrassed, let alone killed, by falling off. Satisfied, he hoisted himself into the saddle, fastened the leg straps, set his bow in its quick release buckle and launched Corella into the air. Glenra was only a heartbeat behind.

At his direction Corella performed a number of different manoeuvres, some easy and some difficult, with Glenra keeping station close behind. After about fifteen minutes, he brought them both in to land. Lelia while looking a little pale was grinning broadly.

"Wow," she said, "that was brilliant."

"Glad you liked it," said Glenra, "but we have only done the baby movements."

"Sir," said a soldier, who had obviously been sent with the message, "we have reports of the enemy at about ten kilometres on each side. They have many dragons with them."

"Remember," Erun said to Lelia and the two dragons, "We may have to kill fellow riders here, who have no idea that what they are doing is wrong. It may hurt us, but do not hesitate. Unless," he added, "we can find the evil that is behind this."

They only had to wait for a little over two hours before the enemy were sighted moving out of the woods, and dragons came into sight circling behind. They did not attack straight away, but seemed to be waiting for something.

Suddenly General D'Arnot stepped forward next to the King, and drawing his sword drove it into the King's side. He flicked his hand and a raging fire leapt forward reducing the stakes in the field to glowing embers and ash. He waved his hand again and Cardoney's army were frozen in place. They still had their minds and it could be seen that they were straining to move, but they could not. The enemy moved forward.

For precious seconds Erun's mouth was open in shock, and then the two dragons leapt into the air. The rogue dragons and riders poured forward. More than sixteen of them, more like thirty Erun noted. It had been Joshua all along. No one had seen it. No one suspected. As he looked downwards he could see the Mage and the Swordmaster rushing forward, to be flicked aside and reduced to dust, as if they had no substance. The power in this wizard was incalculable.

A wash of fire came towards him from the first dragon, which his mind easily and automatically turned away, with the blast washing across an enemy approaching from his left. He watched as the stricken dragon tumbled away. He nocked an arrow, and fired as Corella tumbled sideways between two others. He was gratified to see another roll away with an arrow through its right eye. He hoped Lelia was ok, but could not see her.

"Now," came a thought from Corella, strong and clear

Out of the Dragon Realm they came, flicking into existence all around the developing battle. There were at least fifty riderless dragons in all colours, roaring their defiance and descending upon the unsuspecting enemy. Leaving them to it Erun dropped away, and headed down towards D'Arnot.

"It seems his magic does not work on dragons or for some reason on you." thought Corella, bringing him in to land no more than thirty metres from the wizard.

"**You have foiled me enough**," screamed Joshua, raising both arms in the air. Mighty bolts of crimson fire flashed out to arc upwards and then begin to curve down towards Erun. He looked up at them, and they dissolved into multicoloured raindrops which splattered across the field. From the corner of his eye he saw a free dragon rip a rider from his saddle, and drop him screaming to the ground.

D'Arnot gathered his forces, and a massive halo of light and fire appeared around him. Huge flashes hundreds of metres in length were projected outwards, and the very sky seemed to open in fury. The closest soldiers were blasted away, tumbling into the moat, with the closest to the inferno just ceasing to exist. Still the power built, growing and growing in intensity, and then suddenly it became all of the imagined fires of hell and flashed towards Erun.

His sword was in his hand, and without thought his arm outstretched and pointed it at D'Arnot. Once again Corella's colour flowed from her into the sword, and the massive energies released by the wizard merged with it rather than against it, coming together in all the furies of a solar flare. It was over in one awe-inspiring anticlimactic second. From the tip of the sword came the combined flash of power, and the wizard was reduced to a tiny wisp of smoke rising from a small pile of ash in the centre of a massive crater in the ground. Debris rained down for several seconds, but bounced harmless from the invisible shields that appeared around those closest to the blast.

Hostilities ceased in the air and on the ground almost immediately. Soldiers who had been flung into the moat came struggling and spluttering to its side, having narrowly avoided drowning. Enemy soldiers were laying down their weapons all over the field, and faces red with embarrassment were turning to start the long journey home. The dragon riders withdrew, and everyone's thoughts were full of apologies and horror at what had happened here. Sadness at the loss of friends who hadn't known what they were doing consumed them all, with many a hardened veteran dropping to his knees in grief. The free dragons slipped back into the realm and disappeared.

Lelia and the silver dragon came down to land beside Corella. Quickly Lelia jumped down and ran towards the King. He was still alive, but only just. From a wound such as this there was no hope.

He grasped Lelia's hand and that of Erun as they arrived at his side and whispered,

"Witness"

An officer came forward and knelt down beside them.

"Many years ago," the King whispered, "I was young, and tempted by a young maid. My, she was a beauty was that girl. She was married, but I was a new King, and in my arrogance I would allow no refusal. She cried all through our passion then and on the further six times that I took her. I lived with that shame all my life, but no longer..." he paused, coughing, and blood was starting to trickle from his mouth.

"She was your mother Erun, and she has lived with the secret that you are my son for all of these years. The Throne is yours my son, rule wisely," were his final words.

The news spread around the Kingdom like wildfire, and there was great sadness at the death of King Arunay, but great celebration at the knowledge of who had become heir. Erun's father had long since known who was Erun's real father, and had accepted that it had never been his wife's fault. A girl in her position could never have refused her King. It was to his great delight that he found that there was no condemnation of her amongst the general population in the Kingdom; it was more a case of growing respect and deference.

Erun moved his parents into some of the Castle's finest apartments, and provided them with all they needed and more. His mother tried in vain to stop everyone who passed her from curtsying, bowing or kissing her hand, but her protests made no difference so eventually she gave up. She was from humble beginnings, and for the rest of her life she would still be in awe of the opulent surroundings in which she now found herself.

She had her own maids now, and needed to skivvy no more. Humbly she may have started, but she had always been a lady in Erun's eyes, and very soon the rest of the Kingdom began to see her in the same way.

Only a few weeks passed before Erun's coronation. The whole affair embarrassed the hell out of him. It seemed that everyone who was anyone attended, and all bowed before him. It was also an odd affair, as Erun had insisted that it be held in the open air, so that Corella could stand beside him, and the commoners in the Kingdom could attend on the same footing as the nobility.

Glenra had impossibly formed a bond with Lelia. It had never happened in a pair so old, but they had both known it as they tried to say goodbye. Lelia had started to walk away, and then had suddenly turned and flung her arms around the dragons neck. Glenra had pushed back against her and thought,

"I am not going anywhere my Lelia."

Erun and Lelia were married six months later.

It was a grand affair as befitting a reigning monarch, and it seemed as if the whole world attended. Again the ceremony was held in the Open air, and as the Royal couple took their vows, Glenra and Corella looked on. Both dragons were sniffing and snuffling the whole time, and there were definitely tears in their eyes. Well they *were* both female, and it *was* a wedding.

With the exception of Cardoney, all of the royalty in the rest of the Kingdoms were gone thanks to D'Arnot, and a power vacuum existed in them all. There was a period of considerable confusion as they came to terms with what they had been forced to do, and then they had approached Cardoney with a proposal. So it was that all of the Kingdoms to the South, Amtor, Partonin and Vanticor merged into one, relinquished their sovereign status, and joined with Cardoney. The name chosen by popular acclaim was Cardoney, and all pledged allegiance to its new King.

Erun kept his promise and teams of men were sent to the south to bring life back into the Dragon Hold, and dragons flocked from all over the world to use it again. By Royal decree killing free dragons was outlawed on pain of death, and for the first time in many years, dragons and men found that they could live together in peace.

Erun was a fair and just King, but realising the size of his task in this expanded Kingdom, he formed a '*Council of the People*' to take over a lot of the day to day tasks of government. It was designed to give him more free time, and it worked.

Often if you look to the skies, you can get a glimpse of the brilliant yellow, and the burnished steel of the silver dragon, wheeling in perfect formation, carrying the brand new King and Queen of Cardoney.

The End

Robert A.V. Jacobs

Book Two:

The Diamond Sword of Tor

Chapter One
Missing

King Erun the first of Cardoney awoke to find that his wife was not beside him. At first he was not too worried, because she would often get up early to go flying with her silver dragon, Glenra. Ever since Glenra had agreed to carry her during the war, and they had unaccountably formed a bond, she had never been able to get enough and flew as often as she could. She did love Erun dearly, but flying with Glenra was now in her blood, and was a fact that could not be denied. So when Erun was busy with affairs of state, or early in the morning like now, she would take to the skies with her dragon.

Erun grunted, went to turn over and get some more sleep when, blearily, he realised something was not right. Impinging upon his semi-awake state was the angry bellowing of a dragon outside, and the insistent calls into his mind from Corella his soul mate and the only yellow dragon in existence.

"What ails you Corella," he asked, *"and what is all that commotion?"*

"That's Glenra. Have you not noticed that Lelia is not beside you, and yet Glenra is still here?"

Now he was awake, wide awake, and to his complete surprise dressed. It never ceased to amaze him how this always seemed to happen in times of stress. As the thought went through his mind, his sword in its scabbard lifted from the back of a chair and buckled itself around his waist. The magic was at work again and his subconscious was doing what his conscious mind had never been able to.

Thinking that he should raise the alarm his gaze flicked to the bell pull, and it started to jerk up and down causing an unholy and strident clanging from the bell in the servants' quarters. Within seconds he could hear running footsteps, and his breathless and slightly overweight Butler burst in through the door.

"The Queen is missing Albert." he said, "She hasn't gone flying because her dragon is still here, and she would not go for a walk without informing someone. Alert the Captain of the Guard and get him to organise search parties. Did no-one see her go, or be taken? See what you can find out, and get back to me as quickly as you can."

"At your command Your Majesty," said the

Butler and broke into a run from the room.

"Corella, why can't Glenra sense her?"

"She doesn't know, she is in complete distress and has no idea where to look. It is fortunate that she used to be a free dragon, or I would be afraid for her life."

"Why did you not notice where she went, or if she was taken who took her?"

"We don't know. We did see a trail of fire going away to the south, but put it down to some natural phenomenon and thought no more about it. I only mention it because it was the only odd thing that has happened."

"Well right now, I am dismissing nothing as a coincidence. I will be with you in a few minutes when all is organised here. Meanwhile, do what you can to aid Glenra."

More running feet could be heard approaching his room, but this time they stopped at the door and something heavy beat on the door before it swung open to reveal the Captain of the Guard.

"Your Majesty," said Captain Egmar.

Egmar was only a few months older than Erun and his long-time friend. He had performed valiantly and professionally during the interstate conflicts of a couple of years ago, hence his rapid promotion into the officer ranks. Of course, at such a young age, his position had a lot to do with Erun's influence, but after only a few months in the job he had shown that his appointment was not out of place. He had turned out to be an excellent Captain and soon earned the respect and admiration of his men, even those hardened veterans with longer service.

"Lelia is missing Egmar. The circumstances are unusual and I fear the worst. I can give you no information other than the fact that she is gone. Arrange for the '*Council of the People*' to be informed, and send word to Governor Nordlight in Vanticor that I have need of him."

He paused in thought for a moment.

"It might be wise if he hands over to his deputy before he leaves."

"Ok Eru...um...Your Majesty, I'll get to it."

Erun made his way through the Castle corridors until he reached the main courtyard, and then headed across the drawbridge to Corella. But before he reached her, a knarled and very elderly hand caught his sleeve and stopped him dead in his tracks. He turned towards the hand ready to strike, and was greeted by the sight of a stooped, hooded and very old woman.

"No good will come of this," her toothless mouth spat at him, "I saw a great flash of light travelling to the south. Only the devil could produce its like. There is evil at work here."

He laid his hand on her shoulder,

"I had heard of the strange light, but thank you old mother, your observation will be rewarded."

He turned away and hurried on towards Corella.

"Corella, will Glenra be able to help us given the circumstances?"

4

"If it is to help her find Lelia, then yes I'm sure she will. She is much calmer now."

"Ask her if she will carry another in this cause."

"She agrees."

"I will give her a note for Nordlight in Vanticor. She must deliver it and return with him."

The clatter of hooves on the drawbridge alerted Erun to a rider leaving the castle. His outstretched hand brought the man to a stop, reining in his horse a few feet away from his king.

"You are tasked with conveying a message to Nordlight?" he asked.

"I am, your Majesty."

"There is no need, when I have saddled the Queen's dragon, Glenra will take it in your stead."

He reached up and took the proffered parchment from the messenger, who saluted and turned his horse back towards the castle to report the change of plan to Egmar. It was only the work of a few minutes to fit Glenra with her saddle, and attach the message. Then she was airborne and within seconds had disappeared into the dragons' realm.

By now, soldiers were pouring out of the Castle with Captain Egmar in the lead, and the main alarm which had been tolling away for the last few minutes became silent. Egmar began to efficiently organise them into search teams and directed each team to cover a specific area of the countryside.

Erun felt like a spare part. He was the King and had responsibilities, so he couldn't just up and swan off whenever he felt like it. He could only wait for Nordlight. Nordlight had been heir to the throne, but had indicated his desire not to succeed before his father had died, and had accepted instead the position of Ambassador to Vanticor. King Arunay had confessed in his last moments that Erun was also his son, and had named him as his heir before witnesses.

The Interstate wars had left most countries without Heads of State, and the populations of those countries had voted to join into a single nation under the name of Cardoney, with King Erun as its head. Erun had realised that a Country as large as Cardoney had now become, could not possibly be ruled by a single man unaided. So he had formed a *'Council of the People'* to take over the day to day running of the country and decreed that each new country that joined would become a Region under a Governor appointed by the crown. Nordlight had been the first Governor that he had appointed, and that was of the newly formed Region of Vanticor.

Erun knew that he would have to wait several hours for Nordlight to arrive, because despite Glenra arriving in Vanticor almost immediately via the Dragons' Realm, she could not return the same way carrying a rider. The Dragons' Realm had been the most closely guarded secret of dragon kind for centuries. Not even riders had been told. Through it, dragons were able to cover extreme distances in a fraction of the time it would normally take, but on pain of death were forbidden to carry riders with them. That is, except for the yellow dragon, who according to legend had carried a rider and defeated all attempts to take her life for it. The rest of the dragons had eventually given up and granted her dispensation. Corella had been stunned when she found that the same dispensation was being extended to her.

Several hours later, Lelia had still not been found, and it was apparent that she was also not within five kilometres of the Castle. Erun was beginning to panic, he could not bear the thought that anything could happen to Lelia, and was becoming pretty much useless because of it. He recognised it as did everyone else, and the people around him stopped referring to him to resolve problems. They all knew their jobs and just did them, fervently hoping that they were making the right decisions.

Despite Erun's hopes, no word came from anywhere, not even a rider bearing a ransom note. He could have coped with that, and he would have readily paid any amount asked. It was the silence and the not knowing that was the most difficult to take.

He was beginning to despair, when a silver glint approaching in the sky caught his eye, and it soon resolved into Glenra who swept in to land nearby. On her back was Nordlight, pale as death and lying flat across the dragon's back clinging on for dear life.

"Hi Nord, You can open your eyes now, you are on the ground."

Nordlight opened one eye and looked around cautiously, then began to unbuckle the dozens of straps that were holding him to the saddle. As soon as the last one had been released, he slid off the dragon and hurried to Erun's side.

"Thanks Glenra," he said then turned to Erun, "don't ask me to do that again. That little trip I took from the lake on Corella a couple of years back was bad enough, but this one was in a *hurry.*"

Knowing that the situation had already been explained to Nordlight via the parchment, Erun felt that there was no need to go over it again,

"I can't function at all Nord, not with Lelia missing. I know it and so does everyone else. I can't have them losing confidence in their King so I need to appoint a Regent," he explained, "I just simply can't apply myself fully to my position. I just can't. So I'm afraid that if you agree, it has to be you."

For a second Nordlight looked thoughtful,

"I know that I certainly don't want the job permanently, but for you my friend, I'm sure I can manage it for a little while."

Erun reached out and clasped Nordlight's arm,

"Thanks, you are truly a friend when I am in need, but you can't do it alone, so what say we send Glenra back to Vanticor to fetch your wife?"

"Good idea, Marta was laughing fit to burst when she saw how terrified I was on Glenra. Let us see if *she* can survive the experience."

Glenra had calmed considerably since the morning, and her flight to Vanticor had helped to make her feel useful in the search, so for the first time that day, she spoke,

"I am on my way,"

A mighty flap of her wings and she was airborne. She banked sharply towards Vanticor and once again vanished into the Dragons' Realm.

Chapter Two
South

In Cardoney, all power resided in the King, and The *Council of the People* as created by Erun only had the task of administering that power, and of advising him where possible action or laws should be considered. It debated possible legislation, and then placed the draft laws before him for consideration, saving him a considerable amount of time in the law's detail phase. His signature however, was not a formality and he had to agree fully with the format and content of what was proposed, or it simply did not get signed and never became law. Members of the *Council* were not elected, but appointed by the King on the basis of their service to the community. He had been known to hear a middle aged housewife berating her husband so eloquently for something not done, that he did no more than summon her before him and appoint her to the *Council* Her husband could not stop laughing.

Erun had considered letting his people elect their own members of the *Council*, but in the end the logistics of actually achieving it proved insurmountable. Even with dragons, it was just not possible to carry out an election in a reasonable time scale, but he vowed that it was something that he would achieve in the long run.

So early on the day following Lelia's disappearance, he wandered into the *Council* chamber. He was pale and drawn as a result of the strain that he was feeling, and as he had not had any sleep the night before, his steps were slow and hesitant. All one hundred and forty members immediately stood, and silence fell.

"Please be seated," he said, as he stood before them. His voice a little unsteady at first, but seeing the level of support before him he brought it under control and without further preamble, continued,

"I cannot function as your head of state while the Queen is missing. My mind will always be on that, to the detriment of everything else. Therefore I have appointed a temporary Regent to operate in my stead, and that Regent will be Nordlight. There will be no watering down of his powers, and as my half brother, you will treat him exactly as you would treat me."

He paused to let the information sink in,

"Are there any questions?"

The First Minister stood and said,

"I believe that I speak for us all when I say that we wish you well in your search. If you are ever in need of our help, you only have to ask. Nordlight is a good choice, and we will treat him and his wife as the royal bloodline deserves."

The chamber broke into roars of 'hear hear', as Erun turned and walked unsteadily out.

"I presume that you are taking a guard contingent with you," continued the First Minister.

"No," replied Erun, "The distance is great and there is little time to waste. I need to travel swiftly, and soldiers would just slow me down."

"I am not happy with that, Your Majesty," said the First Minister, "danger lurks at every turn...."

"Your concern is noted," interrupted Erun, "and I thank you for it, but my dragon will protect me with her life."

"Very well, but under protest Your Majesty."

Returning to his quarters, he instructed a tearful maid to fill his two saddle bags with extra clothes, and enough preserved food for a few days. After that, he was pretty sure that provisions from his subjects would be easy to come by as soon as they recognised him. To her complete surprise, he reached out and pulled her into his arms,

"Still your tears and do your duty. I will bring your mistress back to you. Of that you have my promise. Meanwhile, you will have Marta to look after when she arrives."

For a few minutes she clung to him, and then stepped back, curtsied, and hurried off to the kitchens for his supplies.

He had several padded jackets designed to keep him warm during flight and he selected one. For a few moments he stood looking at it then he came to a decision and put it back. Reaching right to the back of his wardrobe he pulled out the first one that Lelia had ever made for him, smiled at the intricate workmanship of the rearing yellow Dragon embroidered on its back, and then put it on. As an afterthought he retrieved a small chest which was in the bottom of the wardrobe and opened it to remove a double handful of coins, which he stuffed into various pockets in his jacket. The chest had been a reward from the old King for his part in saving Nordlight from harming himself, when the prince had been depressed at his part in his brother Darthbold's death, but its contents had never been used, that is until now. Having money for greasing a few palms, was always a good idea.

Only a few minutes passed before the maid returned, laden down with small bags of provisions, and a well wrapped hunk of cheese. All of which she hurriedly packed into his saddle bags with his clothes.

"That'll do fine Katy. Look after the place while I'm gone, and pray for me if you will."

"I will your Majesty, I will."

He hoisted the bags onto his shoulder, let his glance drift around the room for a final moment, and then headed into the corridor towards the main courtyard. He was just in time to catch the second silver glint of the day over the battlements, as Glenra approached. He broke into a trot, and jogged across the drawbridge to join Nordlight who was waiting expectantly for his wife's humiliation.

"Damn!" said Nordlight, as the glint resolved itself into a silver Dragon with a young lady sitting high and proud in the saddle. She held the reins casually in one hand, and was waving to him with the other. What was worse, was that as soon as the Dragon landed, she swung her leg over and jumped down, having not even fastened the leg straps.

"Wow that was awesome," she gasped breathlessly, straightening her skirt, "thanks Glenra."

Then she turned to Erun and curtsied,

"Your Majesty," she said, "my condolences. I hope that Queen Lelia is found soon."

"Thanks Marta, but to you, I will always be Erun, and the queen will always be Lelia." said Erun, "Now go and say sorry to your husband for being braver than he was."

She turned away to Nordlight, and as she hugged him she said sweetly,

"Don't tell me you didn't like flying. Oh you poor thing. Perhaps we should go inside so that I can comfort you."

"Go ahead Nord. I am not fit company at the

moment anyway," said Erun, "I shall stay here and wait for the last of the search parties to return. If there is no news, I shall head south."

"South?" queried Nordlight.

"Corella told me of a light seen travelling south, and this was confirmed by an old woman who accosted me earlier, and also said she had seen something to the south. At least it's somewhere to start."

In a stand of trees, just over an arrow's flight from the castle, there stood an old woman. She pulled her hood closer over her head and wrapped her cloak more tightly around her sparse and stooped body, against the chill of the day. Addressing the tall man standing nearby, if it indeed was a man, she whined,

"I have passed your message such as it was to the King. I don't know if he understood, but I have done what you asked. Now give me my due. Though what an El..."

She had no time to complete her words before the man made a gesture with his hand and she exploded, leaving a cloud of smoke swirling around the place where she had been standing. In the slight breeze it rapidly dispersed, drifting away through the trees, and then there was very little left to show that the old woman had ever been there at all. It was a senseless act and certainly not the due that she had been expecting. But she had seen something that she was not supposed to see, the time for finesse had long passed, and only time for action remained.

It didn't go completely unnoticed, as any explosion releases energy and can't avoid making a noise. The sharp 'crack' alerted the guards that remained in the Castle, and they came boiling out of the Guard House, hastily donning armour and grabbing weapons as they came. A small contingent remained at the drawbridge, with the rest moving into a skirmish line and heading for the trees.

The man eased backwards into the shadow of a tree, muttered a couple of words, made a hand gesture and rapidly became transparent before disappearing completely.

Lelia was seriously peeved. It wasn't the fact that she had been spirited away from her husband that was annoying her, though that was bad enough. It was the fact that she was in her nightdress. It was short, showed far more leg than propriety demanded, and was definitely not the thing for a Queen to be seen wearing in public, particularly when said Queen was not wearing any underwear. The bed-socks were worse however. Castles are cold and draughty places at the best of times, regardless of what you try to do to them. Even roaring fires in the bedroom made little difference, hence the bed-socks.

The maid, either by sense of humour or lack of sight, had laid them out for her. It had been dark except for the light from the fire so she had not seen, as she put them on, that one was green and one was blue. So here she was in a skimpy nightdress, no underwear, and odd socks. Her captives must be... she giggled at the thought... laughing their socks off.

She had no idea how it had happened. One moment she was sleeping peacefully next to her husband and the next she had woken up here. Though where 'here' was, was anyone's guess. She seemed to be alone on a plain that stretched away, seemingly forever, in each direction. She started to wander cautiously forward and walked into a wall, banging her nose and starting a slight nose bleed. She staggered backwards, muttering an expletive that no Queen should even know, and put her hand up to her bumped nose. Not having anything to wipe away the small trickle of blood, she squeezed her nose between finger and thumb for a few seconds until it stopped bleeding, and then wiped away the trickle with her hand. Reaching out in front of her she found the wall, and very carefully felt her way along it. Counting the corners, she stopped when she had passed four, estimating that she had reached her starting point. If she was not disoriented and her hypothesis was correct, she was in a square room that was a little over four metres on a side. The room was either transparent, or someone with immense skill had painted the scenery on the walls. If it was painted, it was so expertly done that even very close examination could not determine the truth.

OK, she thought, *there is always a bright side. If I sit down, at least I have something to lean against. Now though, we have to ask why and how, but more importantly who?*

She knew that despite outward appearances, she was scared to death, but was damned if her captors would see that she was. And there had to be captors, because you don't wake up in a strange place and in a strange room, unless someone put you there. So rather than whingeing about something that was a fait accompli, a bit of bravado was called for.

"My husband *will* come for me," she said loudly, though her voice did wobble a little as she shouted, "and when he does, you won't survive the experience."

But to herself as she looked down at the nightdress, she vowed that when she got out of this predicament, she would take to wearing pyjamas in bed.

The soldiers found nothing when they reached the edge of the woods, except for an area of browned vegetation and a slight scorch mark on the ground. There was a distinct smell of burnt flesh, but as none could be found when a thorough search was carried out to one hundred metres of the scorch mark, they all returned to the castle. The Sergeant reported the findings to Erun and then, when dismissed, followed his men back into the Guard house.

In the woods the air shimmered next to a tree, and a man slowly became visible. It had been an emergency, hence the invisibility. It was not a solution that he would have chosen, had he had more time, because invisible people have invisible retinas, and therefore light passes straight through and they are blind. He was unable to see the soldiers, so it had been necessary to stand close to the tree and be very, very still. He smiled as he watched the soldiers filing back into the Guard House, and then he turned and walked purposefully away through the trees.

By now the regular search parties were starting to return, and each commander marched up to the King, saluted and gave his report. All of the reports were negative, with each specifying the area that he and his men had searched and then adding,

"I'm sorry Your Majesty, but we have found nothing."

When the last had reported to him, he sent out a thought,

"*Corella, we are going south.*"

"*Oww! Don't **do** that.*"

"*Do what?*" he asked.

"*Use your magic toput my saddle on. It hurts. Care and affection was never your magic's strongpoint...*"

"*Oops sorry,But right now, I have no idea what I am doing, or even if I am doing it.*"

With a mighty flap of her wings Corella lifted

from where she had been sitting a few hundred metres away, and swooped in to land beside him. He did a quick check of her saddle, which seemed to be quite properly rigged, and swung up into it. It was only the work of a moment to fix his leg straps, strap his bow into the quick release buckle, and tie his saddle bags, one on each side, just in front of him.

"*Lelia cannot be in this reality, or Glenra would be able to sense her. She's definitely not in the Dragons' Realm, or I would know. I feel that there is magic involved, and magic of a pretty high order. But don't worry, we will find her my Erun. You have my word on it.*" explained Corella.

"Glenra," said Erun, "you must come with us. You can sense Lelia where we cannot. But behave yourself and don't eat anyone."

"As if I would," replied an indignant Glenra.

Chapter Three
The Dragon Inn

Half an hour later the two Dragons, almost wingtip to wingtip, were in the air and heading towards Amtor which was the first Cardoney region to the south. With the equator passing through Partonin to Cardoney's north, it placed Cardoney itself into the southern hemisphere. This resulted in temperatures rapidly falling away as they moved south, so virtually as soon as they started their quest, it started to get colder. It would take them the best part of an hour and a half to get to the border with Amtor, if they kept their speed down to about forty kilometres an hour. Any faster than that and it would not be possible to see anything, in the terrain below, in time to act on it, that is of course if there was anything to act on in the first place.

For a long time they were flying over dense forest, so they could be forgiven for missing the man, sitting astride a very strange winged beast, and sheltering under a clump of trees below. His beast had sensed the two Dragons approaching, and without bidding had dropped down out of sight. It was an odd four legged creature with wings, but not a Dragon. The front half of the beast was feathered like a bird, but the rear half and tail were more in line with a lion. Its head was similar to a bird, with large hooked beak, but it had more prominent ears. Very strange it was, and at least ten metres long with wings to match.

"*Just across the border, there is a tavern that I have heard is called, 'The Dragon and Rider' we'll drop down there, so I can get a drink and ask a few questions,*" Erun thought to Corella.

"*Take care,*" said Corella, "*The fact that these places are frequented by bandits and thieves, is common knowledge.*"

"*Rubbish,*" said Erun, "*they only tell you that to frighten you and keep you out.*"

"*Well apart from the fact that I would never fit through the door, I'm a big fierce Dragon, so how could I be frightened.*"

"*Good point,*" agreed Erun, "*I will take my sword.*"

Corella spotted the tavern nestling in amongst

some trees by the side of the road just as the sky was beginning to darken towards night, and swooped down to land alongside three Dragons that were already there.

The whole day had passed, or Lelia assumed that the whole day had passed. The room was becoming darker, and it was still impossible to tell whether a darkening landscape could be seen through transparent walls, or if by clever use of magic the room itself was darkening. No one had contacted her, and despite going around the room several times she could not find anything resembling a door. In the end she had become so tired that she had curled up into a ball in the corner and gone to sleep.

She awoke suddenly, with the feeling that she had not been alone. Someone had been in the room with her, seconds before she was fully awake. The room had not changed, except that there was a pile in the corner and it was daylight again. Coming to her feet, she stretched the kinks out of herself and then walked across the room to the pile. It turned out to be a heap of clothes with a tray resting on top containing a steaming plate of ham and eggs and a large mug that smelled suspiciously like tea. *At least they are not going to allow me to starve to death*, she thought.

She was so hungry, that she decided to leave

investigating the clothes until later, and make the most of the food while it was still hot. The ham and eggs were cooked to perfection, and she made short work of them, washing them down with large slurps of seriously good tea. Moving the tray from the top of the clothes, she looked up and said,

"Thank you," to her captors, who she was convinced were watching her. She was a Queen after all and giving thanks for some decent food was not a hard thing to do.

The clothes she found to consist of a pair of pyjamas, some matching bed socks, and a couple of blankets. The pyjamas appeared to be made of quite heavy material, but soft to the touch. She quickly pulled on the bottoms, then by some pretty clever contortions managed to put on the top and take off her nightdress without revealing any skin. Next came the bed socks, and then she spread out one of the blankets to sit on. So, in addition to not letting her starve to death, apparently they didn't want her to freeze to death either.

"Just so you know," she said to the air, "there are also other things a lady, and most men I presume, have to do when they wake up."

She didn't expect a response, so was quite surprised when one corner of the room shimmered and a door appeared. She got to her feet, walked across the room, opened it, and found a jug of hot water sitting in a basin, but what surprised her most was to see one of the new flushing toilets. She had only ever seen one before, and that was in the Castle in Cardoney. It had been an experimental model, developed by the King's plumber, and most of the time it worked pretty well. This one however, looked to be far more advanced than the crude one that the plumber had built. She would have to remember to tell him about the wooden seat that this one had. Nice touch that, made for an altogether warmer experience.

She came out of the room feeling much more comfortable, and then realised that the other thing that the door had shown her was the fact that the walls of the room actually were painted. Or so she thought, right up until the moment that this fact was thrown into doubt, when a large rectangle on one wall went blank, and words started to appear on it,

> *"Promise to return the Diamond Sword of Tor and we will let you go."*

The setting sun glinted off Corella emphasising her colour, and the three Dragons moved back with bowed heads in respect and recognition, though they did manage a few aggressive hisses as Glenra settled down beside her.

Erun slid from her back, settled his sword more comfortably at his side, and headed for the Entrance. Turning back to Corella, he pointed to the sign,

"Almost right," he said, "not 'The Dragon and Rider', just 'The Dragon Inn'."

He pushed open the door and entered into hell, or so it seemed. Erun had never been in an inn before so he was unprepared for the crowd, or the noise. The noise stopped however, as soon as he came through the door. A *very* large man, with a very large axe in his belt, which had a wicked looking spike on the top of the handle, staggered forward and placed a hand on Erun's chest.

"Hold," he bellowed, almost anaesthetising Erun with his breath, "we do not allow children in here, even if they are wearing daddy's sword."

"I am no child," said Erun, "remove your hand or though it would pain me because you are drunk, my sword will remove it for you."

The large man did remove his hand, but only to hold his stomach as he doubled over in mirth,

"My, we have a feisty one here for sure."

One man of a group of three hooded men sitting at a table each cradling a large tankard, looked up and spoke,

"Take care Cargan," he said, "You are addressing the King, who also happens to be the rider of the yellow Dragon, and I hear, an expert swordsman."

"Ha! Kaylo, what would you know?" and with a single movement almost too fast to follow, his axe was in his hand. He never completed his intention though, and the axe fell from his fingers as the point of Erun's sword touched his throat. He had no idea where it had come from or how it had managed to be where it was. But it was there and it looked very sharp, so drunk or sober, his survival instinct had taken over and he had dropped the axe on the floor.

"I should kill you now Cargan," said Erun, "but I have seen few men who could wield an axe with such skill. So go to the door, and you will see five Dragons. If you see what I expect you to see, then you will return with your apologies."

Cargan staggered out of the door, to return almost immediately, his face as white as the froth on a tankard of beer. He dropped to his knees in front of Erun, bent his head and muttered,

"I beg your Majesty's forgiveness. I am just a drunken fool."

"You are no one's fool Cargan. Pick up your axe and with the permission of Kaylo and his companions perhaps we can join them," he turned towards the bar, "five tankards to this table if you please innkeeper."

"It would be an honour Your Majesty," said the man Cargan had called Kaylo, and shuffled the chairs around to make room.

"My name is Erun,"

"Of course it is Your Majesty," said Kaylo, "and may hell take my soul the day that I use it."

"You three are Dragon riders?" asked Erun, accepting a tankard from the innkeeper, who had appeared at their table.

"We are," they chorused as they each received a tankard.

Erun reached into his tunic and held out some silver coins to the innkeeper, which were refused.

"I accept no payment from my King," he said.

Erun reached back into his tunic and retrieved a handful of gold coins, and leaned across to place them on the next table.

"I see that someone has left some gold on yon table," he said, "perhaps you can retrieve it and buy drinks for the house to celebrate your good fortune."

The innkeeper scooped the coins into his hand,

"I will indeed," he said, "it was most observant of your majesty to spot them before the many thieves in this place could spirit them away."

"I fear that our good Cargan, may not be conscious long enough to hear the reason that I have come to this place," Erun observed, as Cargan's eyes started to glaze over and he lost the battle to remain awake, slowly toppling forward until his head was stopped by the surface of the table.

The three Dragon riders pushed back their hoods, and introduced themselves:

"I am Kaylo of Pintor."

"My name is Panri of Pintor."

"And I am plain old Johan of Pintor."

All three were clean shaven, and handsome in a rugged outdoorsy way. If Erun had not known otherwise, he could have mistaken them for brothers. He could tell that, even though they were sitting at the moment, when standing they would all be somewhat taller than him, though still nowhere

28

near as large as the massive Cargan.

"Have you heard of Solon of Pintor," he asked softly, as he remembered his friend and teacher who had met his death, together with his Dragon Bethny, during the interstate wars.

"I believe that everyone in Pintor has heard of him and his exploits," said Panri," he was a friend and will be sadly missed."

He raised his tankard as did the other three,

"To Solon," they said together, and the tankards were downed as one.

Chapter Four.
Messages

"I am far from my best at the moment, so let me get to the purpose of my visit here," said Erun, "The Queen has disappeared, kidnapped I believe, in mysterious circumstances. I awoke last morn to find her gone. I am so afraid for her, that I can't concentrate on anything other than finding her. No-one in the Castle saw or heard anything and her Dragon Glenra, who is outside, cannot sense her either. My Dragon witnessed a strange light travelling south and this was confirmed by an old lady who accosted me. It's a slim chance, but it is all I have, so here I am."

The three riders stared at him, the sombre expressions on their faces from the toast to Solon, giving way to puzzlement at first, and then to firm resolve.

"I believe that I speak for all, when I say that with your Majesty's permission we would be honoured to aid you in your search," declared Kaylo.

"Aye that we will," affirmed Panri, "and I warrant that yon mountain of a man will want to come too when he sobers up,"

As he spoke, he gave Cargan a mighty poke in the ribs, eliciting no more than a bemused grunt.

"I accept your offer with grateful thanks," said Erun, "but the hour is late and nothing will be gained by leaving now. If one of you could impose upon the innkeeper for rooms, we can leave at first light."

"I can do that your Majesty," said Johan, "but the rooms here have poor reputation, not at all what you are used to. My feeling is that the night sky may be a more fitting ceiling for a King."

"Before King Arunay admitted his union with my mother, she was a castle skivvy and my father a stable man. Our quarters were poor, as was my clothing. I doubt anything here will be too lowly for my taste."

"I had heard a rumour to this effect," said Kaylo, "but I never believed it until now. Sort the rooms Johan, and then let us get Cargan to a bed before he becomes permanently attached to this table. Then let us all get some sleep, or at least as much as we are able to in this place."

Tor? Never heard of the place, thought Lelia as she stared at the words on the wall*, and as for a diamond sword, it's either very small, or someone has found the biggest diamond that I haven't heard of either.*

The words rippled, and wiped from one end to the other,faded from the wall, only to be replaced by new ones which flowed along as if they were being written one letter at a time,

> *"The how or the why is not your concern, return the sword or suffer the consequences."*

"Ah," thought Lelia, *"so you read my thoughts. Probe deeper and you will see the truth of it. I know of no sword, other than my own."*

Again the words changed,

> *"We cannot probe so deeply, so the knowledge could be easily hidden. We do not believe you."*

"Where is Tor?" Lelia asked, hoping to learn something useful.

"It is where you are."

"Who are you?"

"Your captors."

At this point, Lelia realised that she was wasting her time as they were obviously not going to supply her with any information at all. So she tried another tactic,

"My Dragon Glenra will find me, and she will lead my husband here. I do not believe that he will be happy with you."

"Your Dragon cannot sense you here."

"Erun will find a way,"

"That is impossible, and even if he does he cannot stand against us."

"Don't bet on it, you obviously make mistakes."

"We have made no mistakes."

"So it must have been someone else who lost a sword then?"

There was no reply, and the words were

wiped from the wall.

Lelia sat back down on the pile of blankets and leaned against the wall. She let her mind drift into the place that Erun had shown her, and brick by brick began to erect a wall. It was only symbolic, but she had found it to be the only way that she was able to erect an effective mind block. She was not a Mage, and never would be, but this had turned out to be something that she could learn. Her captors were not going to have the pleasure of little peeks into *her* mind any longer, if she could prevent it.

> *"Quite an effective mind block Lelia, Queen of Cardoney. Unexpectedly, you have managed to surprise us."*

Erun looked around the room. Johan had been right. The room was complete rubbish. Paint was peeling from the walls and spots of damp and mould were everywhere. The bed cover was patched and stained, and one leg of the bed stood on several flat pieces of wood. A very rickety night stand stood to one side, holding a cracked bowl and jug, and a mirror hung above it, tilted and cracked diagonally along its length. The floor covering was unspeakable, but at an unconscious gesture from his right hand, it rippled and became clean and damage free. A second gesture, and the window opened and a succession of bugs began to appear from every nook and cranny and start to march to the window and out through it.

At least I will survive the night bite free, he thought. *Once I've found Lelia, I must do something about this...Perhaps a law setting minimum standards for rented rooms would do.*

He stripped down to his underwear and climbed onto a bed that had somehow become a four poster with some really opulent bed linen, wriggled down under a sheet, and was sound asleep within seconds.

He was awoken the following morning by an insistent banging on his door, and the sound of Kaylo's voice,

"Your Majesty! Your Majesty!"

The door opened a few inches to his grunted "Come in", and Kaylo poked his head through the gap.

"Wow," he said as he looked inside, "we managed to get rid of the bugs, but it seems your magic is just a tad more powerful than ours."

"And good morning to you too Kaylo," replied Erun, "first light I presume."

"No, it's a little earlier than that because I thought we'd get some food inside us before we left," explained Kaylo, "and by the way Cargan has asked if he can come with us. I did explain that we will be riding Dragons, but he rightly said that there is a spare one out there and riding it can't be much different to riding a horse."

"Seems logical, but I will have to ask Glenra. She is the queen's Dragon after all, and whether she would be willing to carry such a monster of a man could be a problem."

"*Corella,*" he thought, "*ask Glenra for me.*"

"*Already have. She agrees, but does point out that he may find the Queen's saddle a little uncomfortable.*"

"Give me five minutes, and I will be down," he said to Kaylo, "and you can tell Cargan that Glenra agrees, but he may find that his enormous backside overlaps the saddle in quite a few places."

"Will do," said Kaylo, and Erun could hear him chuckling as he went down the stairs.

As Erun slid out from under the sheets, he noticed the words on his mirror,

"Return the Diamond Sword of Tor."

What? He thought, but then the words faded and were gone. Deciding it was someone's joke he carried on dressing and put it from his mind. Five minutes later almost to the second, he joined the three Dragon riders and a hugely embarrassed Cargan at a large wooden table which was laden down with plates of sliced bacon, bread, eggs and a massive stack of pancakes. The five ravenous men made short work of the food, and as he washed down the last morsels with a mug of hot sweet tea,

Erun beckoned the landlord to the table,

"I tell you this, because your food is seriously good, but the same observation I cannot make of your accommodations. I intend to make laws compelling minimum standards for rooms put up for rent in establishments such as yours, and I also intend that Dragon riders be asked to police those standards. It may be a number of weeks before I can return and put this in motion. So I am pre-warning you and hope that you make the necessary changes before the laws come into force,"

The landlord inclined his head to Erun,

"Thank you Your Majesty. You have embarrassed me, and I will endeavour to make this place into an example to judge others by."

"I could not ask for more," said Erun, looking round the table at the agreement of his companions.

The five made their way outside to the Dragons, to be met by a protest from Glenra,

"You did not tell me that this man was bigger than me. I will never get off the ground. Perhaps it will be better if I flame him and carry his shrivelled corpse."

"Behave Glenra. He is not much larger than me, and you have a twenty metre wingspan."

"I was just kidding. Come Cargan, mount up and we will get to know one another."

Cargan moved forward without fear, and placed his hand on Glenra's muzzle,

"I like this Dragon," then to Glenra, "I have no fear of you Glenra, you would give all to have your mistress back again."

"And strangely, I sense that you would also," said Glenra, pushing her head into his hand, "Give your instructions firmly in a loud voice, because the wind makes a lot of noise as it rushes past my wings. Also I cannot read your mind as I would with Lelia."

As he swung up into Glenra's saddle, Cargan grinned and said,

"You are right your Majesty, my enormous backside does overlap in several embarrassing places. But I'll live."

Corella leapt from the ground, closely followed by the other four Dragons.

Chapter Five
Followed

The five Dragons wheeled in perfect formation towards the south and across Amtor, heading towards Pintor. Before Pintor would come the Dragon Hold, which by royal decree, was not part of either country, but a place of safety for all Dragons whether they be free or ridden. Amtor covered a considerable area, and it would take most of the day to cross it, and even longer if rest stops were to be allowed for. The plan was to stop for an hour or so mid Amtor, to allow the Dragons time to hunt and provide a short respite for their riders, then to move onwards and spend the night at the Dragon Hold.

Erun was becoming more and more worried as time went on. No word of Lelia had been heard at the 'Dragon Inn', and if truth be known he was terrified, but by steely resolve he managed to keep this from his companions. He was convinced, that through his magic he would know if anything serious was to befall her, but even being convinced of this did not alleviate the worry that he felt. As more time with no news passed, there was a dark place growing in his soul that did not bode well for her captors if he should ever find them.

On they flew, the countryside flowing rapidly past and blurring into a featureless green and brown expanse, with no detail visible for long enough to be focussed on. It was a disorienting experience, making them quite light headed and a little dizzy. So much so, that after a while they stopped looking. The first few minutes soon became hours, stomachs started to protest, and the call of nature became more of a clarion call. Finally, thinking he would not be able to hold on for another minute, Erun signalled the others to find a suitable place for them to land without scaring too many locals to death. For normal folk, one Dragon could be scary enough, but five landing at once would be far too much for most of them, so while he needed to be near people to question them, he didn't want to be so close that they all ran away screaming.

It was not long before they spotted a small village nestling in a large clearing in the forest which covered most of Amtor. Not far away, another small clearing could be seen and they dropped down to land, as a group, inside it. They all dismounted and started to remove the saddles from their Dragons. For most of them this was an easy and routine task, but Cargan found it difficult because by this time he was extremely bow-legged and obviously very sore in embarrassing places. But he made no complaint, just gritted his teeth and carried on with dogged determination. Erun had his saddle off in record time and ran for the woods, followed closely by the others. They all emerged from the trees a couple of minutes later, with intense looks of relief on their faces.

As the five Dragons, no longer restrained by saddles, leapt into the air before separating and flying off in different directions to hunt, Kaylo started to gather wood for a fire and was soon joined in this task by the others,

"Not you Your Majesty," he said as Erun made to gather some wood, "I will not have my King gathering wood for *me.*"

"That's daft Kaylo," said Erun, "but if it makes you happy, I will stay here and start the fire with what we have so far. I will hear no more of you expecting me to be useless."

He piled the sticks into a heap then stared at them for a few seconds, wishing fervently for a flame, any flame, just a little flame. *Don't embarrass me now*, he thought, *just a little smoke*, and was finally rewarded by a coil of smoke coming from the pile before it burst into flames. Even though he was hoping for it, it startled him because he had never managed it before, not even a smoulder, no matter how hard he had concentrated. It must have been that he was daydreaming as he stared at the pile, and his subconscious had stepped in without him realising it. Or perhaps it was his anxiety about Lelia that was giving his magic a boost. Whatever it was, one day he would have to try it again and see if he could repeat the process. *Unlikely to work*, he thought, *but worth a try, and at least right now we have a fire*. He was just reaching for his bow with the intention of trying to bag a couple of rabbits for their meal when Cargan disappeared into the trees. A brief crashing sound was heard and he re-emerged carrying two rabbits by their ears,

"At least we will have meat," Cargan said, grinning.

Panri took over the task of skinning and cleaning the rabbits, which he accomplished expertly and in record time, and both of them were soon roasting over the fire. Erun brought bread and the hunk of cheese that Katy had wrapped from his saddlebags, and laid them on a cloth a little away from the fire.

A kilometre behind them a strange creature and its rider remained unnoticed, and landed silently amongst the trees. Careful the rider might have been, but he must have been overcome by a lapse of concentration when he gathered a pile of sticks, muttered a few words, waved a hand and the pile burst into flames.

*"*I suspect we may have been followed,*"* said Johan, pointing to the wisp of smoke that was rising above the trees to their rear.

"You four have done the bulk of the work gathering the wood and the meat," said Erun, "I will slip back and find out if we are indeed being followed or is coincidence at work here."

He held his hand up as Kaylo was about to protest,

"I will not engage in any hostilities, I will come back and report."

"Very well Your Majesty, but take care,"

Erun checked his sword and bow, and moved away purposely through the trees. When he had disappeared, Kaylo rose to his feet,

"He is my King, and I feel responsible. I'll make sure he comes back safely."

Cargan held up his hand,

"No you stay here, I will go. You know that I am better in the woods than you are. He would hear you a kilometre away."

"Thank you Cargan, but keep out of sight."

He felt a lot better as he watched the back of Cargan disappearing in pursuit of Erun.

Erun moved through the trees silently, going round patches of undergrowth where he could and easing himself carefully through where he couldn't. He had spent most of his waking hours in the forests when he was younger, and had learnt to be able to move through dense undergrowth with virtually no sound. All that he had learnt then was coming back to him and he was putting those lessons to good use now. He didn't need to know in which direction he had to travel as he was guided quite adequately by the smell of wood-smoke. A couple of times he froze in place at a slight noise and listened carefully before moving on again. Eventually coming to a gap in the trees through which he could see the flames flickering from the fire. Nocking an arrow to his bow he started to move forward, but came to an abrupt halt as he spotted the beast. He had never seen anything like it anywhere, *except in a book*, he suddenly remembered. The book had been on fables and fairy tales and he had been very young, so young in fact, that it had been his mother who had read it to him. He let his thoughts wander back and then the memory, aided no doubt by his magic, flooded into his mind. It was a Griffin. He remembered being frightened as his mother read to him, and she had hastily explained that there were some who actually believed that they had existed long ago, but even if they had, they were certainly extinct now. And here he was looking at a real live and very much not extinct one and for a brief moment the fear from long ago washed over him. But now he was much older, and he realised it was only an animal, a strange animal, but an animal nevertheless. Ok so it was as big as a Dragon, but he convinced himself that it was not arrow proof, and felt much better.

The grass rustled and the giant form of Cargan slipped down beside him. *Surprisingly quiet for a man of his size*, thought Erun, who had nearly had a heart attack when he appeared, but had managed to somehow suppress any visible reaction. He turned to him and raised a finger to his lips, but he still heard the sharp intake of breath as Cargan also spotted the Griffin. Then Cargan pointed, and following his pointed finger, Erun saw a man coming back out of the trees carrying an armful of firewood. The man was almost as much of a shock as the Griffin was, from his long thin face to his pointed ears. It was an Elf, and Erun's books had said that Elves had definitely never existed, and were only the figment of adultsimagination to entertain children. Well he wasn't a child anymore, but he was certainly being entertained. He laid a hand on Cargan's arm and pointed back the way that they had come.

A few minutes later, when they were well out

of earshot of the mythical pair, Erun turned to Cargan and not wanting to appear amateurish blatantly lied to him,

"I knew you were behind me. I always know when I am being followed. It's something to do with dragons and magic I think. I'm glad though because if there were to be trouble, there is no man other than you that I would want watching my back. Mind you, if I told them about this without someone to vouch for it,"and he grinned, "they would think I was still drunk."

"I remember reading Elf stories when I was only a child," said Cargan, "I cannot remember the author's name, but I do remember that there was a lot of amusement at the fact that he insisted that his stories were real. Most people thought it was just publicity. They came from Tor he said...."

"What!" exclaimed Erun, interrupting him, "where did you say?"

"Where what?" asked a bemused Cargan,

"Where the Elves were supposed to have come from?"

"Oh that. They come from Tor the author said. Why? Does it mean something to you?"

"It might," said Erun mysteriously, "I'll explain when we get back to the others."

When they arrived back in the clearing, he brought the others up to date with what they had seen. They were not as disbelieving as he had thought they would be, but that was probably because Cargan backed up everything he said. As he accepted a large chunk of rabbit proffered by Panri, he continued with,

"But that's not all," and went on to explain about the message on his mirror at 'The Dragon Inn' and the chance remark that Cargan had made about the Elves.

"So it would seem," said Kaylo thoughtfully, "that the missing Queen, together with Elves, Griffins and diamond swords could be all part of the same puzzle."

"My thoughts also," said Johan, "I remember not being able to get enough of those Elf stories when I was a child too. About six or seven I was then, and I do believe that one of them was about a fabled Diamond Sword. If I remember the right of it, it was one of my favourites."

"Yes, it was mine too. The memory of those books is becoming fresh in my mind again." added Panri, "What is more important, is that I remember a map in one of the books which I believe showed where Tor is."

"We need to find some Children's books then," offered Kaylo, "Let me pop into the village after we've eaten and see what I can find. I'm sure that the villagers won't see me on my own as any threat, and be more likely to talk to me."

The sky above them darkened as the wings of the returning Dragons shut out the sun, and one after the other they swooped in to land.

"*Slight change of plan Corella,*" thought Erun, "*we may be here a little longer than we thought.*"

"*Yes I know. Remember your thoughts are*

mine." replied Corella, *"Not to worry though, we found some rather delicious wild boar only a couple of minutes away, so we won't go hungry."*

Kaylo was away somewhat longer than expected, and Erun and the others had just started to make plans to go and rescue him, when he came trotting breathlessly into the clearing.

"We were about to look for you," commented Panri.

"They were a lot more hospitable than I thought," replied Kaylo, tilting a little as he sat down by the fire. He had a couple of books in his hand, which he handed across to Erun.

"Eventually, after consuming copious quantities of beer so as not to offend, I found this young man who had this couple of books from his younger days. He must have seen how much I wanted them, and haggled far beyond his years. Cost me four gold pieces, which is about ten times what they are worth. And what's more, I only escaped from the clutches of two very buxom young ladies, by the skin of my teeth."

"Well we have decided to stay here for the rest of the day," explained Erun, "so you can always pop back if you feel the need,"

"You have to be joking," said Kaylo, hastily "the attentions of that pair would most likely kill me."

Erun opened the first of the books, and as luck would have it there was the map covering a two page spread at the beginning. He laid the book on the ground and the others gathered around.

"It's there." he said, pointing, "Somewhere to the far south beyond Pintor. From what we have learnt so far, we have to give credence to the author's claim that the place is real. So that's where we start for in the morning."

"That far south looks pretty cold, are we equipped for it?" asked Johan.

"*We* can take very low temperatures," said Corella aloud.

"But we can't." observed Erun, "I vote we give Cargan some money and send him back into the village to get what we need. At least he is more likely than Kaylo to survive the attentions of the two buxom young ladies. In fact, I suspect that he would be more likely to kill them than the other way round."

"We definitely agree on that," chorused Kaylo, Panri and Johan.

Erun reached into his pocket and took out several gold coins which he passed to Cargan,

"I'm sure you know what we need,"

"I do," said Cargan, "I will not be long, notwithstanding the attentions of buxom young ladies of course."

Chapter Six
The Diamond Sword

Cargan didn't return until several hours later, laden down with some large bundles over his shoulder and a silly grin etched on his face.

"Everything we need is in the bundles. I met your young ladies Kaylo, and it happens that they seemed to like me as well, because they brought a couple of friends. They looked after me very well for a couple of hours but then, apparently, they all had to go to sleep. Can't understand it, I don't feel tired at all."

Kaylo's eyes widened at the thought of four young ladies, and silently thanked the lord for his narrow escape.

"I managed to get five heavy jackets that are wool lined, and pants to match. I only had my own hands to judge the gloves by, so they may be a little too big, but I'm sure we'll manage. I also got some fleece lined hats with ear flaps."

"Well seeing as you don't feel tired at all, you can take the first watch," said Kaylo, "wake me in a couple of hours. Then with your permission Your Majesty, as much as it goes against my better instincts, I will wake you to take over from me. I take your point about you not wanting to be useless, but you may have to remind me from time to time. It should be about dawn by the end of your watch, so Panri and Johan can be first at our next stop."

There were mumbles of agreement from around the fire, and then the group started ransacking Cargan's bundles and selecting clothes for themselves. After retrieving some that looked about his size, Erun banked up the fire and then spread a blanket from his pack by his saddle. The jacket, he slipped on as a guard against the night cold, but his saddle was far too big and rigid to act as a pillow, so he rolled up the pants to use instead. Cargan put on his own jacket and moved to the edge of the clearing where he sat down with his back to a tree to commence his watch, his axe ready across his knees. Everyone else had followed Erun's example and soon a variety of snores could be heard joining in with the night life of the forest.

It only seemed like a few minutes had passed, before Erun was awoken by a gentle shake of his shoulder,

"It's time Your Majesty," said Kaylo.

Erun scrambled to his feet, and smiled at Kaylo's surprised look when his sword lifted itself and buckled around his waist,

"I've never seen that before, you will have to teach me."

"I wish I could," whispered Erun, careful not to disturb his companions, "It's taken to doing that every time I get up, No input from me at all, it just happens. An old Mage once told me that apparently it's my subconscious at work, because I have no conscious control over my magic at all."

"What about when you lit the fire?"

"That was hope and wishful thinking. I was just staring at it and wishing like mad. Let me tell you I was quite surprised when it actually lit. Anyway, to bed with you, I have a guard to perform."

Erun settled himself down next to the same tree that Cargan had used and let his mind become one with the noises of the forest. Soon, he was so aware of the natural sounds around him that anything unusual would alert him instantly. So, it came as a bit of a shock to him about half an hour into his watch when, without warning, his sword leapt into his hand. He had heard nothing unusual at all. He came to his feet to find that he was crossing swords with the Elf. To say that the Elf was equally startled would be an understatement. He had seen what he thought was a sleeping man, only to find the man standing at the ready in front of him before he could blink. He was so surprised, that he narrowly avoided dropped his own weapon.

"*Calmyourself Corella, it's alright,*" thought Erun, as he felt her coming to her feet.

"I have no wish to harm you Elf," he said aloud, "In any case you are only in story books and my imagination. Perhaps in reality I am still asleep and dreaming"

"My sword will show you how real I am," snarled the Elf, coming to full readiness.

"May I know why," said Erun quietly, "or must the knowledge die with you?"

"The Diamond Sword of Tor has been lost for several years. We suspected that it was taken by a Dragon slayer, and that it is now in your hands. We want it returned, or you will never see your Queen again."

Erun saw that his companions were now awake, and on their feet with weapons in their hands. He signalled to them to stay their hands, and lowered his own sword,

"This is the only blade that I have. You are welcome to examine it."

"It is indeed the Diamond Sword, I recognise it in that form. Give it to me and I will prove my words."

Erun flipped the sword and handed it hilt first to the Elf, who took it eagerly. He raised it above his head and shouted,

"*Diamond.*"

Nothing happened, except that the light from the fire rippled along the burnished steel of the blade. The Elf looked at the sword in surprise, and then shouted again,

"*Diamond, I command you*."

Still nothing happened,

"I cannot understand this. There is no doubting that this really is the sword, as I said, I recognise it. What has happened? What have you done?"

"Nothing," said Erun, "I first laid eyes on it when I pulled it from a dying Dragon. You are truly mistaken, and I would now like my sword back if you please."

"I have the sword now, and there will be no returning it."

As the Elf spoke the words, the light from the fire reflected in the sword suddenly flared to blinding intensity. His eyes widened in horror as the blinding light enveloped his whole body, and he was thrown back against the tree. The sword was once again in Erun's hand.

The Elf gasped and staggered to his feet,

"This is impossible. No one can master the sword but us. For this you will die,"

He made a peculiar movement with his hand, but Erun was no helpless old woman in the woods, he was a King and protected in ways that even he did not understand. Once more the sword flared to brilliance, and the Elf exploded, to leave nothing in his place but a tiny wisp of smoke that soon dispersed through the trees.

"When you travel with a King, you do see the most amazing things," commented Cargan.

"Bit of overkill really," said Kaylo, "It would

have been really nice to tie him down and slice bits off of him until he told us where the Queen was."

"Sometimes," said Panri, "the way Kaylo's mind works is really worrying, don't you think so Johan."

"Maybe, but in this case I have to agree with him. If I'd had any say, he would have just been disabled," interrupted Erun.

"So now we know why, approximately where, and who is responsible. All we have to do now is find her," said Kaylo.

"There are still at least two hours left until daylight, so I don't know about the rest of you but I am getting some more sleep." declared Cargan.

Erun settled back into his watch position, and as soon as he was sure that they were all asleep, he drew his sword and placed it across his knees. For a long time he sat staring at it. Could it really be the diamond sword? Was such a thing possible? The story of the Dragon slayer stealing the sword certainly tied in with his experience in its recovery. But he was still not sure. So not believing anything was going to happen at all, he whispered,

"Diamond."

He watched in fascination as the blade rippled, and once again the fire light was reflected, but this time it was reflected in the facets of a razor sharp diamond blade. In its present state, it was probably worth more than all of the regions in his kingdom combined. It was an absolutely magnificent piece of work. Though how it could possibly have been made, he had no idea, particularly since he knew of no Journeyman jeweller or Master for that matter capable of such work. The entire blade seemed to be a single piece of diamond, set into another diamond of slightly different colour to form a grip. The Pommel at the end of it consisted of a single large yellow diamond. The Quillon, or cross guard, was a blue diamond, which was slightly curved towards the blade. The whole thing looked carved, rather than cut in the way that diamonds usually are. It was exquisite. Why had it not changed for the Elf, when Elves were obviously its rightful owners? Why had it returned itself to him and protected him from the Elf's magic? These were just two of the many questions that were boiling around in his mind. For the time being, he intended to keep the fact that this really was the Diamond Sword to himself. So he took one last look and whispered...

He did not notice that Kaylo had his head slightly turned towards him and that one eye was open. Kaylo had seen, and could not believe the magnificence of the Diamond sword in Erun's hand. For several moments he was lost in the glory of the vision. It was worth a King's ransom, and any man that possessed it would be the richest in Cardoney, if not the entire world. If it was his, he would want for nothing ever again, and at the very least he would be able to stop flitting around on this silly dragon.

"It is not yours to covet," whispered Fayna's thoughts into his mind, *"you are here to protect your King...and if I'm silly, then what are you?"*

"I'm sorry, of course you are not silly. I was

just tempted for a moment. It meant nothing," he replied, clamping down on the thoughts that gave the lie to his words.

"Let us hope so."

"... *Steel*," he heard Erun say softly, and then watched in fascination as the sword became ordinary again.

This time Erun kept the steel sword in his hand and settled down to become one with the forest again. The rest of the night went without incident except that for a moment the silvery moonlight was dimmed by a large dark shape that flew overhead, heading south. Startled, he could just make out that it was the Griffin. *Probably sensed that it's master is gone and is now heading home*, he thought.

As the sun started to rise, he got silently to his feet and made up the fire, before fetching bacon and eggs from his pack. Never having gone off on adventures such as this before, Erun and his maid, had forgotten to put a pan in his pack to cook his food in, so he quietly filched one from Johan's pack and soon bacon was sizzling in it over the red hot coals.

"I smell bacon," exclaimed Cargan sitting upright.

Another pan appeared from someone else's pack, and the eggs were broken into it as soon as it looked hot enough. They all gathered close around the fire against the morning chill and helped themselves to eggs and bacon. Johan came up with a chunk of bread and split it up amongst the five and they settled down to enjoy their breakfast.

The Dragons seemed to be like minded, and lifted off to go hunting for some more wild boar. The variety of colours was spectacular as they turned away towards the north. Kaylo's Dragon, Fayna, was a classic gold, which unfortunately faded against the glare of Corella's brilliant yellow. Both Panri and Johan's Dragons were both green, with Panri's called Clara and Johan's called Dorna. Glenra of course was silver. They would be away for the better part of an hour, so the friends could look forward to a leisurely breakfast, and at least several mugs of tea.

"I saw the Griffin making its way home during the night. Well I presume it was going home," he told them as they munched on their bacon, "so I don't think we'll have any surprise on our side anymore."

"Well if there was any surprise in the first place," commented Panri, "Elves and magic are pretty closely linked, so he must have been keeping them informed, wouldn't you think?"

"I think you're right," replied Johan, "no point in worrying though. We aren't stopping, so we'll just have to be more careful."

An hour later, Dragons saddled, supplies packed away and the fire thoroughly dowsed with water from a nearby stream, they mounted up ready to continue south.

"We should reach the Dragon Hold by about midday, and then it will be about half a day crossing Pintor," said Kaylo.

"I hadn't realised Pintor was so much smaller

than Amtor," said Erun.

"It's not actually," explained Johan, "it's just not as deep... much wider though. It stretches across the southern part of Vanticor, and a fair bit into the wastelands to the west."

"Right Corella, lead the way," said Erun.

Chapter Seven
Dragon Hold

"Linten's Griffin has returned, but without Linten," the Elf said to the human who was standing next to him.

"I thought he was your best," the human replied.

"He was," said the Elf, "but it seems we may have underestimated this King Erun of Cardoney."

"And the sword is the *only* way that we can open a portal, are you sure?"

"I am sure."

"Then do as you said you would. Do not make the mistake of underestimating us."

The Elf's face took on an ashen look, and his

words faltered,

"... How could I make that mistake... when you keep... reminding me?"

The human turned and walked away towards a small peculiarly shaped building, about fifty metres away. After he had entered it, the Elf watched in fascination as the building suddenly left the ground and streaked away towards the south. He shaded his eyes against the bright light at the rear of the building, and wondered at the power of magic that could achieve this. He knew that such awesome power could never be his nor could it ever belong to Elf-Kind, but that didn't matter. What mattered was getting back the sword so that he could prevent that power from being used to destroy everything he knew.

He had tried using his magic against these humans, but it had no effect. After which he had sought council with an elder Elf to find out why.

"It is a matter of belief," said the elder, "belief is what gives magic its power. If you are convinced down into the very depths of your soul that there is no such thing as magic, then for you it truly does not exist."

"Then these humans do not believe in magic."

"No they don't. They have their own beliefs which control what they can do. Their beliefs are more from the physical world, and magic has no part in it."

But the elder had never really seen what they could do, so surely the incredible things that they had shown him could not have come from the physical world, but from some form of magic much more powerful than his own. They had buildings that could fly. They had special walls that could show pictures and writing. But worst of all they had weapons that could kill from much farther away than an arrow's flight. He could not envisage anything in the physical world that could achieve such miracles... It was time for him to visit the Queen again, but this time it would be in person.

Lelia had just come out of the little room in the corner of her prison. She had no need to use it. She just went in because it was somewhere different and stopped her getting bored. She had examined the wall that had shown the words very carefully, but could see nothing except the tiny dots that all the walls contained. It was these dots that the pictures seemed to be constructed of, but they were so tiny that at first glance they were easy to miss. It was an amazing achievement, and she would love to meet the painter who had created it. The man, or woman, was a genius.

Suddenly a door opened in the opposite corner to the washroom, and an Elf walked in. She knew it was an Elf because stories about Elves had been her favourite during her childhood. As he walked in, '*Elves come from Tor*', jumped into her mind. She remembered the author saying so, and also remembered that no-one believed him. So that was it, she had been drugged or was the victim of magic, and was hallucinating.

"I am hallucinating," she said. "Everyone knows Elves are only stories."

"I am Farno and I am an Elf," the Elf said, "You are not hallucinating. You are in Tor, and yes we really do exist."

"So where is Tor then," asked Lelia.

"It is situated in the frozen wastes far to the south. A complex series of spells keeps a liveable bubble over us, and a by-product of that puts us between realities and consequently invisible in the normal plane of existence. It's not something we could do now, as magic seems to lessen as each generation passes. But we have enough, so we are content."

The explanation was far from the truth, but it was the only thing that he could think of that she might believe. He was not ready to explain about the 'Humans' and their new clear powder yet, nor did he want her to see that he was terrified of them. So the longer such knowledge could be kept from her the better.

"Why have you isolated yourself so?"

"We took the wrong side during the Dragon wars some five hundred years ago, and to survive we had to disappear. Since then there have only been two men who stumbled upon us. And the others of course, which brings me to the sword." He had not meant to mention the 'others', wanting to keep their existence from her, but he realised that she was unlikely to believe anything else that he tried to tell her.

"The others?" she asked, her eyebrows rising.

"They don't need to concern you except in as much as the Sword is vital to them, and they will do anything to get it back. The consequences of not delivering it to them are really something that you would not want to contemplate."

"But I don't have the sword," she insisted.

"Your husband does, and if taking your life is the price we have to pay for it then you can rest assured that your death will be inevitable. He does continue to surprise us though, as he is getting closer every day. The last report we got from our agent before he disappeared, put the King halfway across Amtor."

"You might consider the fact that with me alive you have a chance of getting it back. Without me you have no chance at all. Harm me and the devil himself will not stop him. And believe me that *is* something that *you* really don't want to risk."

The five Dragons were flying in an almost perfect 'V' formation still heading south. The 'V' formation was not for aesthetic reasons, but was the most efficient formation for birds and other creatures to fly in. They were not so far into each other's slipstream, that they were impeded by the flow of air from the Dragon in front, but were rather helped by the movement of air at the edge pulling them forward. Periodically, the leader changed as it was this Dragon that was doing the most work, and needed to rest now and then. Fayna, the golden Dragon of Kaylo was currently in the lead.

They were now five hours into their flight. The Dragon hold should soon be visible ahead, and because of her position in the lead, Fayna would be the first to spot it. A few minutes later she did, and signalled the others with a single thought before started to lose altitude.

"I see the hold ahead."

The five Dragons landed in a valley which was open at one end, with the other three sides forming a great complex of caves in a semi-circle of craggy cliff faces. This was the Dragon Hold. There were hundreds of Dragons here, some with riders and some without. *Very different to the last time I was here, when there was only two*, thought Erun, satisfied that his promise to restore the hold had been kept, *nice to see that it cleaned up pretty well, and the Dragons have started using it again.*

There was a great deal of hissing and posturing amongst the many Dragons there, as they sought to feel out their position. Several standoffs were occurring, though as yet it had not broken into actual violence. Corella took no part, standing aloof of the squabbles. Her position in the pecking order was well known and would never be challenged.

The marks of saddles were very clear on at least fifty percent of those present, and their riders, of which there were at least forty, were gathered in a large group around several camp fires, two of which held sheep roasting on spits.

"I think we should join them," said Kaylo "it's starting to get pretty cold this far south. Besides which those sheep smell better that anything we've eaten so far."

"And you can put your idea to them Your Majesty." he added, "It's not often that you get so many riders in one place."

All of the riders had immediately recognised the King, and if they had been unsure when they saw him, then the presence of the yellow Dragon served to confirm his identity, so he had their attention as soon as he joined the group.

"I am not here to ask the help of the Dragon riders in my present troubles," he announced, "suffice to say that I and my companions are headed south in search of the Queen, who has been kidnapped. But with so many of you here, it is an opportunity that I cannot ignore. We stayed at a hostelry, where the conditions were frankly disgusting, so I propose to set minimum standards for the provision of paid accommodation by Inns and boarding houses. Those standards are simple: Clean rooms, all furnishings in good repair and a comfortable bed with clean linen for each new occupant. I request that you the Dragon Riders of Cardoney monitor those standards and make a point of inspecting offered accommodation when you come across it. You will have the authority to close down establishments that fail to meet those standards after they have been warned and a reasonable period for them to comply has elapsed. What do you say?"

All eyes turned to one elderly white haired rider, who gazed back for a second, but then stepped forward,

"It seems that being the oldest I have been elected to speak for all here Your Majesty. What you suggest has been a long time coming, but it is welcome nevertheless. We would be honoured to be your hand in this, and we would be honoured to be extra eyes in the search for the Queen, and offer condolences for your loss."

"I cannot thank you enough. I will see that you all receive Royal Warrants to reinforce your authority when I return home. Get your Dragons to send any sightings, or information on the Queen, to Corella. She will pass them on to me."

There were murmurs of agreement from around the fires, and Erun accepted a large cut from the roasted sheep. Johan once again produced several large chunks of bread which he distributed as far as they would go. The five sat in a small group a little away from the others to discuss the journey ahead, and try to foresee anything that might arise. Erun started the conversation with a different topic though,

"Johan, how do you do it? Your pack is hardly large enough for the amount of bread you keep producing."

"Ah, I have been found out," he said smiling, "well for the most part I am really rubbish at magic. But what I can do, is conjure up bread, nothing else just bread. At least as long as I can stand a bread only diet I will never go hungry. But the guys here supply other things, so I supply the bread."

"Useful at least," said Erun, "all I seem to be able to do is make Elves explode."

"Well actually," said Panri, "I think he did that to himself."

"Thanks Panri, my confidence has been boosted no end."

"Okay, so what's next?" asked Cargan.

"Well I am sending Corella back to the castle, to keep Nordlight informed, and to get the production of the Royal Warrants underway. It should take her no time at all to get there via the Realm."

"I heard that," thought Corella.

"I know, and having heard all the rest as well you know what to tell him then."

"Right Oh! my liege and love of my life, I'm off."

Corella swept in to land a few feet from the drawbridge of the castle, her claws throwing up great clods of earth. She spread her wings to their maximum extent, let out a mighty roar, and boiled a few thousand gallons of water in the moat with a well aimed fireball just for effct.

"**Nordlight, Regent of Cardoney,**" she roared, **"come on out so that I can eat you."**

Inside the castle there was pandemonium. Armed soldiers deployed along the castle walls. They knew it was Corella, but a Corella the like of which they had never seen before. They were terrified, but they stood their ground and made ready to fire their arrows at this mighty yellow apparition across the other side of the moat.

"What has happened to Erun?" gasped Marta, "It must be something dire for Corella to act so."

Nordlight was the only one who was not panicking, and he smiled at his wife and said,

"Well if she wants to eat me, then I suppose I had better go."

"Are you mad?"

"No, but I do know Corella's sense of humour."

"But are you sure she's joking?"

"We'll find out soon enough," he paused at the door and looked back at his wife, "well are you coming, or do I have to face this horror alone?"

She slipped her hand in his, and together they made their way out of the castle and across the drawbridge to face Corella.

"Corella," he said, "Your sense of humour is going to get yourself killed."

"Probably," she said, "but it did get you out of the castle quite quickly though didn't it?"

"Well if it had been anyone else, they would have filled you full of arrows first."

"I have some information for you, and also a request. Erun is currently at the Dragon Hold, and when I return we will be crossing Pintor to move further south. Elves and Griffins are real; they have been hiding out ever since the great Dragon wars. Apparently the author of all your tales about Elves was right when he said they came from Tor. It seems that our Elfin friends have lost a Sword, called the Diamond Sword of Tor. They believe that Erun has it, which is why they took Lelia to use as a bargaining tool. We have not found Tor yet, but we have a rough idea where it might be."

She thought it better not to tell them that Erun actually *did* have the sword. It would serve no purpose for them to have that information yet. She continued,

"The first Inn that they stayed at was so disgusting, that Erun has set minimum standards for rooms at Inns and boarding houses, and has tasked the Dragon riders with policing those standards. He would like you to prepare a few hundred Royal Warrants to issue to them, giving them the Royal authority that they need to do the job properly. In addition, he wants the *Council of the People* to draft the detail of the law to his requirements, which are..."

And she went on to explain Erun's vision of the provision of accommodation by Inns and boarding houses in all the regions of Cardoney.

"No problem at all," said Nordlight, "I'll get a team of scribes to prepare them, and they should be ready to have names and signatures added when he returns. And I will place it all before the *Council* in the morning, so that they can prepare the right wording for the legislation."

"Thanks, can I eat you now?"

"No you can't. Now, be on your way before I set Marta on to you."

"Oh Err," said Corella, and with one mighty beat of her wings, which almost blew Nordlight and Marta over, leaving them clinging to each other for dear life, she took to the air once more and soon disappeared into the Realm.

Chapter Eight
A Price for Kaylo

Erun did not want to spend too much time at the Dragon Hold and was anxious to be on his way. He kept scanning the skies to the north for Corella's return, and was soon rewarded with the sudden appearance of a brilliant flash of yellow, and the first touch of her thoughts as she emerged from the realm.

"Task completed my liege and love of my life," she thought as she approached.

"I thought we had settled the lovey-dovey stuff," Erun replied, *"just putting 'my liege' in front doesn't make it any better,"*

"Ah, but that was when you were sixteen and

easily embarrassed."

"*I'm not twenty yet, so the same conditions apply.*"

"*Hmm, not when you are with Lelia I'm thinking.*"

Erun chose not to pursue the conversation down that route. It was just too difficult to explain that being totally bonded to a *very*large Dragon just did not seem to be in the natural order of things for a, only nearly, twenty year old King.

When Corella was on the ground and everything was once again packed away, the Dragons were saddled, farewells were said to the many other riders, and the party took to the air again. This time everyone had put on their heavier clothing as a precaution against the increasingly cold atmosphere that they were heading into. Each Dragon was loaded with a bundle of firewood behind the saddle just in case none could be found in the Antarctic wastes. Though in the end, it might have to be magic that kept them warm. It doesn't make a lot of sense to light a fire on an ice floe.

Dusk was approaching as they cleared the southernmost reaches of Pintor. It was time to make landfall again, and consult the map. They did know that it was at least three days flight, if not more, before land gave way to the seas of the Antarctic, but they had not determined whether Tor came before the ice, or whether somehow it existed on it. So knowing how long it had taken to cross Pintor they could now calculate, from the map, how much further they needed to go.

The light covering of snow had started to melt from the heat of the fire, and they hoped that the ground would dry enough for them to get some sleep later. Potatoes, onions and carrots were bubbling away in a pot over the fire, and what was left of the two rabbits from a day earlier were added, as was a large chunk of sheep that Panri had wheedled from the other riders. Johan had produced the inevitable chunks of bread, and Erun was brewing some tea. Kaylo had been given the task of studying the map.

"From what I can determine here, Tor should be just inland of the Antarctic sea. Probably take us the best part of a couple of days, maybe three, even if the Dragons rack up their speed a bit. There are several landmarks which should be easy to spot, like this really weird 'Y' shaped rock. It seems to be the largest of the landmarks. If fact, it's so large that I doubt we could miss it even if we tried." he said pointing to the map, "so we aren't likely to be too far out if we fly south and about five degrees east."

"It doesn't look as if this ground is going to dry up in a hurry," said Cargan glancing critically around, "but I have an idea. Hey Glenra, do you think you and the other Dragons could dry this ground out a bit without blowing the fire to all hell and gone?"

"I think we could," said Glenra, "a few little puffs and it will be as dry as a bone."

"I think that is our cue to withdraw," said Cargan.

They all quickly jumped to their feet, grabbed

their kit, and prudently withdrew to about twenty metres away from the fire. The Dragons positioned themselves on five sides of it, and at a signal from Glenra each gave a small 'cough'. The wash of flame was out of all proportion to the size of the cough, and when it cleared, a gently rising pall of steam was the only sign that the ground in a wide circle around the fire had ever been wet at all.

It had been several hours since the Elf had revealed himself and apart from sleeping, and eating the food that appeared, Lelia was getting bored. There was absolutely nothing for her to do and the hours had started to drag. She was of the firm belief that Erun would find her eventually, but she just hoped that it would be sooner rather than later. There must be a way into Tor despite the fact that it was between realities, a link with the normal reality as it were. After-all the Elf had said that two people had discovered Tor, and the Elves must also have a way to pass backwards and forwards if necessary.

What was it that the Elf said? She asked herself, *Oh yes...the last report from their agent before he disappeared. I'm sure he didn't just disappear, Erun must have found him.*

The Diamond Sword of Tor, what's that all about? I know Erun hasn't got it. The only sword he has is the magic one that he pulled out of the Dragon, and that is steel, certainly not diamond.

And who are 'the others' that the Elf referred to? Whoever they are, they seem to frighten the Elves to death. Where do they come from, and how have they managed to get the Elves so scared. And most importantly why do they want this sword.

Too many questions, not enough answers. I shall drive myself crazy if I don't get something to do soon.

"Hey Elfie," she shouted, **"come to Lelia. I need to ask you something."**

There was only silence, which stretched on for several minutes. When she had begun to despair that they were never going to answer her, the door in the corner swung open and the Elf appeared.

"I am not an 'Elfie', nor am I someone who you can yell at and think I will come running," he said angrily, "my name is Farno."

"Odd that," observed Lelia.

"What is odd about what?"

"The not come running bit. Yet here you are in response to my shout, aren't you?"

*"*Enough!" he snapped, stamping his foot, "What was it you wanted?"

Definitely a petulant Elfie as well, she thought grnning inwardly, but said aloud, "I am bored out of my scull sitting in here with nothing to do. Can't you give me some sewing things or something?"

He visibly calmed down,

"It didn't occur to me. I'm sorry. I will see

what I can find."

"Thank you!" said Lelia to his departing back, as he closed the door behind him.

"So if we head off first thing in the morning," continued Kaylo, as he arranged his blankets by the fire, "and stop about midday for an hour each day, we should be able to make it just before dusk on the third or fourth day... I think."

"What bothers me is the fact that Glenra still can't sense her." said Erun, "That fact alone is enough to give me the jitters. If I were to tell you the truth, I'm frightened to death most of the time, but then the certainty that she is still alive creeps up from somewhere in my mind. These stops... " he faltered, and there was a tremble in his voice "I wouldn't be making them at all if I was alone."

"And then you probably wouldn't have made it all," Panri said gently.

"I know," sighed Erun, "You have kept me focussed to the task in hand, and prevented me from going off on a fool's errand with no thought of the consequences, and I thank you for that."

"We will find her," said Cargan, "and if we have to fight to bring her home, then my friend I will be at your side."

Erun had to fight to stay the tear that started to trickle down his face. It was probably the worst, and the best thing that any man had ever said to him. To declare his King as a friend was unprecedented, and then be prepared to stand by him and to die, if that was what was called for, were the actions of a knight of the highest order. When this was all over, there was no question that he would leave Cargan behind. The only fitting place for such a man was at his King's side.

"Thank you my friend," he said softly.

Johan positioned himself in the dark beyond the fire so that the light from it would not interfere with his watch. He settled himself down in the shadows and wrapped his coat and a couple of blankets around himself to keep out the biting chill of an increasingly blustery wind from the Antarctic. A whispered voice alerted him and he turned to see Glenra a few feet away,

"There is no need Johan," she said, "for what is ahead you need a full night of sleep. We will watch in turn and make a lot of noise if there is trouble."

"Thanks Glenra," he said, "your point is taken and appreciated."

He gathered up his coat and the blankets and returned to the warmth of the fire. A brief explanation to the others and he settled down beside them.

The following morning the sun was just poking over

the horizon in the east, showing as just a tiny strip of fire against the lightening sky, when Corella nudged Erun with her snout. As he struggled to come awake and to sit up, she said,

"Its dawn, and unfortunately I can't cook your breakfast for you, but we have gathered some more wood for your fire. Dorna fetched some water from a stream about a kilometre away. Spilt most of it on the way back, but there is enough I believe."

Finally he managed to become fully conscious and appreciate how bitterly cold it was as he emerged from his blankets. Pulling on everything he had to pull on, he realised that it was only going to get worse, and there was a good chance that even the thick clothes that Cargan had managed to get might not be enough.

"Thanks Corella. I'll get the rest up when I have banked the fire up a bit."

For the next few minutes he bustled about, adding more wood to the fire and putting a good supply of bacon into a pan for when the embers were hot enough. Then he went round and woke each of the others in turn. As he awoke each one, and they struggled up out of their blankets, chattering teeth made conversation difficult.

"Jee-e-eesh b-b-b-but its c-c-c-c-cold," stuttered Johan, making a bee line for the fire, dragging his clothes with him.

"N-N-Never th-th-thought it-t-t-t w-w-would b-b-b-be a-a-as b-b-b-bad a-a-as th-th-this," said Panri through teeth clenched, in a vain effort to stop the chattering as he joined Johan as close to the fire as he could get.

"What's up with you children?" asked Kaylo. "This is pretty mild. Wait until we really hit the Antarctic."

"It's all right for you," said Johan, managing to control his chattering teeth "you only come from just over the border. You are used to it. I come from a lot further north."

"So do I," said Panri.

"If this is mild, then I do believe that we are in need of some arctic clothes." observed Erun, "Perhaps after breakfast you could pop off to this village of yours and pick up some more stuff. I would rather look ridiculous and warm than sensible and cold."

"As long as we can still wield a sword and don't look too ridiculous to fight, because the further south we go, the more likely we are to meet someone unpleasant," said Kaylo, "but at least here we can get some clothes actually designed for the Antarctic."

He was thoughtful for a moment, and then coming to a decision he added,

"Actually I think I'll go now, it'll save a bit of time and I can always pick up a bite to eat in the village."

There was a sudden rush of air, and Fayna landed in response to Kaylo's unspoken request just far enough away from the fire to avoid blowing it everywhere. It was the work of a moment for him to saddle her and then haul himself up into it. He gave a quick wave and then they were in the air and heading away from the camp fire. He glanced backwards as they gained height, but the one thing that consumed his mind was the vision that he had seen. It was a vision, seen through half open eyes as he lay by the fire just over a day ago, of firelight reflecting along the facets of a truly priceless diamond sword held in the hand of his King. They say that every man has his price, and if that was indeed the case, then Kaylo had finally found his. The only problem now, was how he could arrange for it to be paid.

Chapter Nine
Obsession

During the flight to his home village of Dorcutt, Kaylo could not shake what he had seen from his mind. It had been consuming him for over a day now. He could think of nothing else. He knew it was wrong. He knew he might have to kill his King to get it, and he would certainly have to let his friends down, or even kill them too. But none of that mattered against the glory of the sword. He *had* to have it. On the plus side, if they disappeared down there in the wilderness, no one would notice anyway. In another time and another reality what he had would have been called 'gold fever'.

Fayna was getting nervous. Her bond with Kaylo was strong, and she began to despair at the direction in which things were going. She whispered into his mind, trying to point out how wrong his thoughts were, but he dismissed her, and she became afraid that the lure of the sword might just be stronger than their bond. Such a thing was unconscionable, but she knew his mind and his every thought, and knew that the prospect was real, very real indeed.

She spotted the village slightly off to their right and altered course towards it, losing altitude as she did so, and sweeping in for a grand landing in the middle of the village square a few minutes later.

"Hey Kaylo, good to see you," shouted a passing villager.

He acknowledged with a wave and then slid from Fayna's back. In honour of the fact that he was the first ever Dragon rider from the village, the villagers had built an ornate saddle rest in the centre of the square for his use should he decide to visit. He used it now, strapping the saddle firmly in place.

"I shall only be about half an hour. If that's long enough, go hunting, I'll see you back here then."

As a sign or her disapproval, she said nothing, but lifted off to disappear away towards the edge of the village. Kaylo shrugged, and spotting the owner of a clothes shop across the square just opening up his shop, he headed towards him. He had known the man when he had been an apprentice and later as a Journeyman tailor, but he knew that he was now a Master and in fact the President of the guild. He was the perfect person to have the clothes that were needed.

Erun had just finished doling out the large quantities of bacon and eggs that he had cooked to his companions, and they were milking it for all it was worth. It is not every day that your King serves you breakfast.

"Just a bit more bacon if you please Your Majesty," said Panri.

"If there's another egg going spare... " said Cargan hopefully.

"More tea please," said Johan.

Erun laid a cloth across his arm and gave a slight bow,

"Will there be anything else gentlemen?"

They all dissolved into laughter, and then settled down to enjoy their breakfast.

"I hope Kaylo isn't too long, we need to be on our way, or it will be dark before we get anywhere," said Johan.

"I'm sure he'll be back soon, he knows our time scale," observed Panri.

As coincidence would have it, as he finished speaking the shadow of Fayna passed over them, and she circled once before gliding in to land fifty metres away. Kaylo slid from her back and reached up to unfasten several large bundles that were secured behind the saddle. He struggled across the intervening space with the bundles piled precariously in his arms, and then passed one to each of them.

"Sizes are only approximate, but they should fit. The boots may be a little large, but I've included several heavy pairs of socks," he explained breathlessly.

They discovered that the bundles contained very heavy hooded jackets that had a pull string through the waist to close the bottom of the jacket against the cold, and similar pull strings at the wrists and round the hood. The trousers were manufactured in a similar pattern, though the legs were obviously designed to tuck into the boots. But on the whole it all looked perfect. In fact so perfect that they all scrambled into them almost immediately after they had taken their first look. Erun found that luckily, even though he was the smallest, Kaylo's estimation of his size proved to be remarkably accurate, and it only required two pairs of socks to make his boots fit perfectly.

"I shall never take these off," declared Panri, "It's the first time my feet have been warm in a week."

"Well when everyone has finished admiring each other it's time to go," declared Erun.

Lelia cast her eyes critically over her handiwork. When several pieces of cloth and hundreds of different coloured lengths of embroidery yarn had been brought to her, she had wondered what to do with them. There was not enough to actually make anything, but there was ample to embroider some pictures. So here she was, embroidering the picture of an Elf on to a piece of cloth. It was something that she was very good at, so the embroidery was about as lifelike as it is possible to get with needles and yarn.

"As a matter of interest," she asked into the air, "have you asked him for it yet."

"Yes," a disembodied voice coming from all around her replied, "but our agent did not survive the encounter with your husband."

"Well I did tell you what to expect, so you shouldn't be surprised."

"We don't know exactly what happened, because the report from the Griffin is patchy at best. What we do know is that he approached the King, and has not been seen since."

"Well if he was the best you had, you are in real trouble."

Lelia had noticed that the Elf was becoming more and more talkative as the days went by, though the tension in his voice was increasing at the same time. She did get the impression that he was terrified of 'the others' as he called them, but that was one subject that she could not get him to speak about. So she avoided it and tried her best to get him to talk about everything else.

"By the way, where is my husband?" she asked.

"It seems that he has a lot more information that we gave him credit for," said the Elf, "he is now just south of Pintor and is heading this way. It's not accidental. He's deliberately coming this way. Though where he is getting directions from we don't know? It's really very odd."

Lelia didn't reply as she concentrated on working some emerald green thread into the picture of the Elf, but as she pulled the needle through for the last time, she looked up and asked,

"You really are not very good at this kidnapping thing are you?"

She smiled as the door in the corner opened and the Elf walked in. He looked confused and worried, but he walked up to the wall, touched it, and stepped to one side as a chair extruded from it. After it had fully formed, he dropped into the seat and made himself comfortable.

"About five days I've been here," complained Lelia, "and only now you show me this?"

The elf reached across to the wall beside him and touched it again, and a second chair appeared,

"Sit down, make yourself comfortable." he said, "There are a few things you need to know."

"You are right," he continued, "we really are not very good at kidnapping. In fact we have never done it before at all. We never even kidnapped you."

"What!" exclaimed Lelia, "if you didn't, then

who did?"

"It was the others. They went to your Castle to find the sword. They did not recognise it in the form that it had adopted, and in desperation they took you instead." He paused, "It was a terrible risk for us, and still is, that I have not told them that the sword can change its form."

"So Erun does have it then?"

"Yes, he does. We fear that we might not be able to re-acquire it. According to the Elders, the sword chose the Elves hundreds of years ago, but they were always aware that its allegiance could change if it found someone that it perceived as being more fitting. So far it has not happened. But now... after the Griffin's tale we are not so sure. But I didn't quite tell you the truth about that before."

"So what really happened then?"

"Apparently, the agent had the sword in his hand and attempted to keep it, but it returned itself to Erun. He then attempted to use magic against the King, and the sword turned it against him and he was destroyed."

"If it is resisting, then how will you get it back?"

"We can't. Erun will have to be persuaded to hand it back voluntarily."

"Ah I see. Hence the, be nice to Lelia tactic."

The Elf smiled and placed his hand on her arm,

"Well apart from the fact that you are fairly easy to be nice to, you are quite right."

"Well I have a couple of questions, if that's

alright with you. Where did the sword come from in the first place? And who are these 'others' that you keep talking about?"

"We don't know where the sword came from originally, but we do know that it made its first appearance in the early years of the Dragon wars. As for the 'others' well, it's best that you don't ask. It's not something that I want to talk about."

As the kilometres rushed by below, the sky began to darken and take on a distinct feeling of oppression, and then the first snowflakes began to sting their faces as they flew into the storm. The Dragons had worked their speed up to more than eighty kilometres an hour and this speed combined with the speed of the wind, turned the few snowflakes that were falling into a veritable blizzard. The Dragons could have cleared a tunnel through it with their flames, and this would have worked if the journey had been short, but the distance they were travelling made such a solution impractical as their gasses would soon be exhausted. At a signal from Erun, which Corella passed on to the other Dragons, they all began to lose height looking for a suitable landing spot.

A small sheltered spot in a group of rocks became visible as they lost speed and height, and

Corella moved into the lead and angled them down towards it. When they had landed, the Dragons cleared the small amount of snow that was present on the ground before the riders dismounted.

A small rock, about the size of a football was sitting in the centre of the natural rock shelter, and as Erun glanced at it, thinking how bitterly cold it was, it began to glow until it was red hot. *Subconscious at work again*, he thought, *thank god it only does what I would like it to do.* The shelter had turned out to be a tight squeeze for them all, but the Dragons huddled against the rock walls as close together as they could get for mutual warmth, leaving the centre area, by the artificial heat source, clear for the riders.

"That's got to be a really useful trick if you can do it," said Panri, holding his hands towards the heat. "I can heat pans and such up enough to cook food, but I can't do that."

"Yeh," declared Johan, joining him "My ability only stretches as far as setting fire to sticks and stuff, and I certainly can't do that either."

"Well it's OK for you *real*Dragon riders," said Cargan, "my magic just consists of wishful thinking."

They all looked towards Kaylo for one of his usual quips, but he said nothing. His mind was still in turmoil. Nothing seemed to mean anything to him since he had seen the diamond sword. The actual reason for his silence was not known to the others, so his attitude and demeanour did cause some puzzlement.

"Hey Kaylo, are you OK." asked Johan, "You seem very quiet."

"I'm fine," he replied tersely, and turned away to check his saddle.

For a moment Cargan stared at Kaylo's back, a slight frown on his face, and then he turned back to the others, but in that moment he had vowed to himself that he would keep an eye on their friend. Something was not right there, not right at all.

Chapter Ten
A Price for Cargan

A distinct and noticeable chill had started to appear in Fayna's responses to Kaylo. The normal relationship between a Dragon and its rider was complete love and devotion regardless of whatever either should decide to do. It was a bond that permeated into their very souls and was the reason that one could not survive for very long without the other. Even though Kaylo had reached his twenties before being chosen by Fayna, the bond had always been close and strong. That is until now.

Something unusual and previously thought impossible was happening. A Dragon and its rider were drifting apart. Kaylo was so overwhelmed with thoughts of the diamond sword that his bond with Fayna was being pushed into the background, and he didn't notice or didn't care. Fayna could see it though, and was starting to suffer as her devotion was rejected time and time again. For many long hours in the nights of their journey she would sit and tremble. The other Dragons noticed and became concerned that she was not eating properly and was obviously suffering from something. They had no idea what, as she was blocking all attempts from them to delve deeper.

Such was the impossibility of the situation, that none of the other riders noticed or could even comprehend what was happening. Corella did confide her worries to Erun, but he just dismissed it as perhaps a minor Dragon ailment. But, Cargan noticed. Not being a chosen Dragon rider, he had no bond with a Dragon to confuse his thoughts. He could see where the others could not, that here was a Dragon in serious distress. He began to worry that it was the change in Kaylo that was the cause. There was little he could do, except to go to Fayna and try to ease her pain. He took to sitting by her long into the night and as his hand gently stroked her, little by little her trembling eased and she eventually drifted into sleep. With a glittering diamond sword burnt into his vision, Kaylo didn't even notice that either.

So, on this day, in what was turning into a serious snowstorm, in a small rocky enclosure on the way to the Antarctic, Cargan went again to Fayna and sat close by her in the shelter of one of her wings.

"I know you understand Cargan," she whispered, "and I thank you for what you are trying to do. Your presence *is* a comfort to me."

"I cannot watch you suffer," he replied, "so I do what I can, even though it's not much."

"It's not as little as you might think," she said, "you are a big man with a big heart, and where your mind may not know what is right, your heart does."

He leaned his head into her side and for a while they sat together in silence.

"Hey Cargan," shouted Panri, "come on over by the... er... fire, we have some planning to do."

"I'll be back," Cargan whispered to Fayna, and then got up and dashed across the intervening few yards to the glowing rock.

"We are not going to make much headway in this weather, and the further south we go the worse it's going to get." said Johan, "What we need is a shield, and my magic doesn't extend that far."

"Well I can't help there," said Cargan, "because I don't have any at all."

"I've tried," said Panri, "but it's not something I can do either...Hey Kaylo wake up. What about you?"

Kaylo had been sitting staring at the glowing rock and oblivious to all around him when Panri's shout jerked him back to reality.

"... What... sorry wasn't listening... what was it?"

"A shield... you know against the snow... can

you make one?"

"No afraid not," he said abruptly and went back to staring at the rock.

"Well it's down to you then Erun."

"Well I have created shields in the past," said Erun, "but don't know how I'm afraid. They always appeared when me, or my friends, were in danger. But it's not something that I can wave a hand and it will appear."

"Well, we aren't going anywhere if you can't. Give it a go. Think of something that's a threat to you, your way of life or even to a pig in the next field... anything... " said Johan.

"Well I'll try, but don't get your hopes up."

Erun let his thoughts wander, and began to think. What was the worst case scenario that he could imagine? Not being a King? No, that wasn't it. He didn't actually care whether he was or not. Perhaps the loss of his parents? No, it wasn't that either. For many years now, he had reconciled himself to the fact that one day they would be gone. Then he knew. Life without Lelia was the worst thing that he could think of. He knew without a shadow of doubt that he could not live without her, in the same way that he could not live without Corella. He felt the wash of fear crawl up his back at the thought, and shuddered. He opened his eyes. At least it had stopped snowing. Then he noticed that his friends all had broad grins on their faces as they looked upwards. He shifted his gaze to follow theirs, and sighed as he saw the shimmering dome of the shield which arced over them all.

"I think it will stay there until I am not afraid anymore," he said, "we may as well eat, and then we can move on."

Thirty minutes or so later, they were airborne again. This time though, the formation was a rough 'H' shape with Erun at the centre to ensure that they were all inside the shield. It took a couple of circuits before the Dragons stopped bumping into the shield and managed to synchronise their flight. The shield was efficiently performing the double function of protecting them, and at the same time slicing cleanly through the wall of white ahead. Their speed was gradually increasing as the Dragons got into their stride, and they were soon exceeding their previous maximum of eighty kilometres an hour.

They had eaten early that day, so they decided to press on past midday and see how far they could get before dark. Ahead nothing at all could be seen, and they only knew that they were going the right way by Panri's unerring sense of direction. It was a vital talent that he had that the others did not, with even the Dragons being confused by the snow. So he was elected point and was relishing the feeling of being indispensable.

Being in a bubble in a sea of white, with no points of reference is disorienting, confusing and even removes the sense of up and down. It's not something that a normal person can tolerate for very long without turning into a gibbering wreck, so four hours into the flight Panri signalled that they needed to land.

They came down into an area of utter desolation. The snow lay thickly on the ground almost a metre deep in places and their weight, in the bubble, compacted it below them. As far as they could see, which wasn't far anyway, it was a flat expanse littered here and there with outcrops of rock and boulders. There was no vegetation, no animal life and it was eerily quiet except for the whistle of the wind, and the soft rustle that the snow made as it fell.

Orientation quickly returned when they felt the ground beneath their feet, giving them a tangible point of reference. They all quickly dismounted and started to wander around, stretching and stamping their feet to restore impaired blood flow. Finally, all the kinks removed, they began to open their packs for the precooked cold rations that were in them. For the first time in days, Kaylo was the first to speak,

"I have been looking at the map again in this book, and I noticed something odd. All of these little dots around the area where Tor is, I assumed to be Elves. But now I am not so sure. See if you look here," he said, opening the book and pointing, "it shows the Elves grouped inside Tor and the dots outside are definitely separate."

"I do believe you are right," observed Panri, "but what does it mean?"

"That's the big question, but whatever it means I think we need to be on our guard before we get there."

"Well, it looks as if four hours flight followed by a couple of hours on the ground is the best we will be able to manage in this soup, without losing our senses. So it's probably going to take as another three days before we are even close to reaching our destination." observed Erun.

"You're right," agreed Johan, "So let's relax for an hour or so, and then be on our way."

"Good plan," said Cargan, "I'll just pop over and check on the Dragons."

"For a non-rider, you have developed an uncommon affection for the beasts," commented Panri to his departing back.

The door in the corner opened once more and Farno walked in. He looked considerably brighter than he had on the previous occasions that he had visited her, as if he had come to an accommodation with himself.

"Your Highness," he said, causing Lelia's eyebrows to raise. He had never addressed her by her title before.

"What can I do for you?" she asked.

"I have no quarrel with you, or your husband. I never have had. I am ashamed of the way that you have been treated, and I intend to see that it is put right. I cannot return you home as it would be against the wishes of the others, but I can give you a measure of freedom."

"I would appreciate that," said Lelia.

"Think of this as your room. We will ensure that it is furnished properly, and that everything you need is here. The door however, will not be locked and you may come and go, exploring as you wish."

"What if I run off?"

"Not possible I'm afraid. There is nowhere for you to go. The exit from this between realities is guarded, and there is no other way out."

"That is reasonable under the circumstances," said Lelia, accepting the inevitable, "but what about your agent. From what you have told me, he did not seem like a particularly nice Elf."

"He was not. Not many are fitted for tasks such as his, and from time to time he has had to do things which were abhorrent even to him. Circumstances and the world have made his type necessary, but may a time come one day when they are not."

"That is my hope also. I appreciate your candour, and I will conduct myself accordingly."

"When my wife returns she will come and help you choose some appropriate clothing. She is a school teacher, and should be home in about two hours. I will see you later."

She noticed that when he went out, he left the door open behind him. So she settled back to wait for his wife. She thought it best not to go wandering around yet, because pyjamas are not the best clothes to meet new people in. The two hours stretched into three, but passed surprisingly quickly now that the door was left open.

She had actually started to doze off, when a timid knock on the door jerked her back to full awareness,

"Come in," she said.

The door was pushed open and an absolutely stunning woman walked in. She did have the characteristic features of an Elf, and the pointed ears, but apart from that she was one of the most beautiful women that Lelia had ever seen. When she spoke, her voice was soft but left you with the impression of distant tinkling bells.

"My name is Kirnina. I am Farno's wife."

The hour passed uneventfully, but soon Erun decided that they needed to move, and started to gather everything up ready to pack on to the Dragons. The others soon joined him and it was only a matter of minutes before they were all mounted and ready to leave.

"Hold for a moment," said Cargan, "I need to rearrange things on Glenra."

He slid off her back and removed her saddle, packing everything on to it and then fastening it a little further back.

"I will never walk again, if I spend another minute on that saddle," he said, then to Glenra added "I hope you have no objections to me riding bareback."

"None at all," she replied, "I hear you are a good horseman, so there should be no problem."

He swung up on to her back, and with a wave of his hand signalled that he was ready to go.

Taking off together so as to remain inside the shield turned out to be just as difficult as it had been the first time, with the Dragons on the outside continually colliding with the wall as they gained height. Eventually, order emerged from the chaos and they were once more moving rapidly south in their bubble. Erun was becoming more anxious as the hours passed, and unknown to his conscious self, his magic started to push the bubble forward at an ever increasing speed. None of them knew it, but their forward momentum had soon reached and passed three hundred kilometres an hour. After a couple of hours, Panri was the first to notice, and sent a message via his Dragon to everyone else.

"*Panri says that his directional sense is indicating that we are travelling at more than four times our normal speed and it's still increasing,*" Corella thought to Erun.

"*Pass back to him that I have been getting impatient, so it's probably me,*" he replied.

"*He says that was his thought also. He adds that at this rate we should be there before nightfall.*" she paused, "*he says keep up the good work.*"

When about four hours had elapsed since

they had taken off, Panri signalled to them all that he intended to land, and Corella angled herself and the bubble downwards. As they slowed and began to descend, the curtain of snow began to thin out, and soon they were able to see the weird 'Y' shaped rock that towered into the sky. It was only roughly in the form of a 'Y' with its two arms stretched upwards. It was a jagged stark rock that certainly looked impossible to climb without seriously good climbing gear, and some experts to use it. The arms of the 'Y' were angled in such a way that it was not possible to see between them without either climbing up to them or flying out over the sea.

When they were on the ground, Panri estimated that they had covered more than two thousand kilometres in the four hours. He found that his estimation was falling on deaf ears as everyone else was staring around in disappointment. Apart from the massive rock, there was nothing except a sheet of ice stretching away towards the glint of an ocean in the distance. No Tor, no Elves, no Griffins, nothing. Well a few large rocks scattered around, but apart from that... nothing.

"Well, what now?" asked Johan.

"The book says it's here, and I believe the book," said Panri.

"There is something here," said Corella, "but it is not completely in this reality. I cannot see it but I can feel it."

They had started to spread out looking in different directions, when an ear splitting scream shattered the silence. From between two rocky outcrops a young girl came. Her clothes were in rags, leaving her virtually naked, and she was running as if pursued by the devil. She ran into Cargan before she saw him, and then her screams went up a notch before stopping abruptly as his axe almost split the thing, that was running after her, into two pieces. His arm went around the girl, lifting her off her feet and moving her to one side as the point on the shaft of his axe entered another's throat, lifting him from his feet, before flinging him to one side.

Within seconds his friends, with weapons drawn, had ranged themselves to each side of him, and the Dragons moved in to flank them. Hundreds of the monsters seemed to be pouring from the rocks, only to perish in their hundreds in the wash of fire from the Dragons. The few that did manage to avoid the flames lasted only a few seconds as the five riders cut them down. Erun's sword seemed to have a mind of its own, as it disembowelled the first, before removing the heads from two more and leaving several writhing on the ground screaming for their lost limbs. It was over almost before it had started, as the remainder of the monsters melted away into the rocks. Erun turned aside and was violently sick.

"Are you Ok Erun," asked a concerned Panri.

Erun wiped his mouth on a handkerchief from his pocket,

"Yes, I'm fine. I have this problem that I get sick when I kill people."

"That's odd, you weren't sick when the Elf

exploded."

"No, as you quite rightly said, it wasn't me it was himself."

"True, very true."

During the whole time, Cargan had never let go of the girl. He had tried, but she clung to him and wouldn't be moved. Even now that it was over, she still wouldn't let go. Cargan was not the brightest of men, but he knew a good thing when he saw it, so gave up on what had become an unequal struggle. He finally had a chance to really look at her and saw that her clothes, or what little was left of them, left very little to the imagination. He decided that he really, really, liked what he saw, and frankly he was quite happy to hang on to her, albeit a little tighter than before.

When he was sure that the immediate threat was over, he carried her over to Glenra and dragged his spare jacket from his pack. It was with some reluctance that he released her so that she could put it on. Cargan was a big man. The girl, while quite buxom, was small, so his jacket almost reached the ground and virtually wrapped around her twice. As soon as she had it on, she wrapped herself around him once again. He did observe that it certainly looked as if she intended to stay there for good.

When he had a chance to look at her head instead of her delectable other parts he realised,

"You are an Elf," he exclaimed.

"And you are lovely," she whispered in a voice that, if he had not been already, would surely have captured him forever.

So another of the five had found his price, but unlike the price that was Kaylo's, his seemed to be freely offered and with the prospect of its payment, his soul soared.

Chapter Eleven
Treachery

"So these are your friends," she said, as the four joined Cargan by the Dragons. A shudder went up his back at the sound of her voice, and he wondered if it would be the case for the rest of their lives. *For the rest of our lives,* he thought, *what am I thinking? She's probably only holding on to me because she's frightened. Why would such a woman want me? All I am is a big thick Ox.*

"Will they be living near us?" she asked.

"... Living... near... us...?" he stuttered in shock, "You can't mean... ?"

"Why not? I have found you now. Why

would I let you go?" she hesitated, "I thought... well it seemed... you looked... as if you felt the same way." she finished in a rush.

He reached for her and pulled her towards him. Leaning down he kissed her on the forehead.

"If you would be happy with a big Ox like me, then I can't imagine life without you now, because I love you already."

She disappeared into his arms and her lips seemed to be glued to his. Then she was kissing all the parts of his face that she could see.

"Well, I never really believed in love at first sight before," said Panri, "In fact I thought it was some sort of myth. But now I have seen it all."

"And they haven't even asked each other their names," observed Johan.

Cargan pulled back reluctantly from the embrace, his face flaming,

"I am Cargan," he said.

"And I am Wispet," she replied, and dragged him back to her.

"I truly understand how you two feel, because I felt the same way when I saw Lelia. But we are here for a purpose, so when you have a moment... " said Erun.

Kaylo said nothing, having to force himself to tear his gaze away from Erun's sword. *It would not do to make him suspicious,* he thought, *when I move surprise must be absolute. I'll only get one chance at this.*

"This is Glenra," said Cargan, gasping for air and pointing to the Dragon, "I am not a rider like the others. She is the Queens Dragon, and has agreed to carry me until we find the Queen."

"And this," he continued, pointing to Erun, "is the King, and the rider of the Yellow Dragon. My other friends are Kaylo, Panri and Johan," he finished, pointing each of them out in turn.

"Until you find the Queen? What happened? Is she lost?" asked Wispet.

"No she was kidnapped and is being held in Tor," explained Cargan.

"How would that be possible? My people are not like that. They don't kidnap people." She paused in thought for a moment, "I get it. It must have been the others. They must be getting desperate."

"Ok, I won't ask who the 'others' are yet. That can come later," said Erun, "but for now let me see if I can heat up a rock. It seems that we have a lot to talk about."

"Try this one," said Cargan picking up a football sized rock from the side of a rock fall and carrying it to a clear spot.

Erun was just about to concentrate and stare at it, when it began to glow, gradually getting hotter and hotter until it reached a satisfying cherry red.

"Seems to be getting easier," he said.

"Or becoming second nature," observed Panri.

"*Corella,*" thought Erun, "*keep a watch out for those monster man things, or whatever they are.*"

"*Don't worry,*" she replied, "*weDragons will take care of it.*"

Soon, pans and food were removed from

packs, and placed closely around the rock to heat up with a little help from Panri's magic. He couldn't heat up rocks, but he could certainly heat up a pan enough to cook in. Wispet insisted on taking over, saying that she was a woman, and after all it was a woman's work.

[*Apologies to all the ladies, but equal rights haven't reached this reality yet.*]

When the food had been prepared, distributed and consumed, Erun started in with the first question.

"How is it that you are not in Tor, Wispet?" he asked.

"I was out on a Griffin," she said, "we actually aren't really allowed to leave without permission, but I did and the Griffin was startled by something and left me. Elves don't get to bond with Griffins, we just ride them. I dread to think what would have become of me if you had not happened along."

"But how did you get out, when my understanding is that the exit is guarded?"

"I don't really know. I picked a Griffin that knew the way. It was my first time and I'm afraid I closed my eyes until he landed."

"Ok, but from here, where is Tor?"

"It's between realities, with only a single exit to this one, but I don't know where it is."

"What about these monster things that were chasing you? What are they, and where are they from?"

"I can only tell you what I know from

history," she said.

"Fair enough," said Erun.

"We were taught that when our very existence was threatened at the end of the great Dragon wars, a wizard of immense power moved Tor out of this reality. Apparently that action released some sort of poison in the atmosphere, which affected several human villages that were around the outskirts. Whatever happened seems to be...what did they call it? ...oh yes...genetic, and passed on through the generations. They are virtually mindless. They only seem to be able to breed and kill anything that is not one of them."

"So, if they can breed, it seems that they could be a danger to us humans," observed Panri, "so if we can't cure them by magic, we might just have to kill them all."

"As a last resort... only as a last resort," said Johan.

Erun turned back to Wispet, to continue his questioning, though it was a bit hard to see her, wrapped in Cargan's arms as she was.

"Who or what are these 'others' that you mentioned?"

"I can't tell you very much at all, except that one day they appeared. That was about three or four years ago. They have buildings that fly, walls that show pictures and things that they hold in their hand that kill at tremendous distances. At least ten times an arrow's flight. They also talk into little boxes that answer back at them."

"That sounds like damn powerful magic to

me," said Johan.

"I'm not so sure," said Erun thoughtfully, "none of that would seem to be the sort of thing that you would use magic for. One of my alchemists has invented a powder which if packed tightly, explodes when ignited, and it's got nothing to do with magic. Apparently it is the mix of ingredients, and if you know what they are, and the quantities of each, anyone can make it."

"So then, all we have to do now is find the entrance, stay alive against people that can kill us before we see them, and then rescue the Queen." said Panri.

Finally she was outside and could walk about without fear. Kirnina had lent her some clothes which had fitted fine but a little tight, and then had taken her out to some shops. Even if she had possessed any money, it would not have been of any use as the Elves used entirely different currency. Kirnina had given her some, saying that Farno had advanced it as some compensation for her capture. So she was happily shopping for anything that looked feminine enough for her taste. So far she had found several outfits that she liked, and was surprised at how little of her finances were used to buy them. It was a little disconcerting in the way that the Elves looked at her, but it was something she could live with, so she gave up worrying about it, and just smiled sweetly.

She always had been an observant girl, and her eyes missed nothing, with it all being filed away for possible future use. Tor was unremarkable and seemed like a rather large and ordinary town. Many shops were scattered about, offering a variety of products for sale, and interspersed with these could be seen cafes, restaurants and the inevitable drinking establishments. Most of the living quarters were on the outskirts of the commercial district and consisted of small houses and apartment buildings. As she was straining her eyes against what seemed to be an artificial sun, there was a sudden roar and something flashed by overhead trailing a thin pencil of fire.

"The 'others' I presume?" she said to Kirnina, "very odd building though. It has wings like a bird, but they don't flap."

"Yes it is. We had better get you back. They have magic that can see everything, and Farno is really sticking his neck out by releasing you like this."

"Ok let's get back then, Farno is being fair, and I wouldn't want to see him hurt because of me."

As they turned to head back, something hit Lelia like a physical blow,

"Glenra," she gasped, "my Dragon, she is here."

"You must be mistaken," said Kirnina, "quickly we must hurry."

It was obvious that Kirnina did not fully appreciate the bond between a human and a Dragon, or she would not have dismissed Lelia so easily. Lelia however, thought it best not to argue with Kirnina who knew more about the situation here than she did. So she quickly fell in bedside her and they broth broke into a jog, keeping as much to the shadows as they were able.

When they got back to her prison, it was transformed. Several easy chairs were set against the wall with a small table placed in front of them, and a very comfortable looking bed was positioned between the entrance and the wash room. Windows had appeared in the walls, and tasteful drapes adorned them. It looked quite comfortable. A young elfin girl was stood by the bed as she entered,

"My name is Darlelia, but I will answer to Lelia or Dar. I am here to be your maid."

"I think I will call you Dar. My name is Lelia as well and we don't want any confusion now do we?"

Dar smiled,

"No we don't."

Then she pointed to a small square glowing patch on the wall,

"Touch that... just touch it, no need to press or bang or anything, and I will come... any time of day or night."

"Thank you Dar, might I have some tea before you go?"

"Of course," she said, curtsied and hurried from the room.

"Two of us at a time are going to stay airborne to keep watch, because we can see more from up there." Corella explained to Erun, "The rest of us will be down here as a close guard. With a bit of luck we should get enough early warning of any approaching trouble."

Corella and Glenra were the first to take the aerial watch, and circled out over the frozen sea before sweeping around in a large circle and heading back to circle inland past the campsite. They had only got a little way out over the ice flow when Glenra suddenly dipped a wing and dropped like a stone. She fortunately recovered after falling only a few hundred feet, and with a few flaps rejoined Corella. They both turned and headed back towards the camp. Corella's thoughts went ahead of her,

"Glenra has sensed Lelia. It was only a brief contact, but the shock was considerable."

"Is she able to pinpoint the direction?" asked Erun.

"Not yet, the shock of the sudden contact was too much, she will need to recover first."

Erun let the sight of the Dragon suddenly falling from the sky run through his mind, and remembered where it was,

"It's Ok. I have it. I know where it came from. It's the 'Y'. The entrance is between the arms of the 'Y'," in his excitement he spoke aloud, "Glenra picked up Lelia's thoughts when she flew past."

"Well wherever that came from, it's a welcome development," said Johan.

It has to be soon, thought Kaylo.

"We have movement in the rocks," roared Dorna.

There was a scramble for their arms and the men took up positions facing the oncoming threat. Kaylo, sensing that this was his opportunity, moved in immediately to the left of Erun and signalled for Johan and Panri to move to his left and Cargan to take position on Erun's right. Wispet moved out of sight behind them. The deployment didn't seem to concern the others, but it did Cargan. It made no sense. Erun was the King. Two should be positioned to each side of him for maximum protection. He was just about to protest when the monsters came boiling out of the rocks.

They were all carrying clubs and various sharp objects, which did not make efficient fighting instruments against five experienced arms men, but chaos reigned supreme for some savage moments. Dragons were coughing out great gouts of fire where they could without frying their own riders, while those riders were parrying wild swings and despatching monsters to their maker almost as fast as they made contact. It was a one sided conflict, even given the number of the monsters that came at them, and consequently it did not last long.

As the last one turned and ran off back into

the rocks, Cargan was stunned to receive a whispered thought into his mind,

"Move Cargan, move now past Erun. Move to your left."

He did not hesitate, but moved quickly to his left and across the back of Erun, who had stuck his sword in the ground in disgust and moved away from it. The Killing had sickened Erun's stomach, so senseless in the way that it was. These monsters did not know what they were doing, and it was tantamount to murder being able to cut them down so easily. He leaned over to vomit on the ground. He would never get used to it, but if it had to be done then he would have to put up with being sick.

As Cargan moved, he came into just the right place in time to see Kaylo drive his sword into Erun's side as he was bent over vomiting, wrench it out and dive for the diamond sword. By his plan Kaylo should have made it, but he had not counted on the watchfulness of Cargan and never even felt it as Cargan's axe head split his spine. As he fell to the ground, just one word whispered from his mouth,

"Erun," and then he died.

Cargan turned back to see Johan and Panri kneeling by the kings side,

"Too late he's gone," and then they sprang backwards as the screaming, shrieking shape of Corella crashed down beside them.

"**Cargan, get the sword, get the sword quickly bring it here,**" she roared.

Cargan grabbed the sword from where it was stuck in the ground and rushed towards Corella,

"No take it to him. Hold it in both hands, point it at him. Quickly now."

Cargan held the sword in both hands pointing it towards Erun and closed his eyes as the sword flared with a brilliance that none of the four had seen before. Corella's colour streamed into the sword, and the flare reached out and bathed Erun in a light so bright, that for a moment the sun was dimmed into insignificance. On and on it went for what seemed like an eternity and then as fast as it had appeared it was gone. All that remained was a small wisp of colour that trickled from the sword and gradually brought Corella back to her former glory. Erun groaned and sat up.

"What happened?"

"Kaylo killed you, and the sword brought you back," said Johan as if he didn't really believe it.

"Cargan, Fayna is dying. Go to her. You may be able to soften her passing," said Corella.

Cargan hurried away to where Fayna was laying on the ground with her wings crumpled under her, and knelt down to cradle her head in his arms. She shuddered and one eye opened to look at him. Her voice was strained and weak as she spoke, but clear enough for Cargan to hear.

"It was me that warned you. I could not let it happen. I did not know whether I could, but I had to try. We had drifted apart, me and Kaylo, and that doesn't happen, but it did. I did not agree with his intentions and he was so consumed, that he did not see that I was there for him. Your presence on all those long nights, were more of a comfort to me than you can imagine. The pain is still great but given time I think I will live. But I need you Cargan. We are compatible or my thoughts would not have reached you. I need you to be my rider. Your heart is amongst the purest that I have known among men, and I feel a bond forming already."

Cargan was stunned into silence. As Wispet came up behind him, and wrapped her arms around his neck, he could only sit with his mouth open.

"It would be my privilege," was all he was able to mutter.

Fayna sighed,

"Then I will sleep now and if in time I awaken, then it will be done," and her eye closed.

"Sit with me Wispet," said Cargan, gulping as emotion caught up with him, "I have to stay with her. She needs me, and I need her. Without me here, she will die."

Wispet came round beside him and gently stroked the Dragon's head where it still rested in Cargan's lap. Then she leaned to him and kissed his cheek.

"Should it be forever, I'll be here to care for you both," she said softly.

"Of course," said Erun disbelievingly, "now tell me what really happened."

"Johan told the truth," said Panri, "Kaylo truly did kill you, and the sword did give you back your life."

"Why? Why would he do something like that?"

"Fayna told me, but too late for me to act." said Corella, "Apparently Kaylo was awake when you changed the sword, and has been consumed by it ever since. He planned to kill you and then seize it, and if necessary use it to despatch Panri and Johan. He thought he would have no trouble with Cargan. He was mistaken, and Cargan killed him."

"But how did Cargan know?"

"It was Fayna. She thought she was committing suicide. But she could not live with what Kaylo was about to do. So she warned Cargan," explained Corella.

"How could she do that? Dragons cannot communicate mentally with anyone except their rider."

"It seems," said Corella, "that fate has intervened and decreed that her true rider should be Cargan. She will take time to recover, because the shock was great, but at least she *will* live."

"Did... " Erun hesitated, "did Kaylo say anything before he died."

"One word," said Panri.

"I know what it was," said Erun, "he said 'Erun', didn't he?"

"Yes."

"Well he did say 'may hell take my soul the day that I use it', and I think in this case that it certainly did," said Johan.

"Help me up and take me to Cargan,"

Panri and Johan helped him to his feet. At first he staggered a little but gradually became stronger, until finally they could release him to walk on his own. He opened his hand and his sword lifted from the ground into it. Then he walked with confidence to where Cargan sat cradling Fayna's head in his lap.

Standing by the Dragon's wing, he faced Cargan,

"No man has served me more faithfully than you Cargan of Amtor. Without you saying it, I know that you would give your life and gladly if I were to ask,"

Cargan started to struggle to his feet, but Erun's hand on his shoulder stopped him.

"Stay with your Dragon Cargan, what I have to do is more normally accomplished with the subject in a kneeling position, but nothing in the code says that I cannot perform it while you are sitting."

He touched Cargan's shoulders with the blade of his sword, first the left and then the right,"

"Here, I would normally say 'Arise Sir Cargan of Amtor' but instead I will say 'stay seated with Fayna Sir Cargan of Amtor, Knight of Cardoney, Dragon Rider and Protector of the King'."

Cargan looked up at his King, his eyes wide. He was not sure whether he could take any more shocks in one day. He had met the love of his life. He had become a Dragon rider for real, and now here he was a knight of the realm.

Erun smiled. He understood completely. It had not happened quite so quickly for him, and apart from him becoming a King instead of a Knight, the similarity was unmistakeable. He turned to Wispet,

"Look after your man Lady Wispet, which is what you will be as soon as we find someone to marry the two of you."

Wispet stood up and curtsied to the King,

"Thank you Your Majesty. I have only known him for a short while, but in my opinion there is no man more deserving."

Erun slipped his sword back into its scabbard and looped an arm around the shoulders of Johan and Panri,

"Come my friends, we have preparations to make for the storming of Tor."

Chapter Twelve
Invasion

"We will wait," said Erun, "Lelia now knows we are here, and Glenra sensed no distress when she touched her mind. And I am not going anywhere without Cargan by my side."

"We understand Your Majesty," said Johan speaking for himself and Panri. "I think we are probably pretty safe here now, as two resounding defeats must surely have penetrated the minds of even these monsters."

Surprisingly, Fayna woke up after only a few hours. But it took three days for her to rebuild her strength, particularly since she had been neglecting her health anyway for the past few days. The other

Dragons helped by returning to the forested regions of Amtor via the Dragons' realm to hunt for food and bringing a portion of that food back to her. It was on the third day after Kaylo's treachery that she felt strong enough to join them in the hunt, and on the fourth she declared that she was ready. During this last day, Cargan also discovered that his bond with her was complete, and finally understood what all other riders already knew. The Dragon was part of him and he a part of her, and neither could survive if the other was lost. Impossible as it should have been, he really was a Dragon rider.

"Johan and I will go ahead when we enter Tor," said Panri, "Sir Cargan you stay close to the King, which will be your place from now on. And Glenra, you have no rider now until we retrieve the Queen. So stay to the rear and watch our backs."

"What about Wispet?" asked Johan.

"No problem," said Sir Cargan, "she will be riding with me."

"It's getting late in the day now, "said Erun, "so, we go first thing in the morning. Dorna reported that no gap appears between the arms of the 'Y' on the land side, so we have to approach from the sea. Wispet confirms that the entrance is guarded, so watch out for that."

Lelia awoke in the morning, from one of the best night's sleep that she had had since her captivity.

She had been sleeping in a proper bed now for four days and stretched luxuriously in it, vowing to spend the whole day there if she was not disturbed. A timid knock on the door dashed her hopes, and Dar entered at her shouted 'Come in'. She was bearing a tray containing breakfast and more importantly a steaming mug of tea. It had only taken Lelia a day or so to persuade Dar to bring her a mug instead of a fancy cup.

"But you are a Queen. You shouldn't be drinking out of a common mug."

"I like tea. I don't like to keep pouring it out, and cups are not big enough."

"Ok then a mug it is."

"When this is all over, would you like to come and work for me?"

"Well if we are all still alive, I would have to ask my dad, but other than that I would love to."

"Who is your father?"

"Why Farno of course, I thought you realised."

"No," said Lelia, "actually I never did."

The door suddenly flew open and Farno staggered in, being savagely pushed by a human behind him, obviously he was one of those that the Elves described as 'The Others'. The human looked at Lelia and his lip curled,

"How is the little primitive Queen today now that she has a little comfort?"

Darlelia was trying very hard to disappear

into the wall, obviously terrified, and Lelia laid a hand gently on her arm. She turned her gaze on the human, and put on what she thought was her haughtiest look.

"Primitive or not, I am still a Queen, and I would thank you sir to act accordingly."

The man said nothing, but stepped forward his arm raised to strike, but Lelia had not spent long hours in unarmed combat training with Erun for nothing, and she ducked under his arm, giving a little push as it passed and he spun staggering against the wall. Farno sniggered. He couldn't help it, and the man turned. Something in his hand flashed and Farno was thrown backwards to hit the floor and slide up to the wall. Dar screamed and leapt at the man, but the object flashed again and she never reached him, but ended as a crumpled heap by the bed.

"You animal," spat Lelia, "You had no cause to kill them."

"Oh don't worry Queenie," the man laughed, "they are not dead. They will wake up in about an hour with a right," and again he laughed, "royal headache."

He then sobered, and his glance narrowed as he looked at her,

"But if you try anything like that again, they *will* be dead and so will you."

"What do you want from me, you excuse for excrement?" asked Lelia, without showing the slightest sign of fear at his tone.

"Nothing, but I do want something from your

husband. And if I don't get it then your worries will be over, because dead people don't get worried."

"You like threatening people don't you. You are a disgrace to the human race."

"Not to mine I'm not, and yours is too primitive to count."

"If being primitive is judged by actions, then yours make you a savage."

He laughed again and turned towards the door,

"Quite a feisty little Queen," he said as he left.

Lelia did not have the strength to lift Farno, but she got a pillow from the bed to place under his head and covered him in a blanket to keep him warm. She was able to lift Darlelia and she did so, gently placing her on the bed before covering her with a blanket as well. Then she went to look for Kirnina.

As she went to the door, it struck her. It was Glenra again. They were on their way. They would be here soon. They had found the entrance. She sent out one desperate thought, "*Don't harm the Elves. Whatever happens, do not harm the Elves.*", before the contact was lost again. She ran as quickly as she could to the school, and a quick question to a wide eyed Elfin, pointed her to Kirnina.

Kirnina gasped as she saw her, but thinking of her pupils first she turned to a sea of stunned faces and said,

"This is a human. She is a Queen, so treat her with respect."

"Good morning Madam Queen," they all chorused.

"Good morning children," said Lelia then turning to Kirnina, she quickly explained the situation.

"I have to go children. The oldest, which is you Pernol," she said addressing an earnest looking boy at the back of the class, "go to the head teacher and explain. She will send someone to take over the class."

She grabbed Lelia's hand and together they hurried from the building, but just as they reached the edge of the school complex, Lelia came to an abrupt stop,

"Glenra my Dragon really is here now and she has brought my husband and some friends."

"No it can't be... " said Kirnina, and then she gasped as she looked skywards and saw the bright colours of the Dragons approaching.

The invasion fleet flew in formation past the massive rock entrance to Tor, with the intention of turning out to sea before coming back at high speed in the hope of getting surprise on their side. As they did so, Glenra staggered again in the air, but recovered and shouted to the others,

"Lelia says, do not harm the Elves. Whatever happens, do not harm the Elves."

They swept around in a huge circle and then began to rack up speed as they headed for the entrance. They shot between the arms of the 'Y' and were surprised to see several hundred Elves who were obviously guards, standing up cheering and waving their arms. Then the rocky entrance was behind them and they were inside Tor. Glenra suddenly turned and headed away to the right sending '*this way*' to the other Dragons, who wheeled to follow.

Lelia stood still as she watched her beloved Glenra sweeping in towards her. She was already in mind to mind contact, so she let her gaze turn to Corella and the love of her life astride her. He had come, as she never doubted for a second that he would, and now he was here.

Erun was off the Dragon almost before it had hit the ground and was sweeping Lelia into his arms as Kirnina cowered back against the wall in terror. It had been a lot of years since Tor had seen Dragons, having been shifted out of the reality precisely because of them.

Corella moved up until she was close to the quivering Kirnina,

"You need not fear us," she said gently, "most of us have forgotten, and those that haven't, have forgiven."

Kirnina stepped forward hesitantly and reached up a hand to touch Corella's nose.

"Thank you, I did not know that Dragons were so beautiful. It seems we truly chose the wrong side. But we must hurry. My husband and daughter are hurt."

"Hello my sister," said Wispet, walking up.

"**Wispet,**" Kirnina almost screamed, grabbing her sister in a bear hug "we thought you were dead."

Struggled out of her sister's strangle hold, Wispet stepped back,

"We must hurry to Farno. I will make introductions later."

When they reached Kirnina's house, and Lelia's prison, the Dragons ranged themselves outside on guard, while everyone else trooped in through the door,

"I think there is little to be done," said Lelia, "the human told me that they were not dead, but would awaken in a while. I think we just keep them warm until they wake up."

Kirnina made a quick examination of her husband and daughter, and then nodded,

"I have seen this before in Elves who have irritated the humans. They will wake up, but won't feel good for a while when they do."

She turned to Wispet,

"And now my sister, introduce me to these fine young men that you have brought into my house."

"This is Panri," she said pointing to him, "who rides the lovely green Clara."

"And this is Johan who rides the other green Dragon, the lovely Dorna."

"And this beautiful man," she said, wrapping her arms around Sir Cargan, "Is Sir Cargan, rider of the golden Fayna, knight of the realm and my husband in *every* way, but ceremony. And that we intend to fix as soon as we can."

Kirnina's eyebrows raised at the *every,* but all she said was,

"We will have to see what we can do."

Seeing Erun wrapped around Lelia, she added,

"I do not need to ask who this is. Welcome to my home Your Majesty."

"Thank you er... "

"Kirnina," prompted Lelia

"Kirnina," Erun finished lamely, "but what I need to know is about the 'others'. Everything, so what can you tell me."

"Come let us move into one of my more comfortable rooms, and I will tell you everything I know."

She turned and led the way into a quite tastefully furnished living room that contained more than enough comfortable chairs for them all. When everyone was seated, Kirnina disappeared into what was obviously a kitchen and surprisingly quickly returned with a tray of tea. She set it down on a table, and indicating that everyone should help themselves, she sat down as well.

"I don't know a great deal, and you must forgive me for using words that you may not understand. Frankly, I don't understand them either, but they are all I have."

"Go On," Erun prompted.

"The others say that they come from a

parallel reality, through a portal which suddenly opened. They say that they are much more advanced scientifically, whatever that means, than we are. They say that magic is just in our imagination and is not real. In fact it does not work against them anyway. Our elders say that they have no place in their lives for magic, so for them it really does not exist."

She paused, and everyone waited expectantly.

"Five hundred years or so ago, they discovered that there were other realities, and created a talisman that could open a portal. They did not call it a talisman, but I cannot remember its real name. Anyway, they opened a portal between realities, and a large number of them came through it. The Dragons moved against them, and we sided with these new humans. There were a *great* many Dragons in those days, and not enough of us or the 'other' humans here. Dragons died in their millions, but it was obvious that our side could not win. So the 'other' humans decided to return to their own reality, but refused to take us. By the use of *something* which they called new clear powder, I think that was its name but I'm not sure, they shifted Tor between realities. They made mistakes, and the bulk of the force went through the open portal. I don't know what damage it caused to them, but it must have been considerable. The portal closed leaving one human behind. He was outside of Tor and tried to make it back with several Elves in one of their aircraft as they call them. Before they reached the gateway into Tor, they were flamed by several Dragons, but made it through before crashing in flames on the inside. None of the Elves made it alive, but the human survived, though only for a few minutes. Before he died, he gave us the diamond sword, calling it a reality key, and also explained that it would be dangerous for us out there because the population had been contaminated by raider action, again I'm not sure if that is the correct term."

Again she paused, taking a sip of her tea and arranging her thoughts.

"We had a really powerful mage in those days, and he spent hours trying to fathom the sword's purpose. One day he projected a force at it, and in the flare that followed, it turned from its glittering diamond form, into the normal sword that you see now. He kept quiet for the forty or so years that he remained alive. Then on his death bed he confessed that the sword was intelligent. Not alive he hastened to add. Well it wasn't when he first looked at it. But something happened in the force that he used and that force merged with the intelligence, and something living emerged. And that something had more power than had been its original purpose. We kept it as a symbol. Up until now, it would not take on its diamond form, or use its power for anyone but us."

"But it does for me," said Erun.

"Yes, it does," agreed Kirnina, "It seems that you have been chosen over us."

"Scientifically, Aircraft, raider action, reality key, new clear powder," said Johan, "They all mean nothing to me."

"Not to me either," said Kirnina, "but they are the words they used."

"How did the 'other' humans get here then?"

Kirnina sighed,

"It was forbidden, but you know how children are. A small child thought she could play with the sword, and she opened a portal. A man, a Dragon slayer, that had found Tor was passing and took the sword from the child. It immediately turned to its metal form and the portal closed, but not before an aircraft had come through. He escaped with the sword, and we have been searching for it ever since."

Erun closed his eyes, as a far away voice started to speak to him. It had happened several times since he had acquired the sword, and he had thought nothing of it until now. The schematics of an aircraft appeared as a picture against his closed eyelids and a quiet voice started to explain each of the parts in detail. Every time his mind seemed confused the voice would change and using simpler words would explain those that he did not understand. Halfway through, he was jerked back by a hand touching his arm.

"Are you Ok Erun?" asked Panri.

"Yes, I was just having a lesson. By the sword, I'm pretty sure. It was about halfway through a detailed explanation of what an aircraft is. It is also quite clear to me now, that the sword creates the shield, and it really is intelligent. It also seems that it has a method of utilising Corella's colour and her magic, and that is probably how it managed to revive me."

"Did you understand any of it?"

"About the aircraft? Yes, but very little. The principles of operation seem clear enough though."

"What is it then?"

"Briefly. A bird flies by flapping its wings and pushing against the air. The flapping is a rotating motion that pulls the air backwards causing the bird to move forward. An aircraft has a wing that is shaped to move upwards in the air if you push it forward. It needs some pretty powerful pushing, hence the fire coming out of the back."

"That seems clear enough, what about the rest,"

"Use your imagination. It gives me a headache,"

"It seems obvious then that the 'others' need the sword to open the portal, so that they can go home," observed Johan.

"Nothing significantly new, has been produced by us in generations," said Erun, "we haven't needed to, having access to magic. Oh little things like the exploding powder, and better toilets, but nothing significant. But I wonder, these humans rely upon what they can learn from the physical world, and they obviously made the key and opened the portal five hundred years ago. That flash of power through the portal must have caused more damage to them than we can imagine, or they would have been able to reproduce the key, and would certainly have much more knowledge of the physical world than they seem to have at the moment."

He turned to Kirnina,

"From your history, is what they had then, much the same as what they have now?"

"Yes, but I am pretty sure that some things they had then, they don't have now. The history books are clear on one point. Their aircraft had no wings and did not project fire out of the back."

"I do believe that I hear groans from the back room," said Wispet.

Chapter Thirteen
Reinforcements

"It's hard to decide how many of us it will take to get the upper hand in the conflict that I know will come," said Erun, "I have no intention that the sword be used to reopen the portal. We do not want more of them coming through, or we stand the danger of ending up like we did five hundred years ago. If we are only dealing with one aircraft, surely if there are enough of us we can win."

"But how can we get more of us here in time?" asked Sir Cargan.

"I will talk to Corella," he said.

"*Corella,*" he thought, "*we are in trouble*

here unless we can get some reinforcements. How can we do it?"

"I have been monitoring the conversation through you," she replied, *"and the only way I can see is via the Dragons' realm. It is about time that this secret became public. I will have to go to them and try to get them to agree to riders entering the realm."*

"How much hope is there?"

"Very little, but I have to try."

"Go then, there is little enough time as it is."

Kirnina came into the room with her arm around Farno supporting him, so that he did not fall flat on his face from some seriously wobbly legs. She was followed by Wispet holding up Darlelia.

"They'll get their strength back in five or ten minutes," said Kirnina, "I have brought them up-to-date with our conversation so far."

"One question that still remains, Kirnina, is how many are there in one of these aircraft things. Do you have any idea?"

"I do," groaned Farno, who was still suffering from the effects of the stun gun. Not that he knew it was a stun gun of course. He just thought that he had been struck down by some sort of a spell.

"There are exactly fifty six. Their leader let it slip once, though I don't think he really cared whether we knew or not."

"Well at least we know the size of the problem, even though it's a little larger than I had hoped. With that many we definitely need help. I have already sent Corella back to the Dragon hold for reinforcements. Whether she will be successful only time will tell, and even if she is, I've no idea how long it will take them to get here. So, whatever happens, we will have to hold for some time and just hope."

"Fayna, has just told me that the 'others' are coming," announced Sir Cargan.

"Not sure what we can do, but we will try to hold them away from your house as long as we can," said Erun to Kirnina.

He led the way outside, sword in hand and was rewarded by the sight of the characteristic glitter as the shield formed around them all.

"All of you Dragons," he shouted, "don't go spitting fireballs. They won't go through the shield and you will fry us as likely as not. If the shield is not effective against them, I'll drop it and you can have a field day."

The aircraft had landed vertically some four or five hundred metres away, and at least twenty humans had emerged from it. Knowing that there was more than twice this in their actual numbers, Erun surmised, correctly as it happens, that this was only a probing mission and not the full, all or nothing, attack that he had been expecting. All of them seemed to be armed with some sort of weapon in their hands, and had deployed down each side of the street. They were taking no chances, and were moving forward efficiently, seeking to cover each other and use whatever concealment that was available. They were certainly not amateurs as the trailing four men covered their rear in a most professional manner. They had covered about fifty metres before half a dozen Elves suddenly appeared and unleashed a volley of arrows. The volley of arrows turned into a falling rain of ashes as the weapons of the rearguard flashed some sort of energy beam. A split second later the archers suffered the same fate, and the advance continued. It was brutal and unnecessary given the power of the weapons that they were using, but it did bring home to Erun the ruthlessness of the enemy that they were facing.

"**Farno, if you can contact anyone, get them away. They don't stand a chance**," shouted Erun.

At about two hundred metres the first of the humans emerged from cover and sent coordinated beams at the shield. The shield did not absorb energy in the same way that magically generated ones did, but acted as an energy mirror sending it back the way it came. Two of the 'others' were unlucky, and were caught in ricochets and left as smouldering heaps on the floor. The Shield held.

"This shield has to be a product of the sword," said Erun, "It can't be magic, because apart from a magic shield absorbing energy and not bouncing it off, it's not supposed to be able to affect them anyway. That must be why I was never able to erect one myself. I was just never capable and the sword picked up my need and obliged me by creating it."

The humans learnt quickly, and seeing the effectiveness of the shield together with the loss of two of their own, they beat a hasty retreat back to their aircraft. Almost as soon as the last had boarded they were airborne and turning to accelerate away to the south.

Erun lifted his sword, studied it for a moment and then decided to test his hypothesis.

"We seem to be safe now, so you can bring down the shield."

A ripple ran along the blade and the shield vanished.

"Well I guess that answers our questions," observed Panri.

"Let us test some more," said Erun.

"Are you the diamond sword of Tor?" he asked.

There was no discernible reaction from the sword.

"Are you Erun's diamond sword?" interrupted Johan.

A ripple ran along the blade.

"Are you a reality key?"

Again a there was a ripple in response.

"Were you once the diamond sword of Tor?" asked Erun.

The blade rippled.

"I think that's enough for now," said Erun sliding the sword back into its scabbard, "Our problem is that we don't know the right questions to ask, that only have a yes or no answer."

"I am not sure that I can hold the shield against a coordinated assault of as many weapons as they possess," whispered into his mind. Then he

sensed amusement as it continued, "*and not all the questions need to have a 'yes' or 'no' answer.*"

"Farno, something has been bothering me." Erun said as they all moved back into the house. "Mostly your house is much like houses that we live in, but the room that Lelia was kept in is different."

"Yes, that's true," Farno replied, "The others built it with something they call 'tek know lodgy'. It does all sorts of things, most of which I have no idea how. It seems like magic to me, even though they insisted that it's not. Come with me."

He led the way into a small room that was situated adjacent to Lelia's prison. It contained several large rectangular pictures of the inside of the prison room. He hadn't realised that it was showing everything as it actually happened, until he saw Wispet suddenly appear on one of them as she went back to get something she had forgotten It came as a bit of a shock to him and he jumped back in alarm.

"It's not dangerous," said Farno, "they just let you see inside the room. And here," he continued, pointing to an oblong board that contained small squares with letters on them, "is a thing they call a keyboard. You can touch the letters to make up words, and they appear on the wall in the room as you are doing it. Now if none of this is magic, then you could have fooled me."

"So that is how those messages appeared on the wall, I just thought there was some mage at work," said Lelia, "but what about my mind being read?"

Farno smiled,

"A little subterfuge there I'm afraid. From the expression on your face we had a good idea of what you were thinking. We guessed really, and remarkably accurate were we not? In the same way, when you were concentrating, the only explanation was that you were erecting a shield."

"Well that's a relief," said Lelia, "but how did you know that I was embarrassed about my nightdress."

"You took great care when you sat down, and every time you moved you kept pulling your nightdress down while, at the same time, blushing an extremely attractive shade of pink."

"While we are getting explanations, what about those words that appeared on my mirror in the Dragon Inn?" interrupted Erun.

"Ah yes, that," said Farno, "one of my favourites actually. They have this thing that sends out a beam of light and the words appear on anything that it touches. The beam was sent through your room window."

"*There is movement again at the far end of the street,*" came from Corella.

"Come on soldiers, Corella reports movement," Erun said aloud, and led the way to the outside door.

At the far end of the street, one man detached himself from the others. First he took his jacket off, and then laid his weapon on the ground. Turning slowly to make sure that the defenders realised that he was unarmed, he started down the street towards them. Eventually he arrived at the edge of the shield that the sword had automatically re-erected, and seeming to recognise Erun, addressed himself to him.

"Well I have no intention of standing out here and shouting at you. I want to talk, but I need to come in to do it."

"I will remove the shield to allow you to enter, but if your friends are foolish enough to twitch, then you will be dead before the twitch is complete."

"I understand," he said, and moved across the shield line as it flicked off. As soon as he was clear, the sword re-established it.

Erun moved to one side to allow the 'other' human to enter the house in front of him, and soon as they were inside and seated, he said what he had needed to say for a good few days now.

"You can count yourself lucky, that I have a mother who does not believe in revenge. You took my wife, when all you had to do was ask, and I am sorely tempted to kill you for that. You are welcome to the sword, in fact... " he drew the sword from its scabbard and handed it hilt first to the man. As he did so, the shield outside disappeared.

The human reached out, a surprised look on his face, and gingerly took the sword from Erun's hand.

"You people continually manage to surprise me. This was unexpected. Why so generous?"

"I don't know what people are like where you come from, but we do not go looking for trouble. Besides which, I hope you will remember to give it back when you find out that it doesn't work."

The shocked look on his face did Erun's heart good. He couldn't bring himself to kill the man, but at least some measure of revenge was being realised.

"What do you mean it doesn't work?"

"Well strictly speaking that statement was not true. I should have said 'doesn't work *for you*'."

"Why would it not work for me, it is only a tool after all."

"Ah well, a long time ago, one of our mages got his hands on it, and applied some of his magic to it. You know; that magic that you don't believe in. Its intelligence got a metaphorical kick up the backside and it became self aware. I hope I have managed to use the right words. And to cap it all, it seems to like me and won't work for anyone else."

The man looked hard at Erun,

"You are really enjoying this aren't you?"

"You kidnapped my wife. What's not to enjoy? I appreciate no end any, and all, of the discomfort that you and your fellows must be experiencing. You should not have done it. It was a mistake that you surely must be regretting by now."

"What the hell, it got you here didn't it?"

"Yes it did, but not in any frame of mind to cooperate. In fact, I am seriously disposed to be as difficult as I can. You need me to activate it because it really will *not* work for you, but what if I say no? What happens then?"

"The simple answer would be that we will do that which we promised the Elves. We will raze every building on this planet to the ground and then go hunting every living thing, until there aren't any left anymore."

"Well in the first place, I am not sure there are enough of you. And secondly, what if we come hunting you? Can you stay awake all of the time? Oh, and thirdly don't forget who has control of the most potent weapon that this world, or yours, has ever seen."

"When you two have finished posturing at each other, can we stop threatening and work together for a solution?" interrupted Lelia.

The man stood, and held out his hand towards Erun,

"Your wife has a good point. I am willing to put aside differences. Would you take my hand on it?"

Erun ignored the outstretched hand and eventually the man let it drop to his side.

"I will not shake hands with you. Because, in truth, I would rather stand and be flamed by my Dragon, but until we see the back of you, I will cooperate. You have *my* word on that."

"Ok, that's fair enough. May I take the sword and let our people look at it. I am a little sceptical about your statement that it has become self aware. But if you would stay here for a few more days I'm sure we can sort this out. My name by the way, so that you have something to call me, is Simon."

"I'm sure I can do that Simon. As soon as my Dragon returns, I can send her off to brief my Regent."

"Returns? I thought all your Dragons were

here."

"Oh no," said Erun smiling, and lying a little, "I sent her for reinforcements, and I expect her to arrive back here any minute now with about forty others."

"Would you believe that I was successful?" Corella's thoughts broke into his conversation, *"There are forty six and me coming through the entrance now."*

"You can brief me about it later. I'm talking to the human at the moment."

"And as I speak," he continued aloud, relieved that his previous statement had been vindicated "They are coming in through the entrance now."

"Farno, get the word out as quickly as you can that there is no danger to the Elves here. And you," he said to Simon, "get back to your own people. The sooner you fully understand that the sword is of no use to you the better.

Chapter Fourteen
The Return of the Sword

At this distance from the entrance, the swarm of Dragons appeared as a cloud of multicoloured autumn leaves, but soon began to resolve into their individual shapes as they approached.

"How did you manage it Corella," asked Erun, *"I thought it was the next best thing to the word of god."*

"It was rather simple I'm ashamed to say," Corella's soft thought whispered into his mind, *"It seems the whole of Dragon-Kind have been monitoring the situation through me and the other Dragons here. Their assessment of the situation was, in fact, more pessimistic than our own, and*

collectively we came to the decision as I was on my way there. The Dragon's Realm is now open to all Dragons, whether they be ridden or not."

"Well that will certainly make getting around much quicker."

"Erun Oncant, a decision as monumental as this and that is all you have to say."

Farno rushed breathlessly through the door,

"We've passed the word, and all the Elves I have spoken to are eager to offer accommodation to the riders when they arrive."

"I'm sure that will be appreciated," said Erun, "only one stipulation. Just make sure that they are all close to here."

The all moved outside, to watch the approach, Wispet in her usual hiding place in Sir Cargan's' arms and Erun clasping Lelia's hand as if his life depended upon it, which in a metaphysical sense it probably did.

The Dragons began to circle, peeling off one at a time to come down into any empty spot that was available. It was probably the best tactic, as Dragon flight is only a hit and miss affair at the best of times, and a mass approach could only have ended in disaster. The whole affair took almost an hour, if you included the time taken in unsaddling and stowing gear. Elves started to appear from everywhere, seeming to have the same idea and laden down with trays of tea and coffee mugs.

One little boy Elf, of no more than five or six, wandered up to the most ferocious looking Dragon he could see and was happily pulling up its eyelid to look into its eye.

"Are you not afraid that I will eat you," asked the Dragon, staring back.

"Not worth it," said the boy, "the gaps between your teeth are bigger than me."

"True," said the Dragon, "My name is Jaline, what's yours?"

"Welknit I was given when I was born, but sometimes my mother calls me other things,"

"*I bet she does,*" the Dragon muttered under its breath, but aloud she said, "Welknit, that's a nice name. Would you like to climb on my back?"

The young Elf must have been closely related to a monkey, given the speed with which he went up the side of Jaline as if her scales were a ladder. Then there he sat waving excitedly to his friends below, who had been too timid to approach with him.

"**I'm a Dragon rider**," he was screaming

Suddenly all of the Dragons' heads came up, and they rose to their feet as one. Virtually instantly, riders were grabbing saddles and heading towards their own, as their symbiosis with their Dragon brought the same feeling washing over them.

"What's wrong?" asked Farno, as Erun threw his saddle onto Corella, while Lelia was doing the same with Glenra.

"Get everyone away from here, there is danger,"

Welknit did not need to be told, he was quite bright and saw that this was not the place for him to be right at this moment, so he quickly slid down the side of Jaline to the ground.

"Another time," she said, as he hurried away to join his friends, who had already started to disperse towards their homes.

The first Dragon and rider to rise above the roofline of the houses disappeared in a flare of light, with only a light rain of ash to mark where they had been a second before.

"**Keep below the roofs. Use the houses as cover,**" yelled Erun as Corella lifted from the ground.

"*It would seem that they are not happy with us.Not happy at all,*" thought Corella.

"*Look up.*" said Erun, "*I think that's their first mistake.*"

Corella brought her head up, and actually faltered in flight, before recovering, as she saw at least three dozen humans, with no visible means of support, zooming about above their heads. The sight startled Erun for a second, but there was no time to ponder on the 'how' of this phenomenon, only time to act. So he snatched his bow from its quick release buckle, quickly nocked an arrow, loosed it in one easy movement, and was gratified to see the human he had aimed at transfixed through the throat. His small victory didn't go unnoticed though, but was witnessed by the closest of the flying men who turned towards him raising their weapons. Corella dipped a wing and shot between two houses as a dozen bolts of energy destroyed most of the street behind her.

There was fire and running Elves everywhere, as Dragons coughed flames in all directions, partly as attack, partly as defence, but mostly to provide a smokescreen for concealment. Even in the heat of this battle, they were being careful to avoid any danger to the Elves where they could. Frun saw the glint of a silver Dragon transfixed by a beam of light and disintegrate as he watched. His heart stopped...

"*It was not Glenra,*" thought Corella

His heart started again... though a huge sadness at the loss of a brother sent a shiver through his body. Glenra suddenly appeared just above him and coughed a huge ball of fire away to his left. He looked, just in time to see a figure engulfed in flame tumbling away end over end to eventually smash into the side of a house. A second later both figure, and house, vanished in a massive explosion.

From reports coming to him via Corella, he knew that they were having some success, but not enough to balance their own losses. Fifteen Dragons and riders had already perished for the gain to them of only four of the enemy. He knew that the enemy's numbers had been fifty six at the start, but it was difficult to tell whether they all had been deployed or only just a portion. With this rate of exchange the others stood a good chance of winning, so something needed to be done, and quickly, if Tor and the Dragon riders were to survive.

"*I need the sword.*"

"*Then we must find...*" Corella started, but then another soft and remote thought intruded,

"*I am coming.*"

Far away to the south, but still within the

reality that was Tor, a brilliant flare lit up the horizon and a bright finger of light arced up from it and streaked towards them. The humans that he could see suddenly broke away, and started moving rapidly back towards the glow that was still pulsating in the South. Something nasty was obviously happening back where they had come from. The finger of light was getting rapidly closer, and then transposed itself into the diamond sword travelling towards them hilt first. Erun lifted his hand into the air, and closed his fingers around the hilt, as the sword arrived.

"*Their aircraft is no more*," echoed in his mind.

Erun glanced at the Diamond Sword in his hand and thought, *steel* and watched as a ripple ran along it, transforming it into its plainer form.

He gazed at the desolation around him. There had been considerable loss of life here, amongst the Elves who could not get away in time, and also the Dragon riders. The Elves were paying a high price for the actions of their ancestors, and that did not rest easy with Erun. Somehow they had to win this conflict and somehow Tor had to be brought back into the world, and somehow the Elves had to be persuaded to forgive themselves. It was too much to heap upon the shoulders of a twenty year old King.

"But you are all they have," said Corella quietly.

"I wish there was someone else, because if they come again it will be all over for us."

All of the remaining Dragons and riders

landed in the streets facing Farno's house which was miraculously still standing. Of the fifty two that had started into battle together, only thirty six remained, and of those that were left at least half had some sort of injury. Elves were appearing from everywhere, most were carrying bandages and various pots of ointment for soothing the more minor burns, and they hurried to the injured to administer what help they could.

Welknit appeared, shaking off the hand of his mother. He ran forward, his eyes searching the crowd, and not being able to pinpoint her he started yelling,

"Jaline, Jaline, Jaline,"

There was no answer, and floods of tears began to pour down his face. A large Dragon, browny-green in colour came forward to stand before him. The Dragon leaned down to be level with him and its tongue licked out and took away the tears from his face.

"There is no need for tears young Elf. Jaline died as she lived, with her soul mate and the love of her life. Her only regret, as she died, was that she could not fulfil her promise to you. So she asked me if I would come and do that for her. So Welknit, my name is Falini and it would be my pleasure for us to take a ride together when you are ready."

The young Elf leaned forward and wrapped his arms around the Dragon's neck as far as they would go and pressed his face, sobbing, into her scales.

"Thank you Falini, I would like that, but not

yet it hurts too much."

He turned, and wiping away his tears, he walked back to his mother, who had been watching her son hugging a Dragon with wide eyed disbelief.

"Mum, are all Dragons as kind as that. I saw how most of them died. Jaline really didn't have time to regret anything at all, did she?"

His mother placed her arm around his shoulders.

"Maybe Dragons have links to the hereafter, who knows? But they certainly seem to be much kinder than we gave them credit for. Come my son, it's pretty much of a mess around here, and we have a bit of cleaning up to do," she said in a typical mother's understatement, and then added, "You can always come back later."

"*That was a good thing you did my love,*" thought Jackbert of Amtor, rider of Falini.

"*It was the least I could do. We cannot blame the little ones for the sins of their fathers. Besides which, I sense this little one is special.*"

Jackbert, like all riders shared his thoughts with his Dragon, so the sense that this child was special ran through his mind as well, and the 'why' of the statement did not need to be asked.

Erun stood before the assembled survivors, took the sword from its scabbard, and explained what it was and how it communicated with him sometimes. Most of them knew the story second-hand, so it was of interest to them when it was confirmed and some of the misconceptions that they all had were removed.

"It has told me that it can erect its protective shield over no more than a dozen Dragons. It has also said that the shield *will* protect against their beam weapons. So I have asked Panri of Pintor to organise a drawing of sticks among the uninjured to say who stays and who will leave. It goes without saying, that those of you who are injured will not be expected to face these monsters again. My companions *will* stay, so another seven will be selected by the draw. My thanks to the rest of you, and may God go with you."

He turned to Lelia, and spoke quietly so no-one else would hear,

"Come my love, we have been away from each other too long, so while it's quiet we have some catching up to do."

"If we can find a space not occupied by Sir Cargan and Wispet." She said, and grabbed his hand to drag him towards the house. Hoots and whistles from the other riders echoed around the streets, and followed them as they hurried away.

Chapter Fifteen
The Death of a Sword

The glow to the south had subsided, and eventually disappeared as whatever it was, was brought under control by the invaders. Several hours had passed, the seven Dragon riders who were to remain had been selected, and the rest had headed for home, with the uninjured acting as escort for the injured. They would once more be travelling via the Dragons' realm, so everyone was satisfied that they would be in the hands of healers quickly enough to prevent their injuries from getting any worse.

Falini had been one of the Dragons sent home, so Jackbert without being asked, sought out

Welknit and gave his word that when the crisis was over they would return and give him the ride that had been promised.

All twelve Dragons and riders gathered together in the street outside of Farno's house. Admittedly it was a tight squeeze and would make taking off difficult, but at least this close together made the sword's task of providing a shield that much easier. They knew that the humans would come again but not when, and the waiting and not knowing was always the most difficult part.

When the attack finally came, it was pretty much an anticlimax. The sword had explained to Erun about antigravity belts. It had explained that hundreds of years ago the humans' aircraft had been powered in the same way but that technology, had been lost in the great disaster, and only recently re-discovered. Its stage of development was still very primitive and so far restricted to the belts. The sword tried to explain the technical details, but when it found it was getting nowhere, it just said that it was the belts that made them fly, and left it at that.

It was Johan who first saw them, and shouted a warning to the others. The shield snapped on over them and they sat back to watch the approach. The human swarm poured in towards them, and had just brought their weapons to bear ready to fire when the voice spoke.

"Hold," was all it said, but it resonated through everything and seemed to go on and on. The humans came to a halt... waiting, not quite sure what it was or where it had come from, but then it spoke again.

"I am the Diamond Sword of Tor. I was created over five hundred years ago as a dimensional key. I can open portals between realities and also between dimensions. But hear this humans. *I will not open one for you.* I was given life by an elfin mage, even though he did not realise what he had done. But it was then, at that point, that I fully comprehended what the first humans had done, with the complicity of the Elves. It appears that I have integrity, though where that came from I don't know, but I have it nevertheless and I made a vow back then that if a more fitting person were to appear then I would work only for them."

There was a slight pause and then the sword continued.

"That more fitting person is Erun of Cardoney. You can go nowhere. I would advise that you try to integrate yourself into this society, because you certainly will not be allowed to leave or to damage it while you are here."

Virtually all of the humans screamed their protest and several of them let fly a blast at the shield.

"Look," said Panri

All of the belts on the humans began to glow, the glow getting brighter and brighter. Panic stricken hands began to tear at fastenings, trying to release them, not caring that they were several hundred feet in the air. Then there was a series of flashes and a shock wave which brought with it the sound of multiple concussions. All across the sky, all that could be seen was the small expanding clouds of individual explosions, which slowly dispersed leaving no trace of the humans behind.

"The belts were their undoing. Without them I could do nothing. But now I have one more task to perform," thought the sword to Erun, *"It will be my last."*

"What task is that?" asked Erun.

"I need to restore Tor into your reality. It will take all of my power and all that I am, but I believe that I can do it. Either way, when it is all over, I will just be a sword. Nothing more than that will remain."

"But that's suicide," protested Erun.

"Not really," replied the sword, *"I should not be alive anyway. And tell me, would you want to be a living thinking intelligence stuck in here?"*

"I understand," thought Erun,* " I really do. What do you want us to do?"*

"You will have to evacuate everyone from Tor, but leave me here when you leave."

"Evacuate? But there has to be a million Elves here. How can we possibly manage that? It will take months."

"They don't need to take anything. With some luck, they may only be away for a few hours. Use all of the Griffins here, and get as many Dragons back as you can. Any elves that are fit enough to walk, get them started now."

"I hear you." then to Farno, he said, "We have to evacuate Tor, *now*. There is no time to discuss this. It is vital, we have to move."

Farno looked at him for no more than a second, and then shouting instructions to Kirnina and Wispet to follow him he headed away from the house. After a few paces and more shouted instruction s they split up and started off in different directions.

"Corella, we need as many Dragons here as we can get, hundreds, no, thousands and quickly."

"The call has already gone out, my Erun."

"I'm not sure why I keep doing that Corella, I already knew didn't I?"

"Habit Erun, habit."

A few Elves started to come out of the houses to receive hasty explanations, and they would move away to pass those explanations on to more Elves as they appeared. The dribble became a flood and soon thousands were hurrying towards the entrance to Tor. Those that had access to Griffins were hurriedly mounting them, taking a friend and then heading out. Dragons had started to appear just outside of the Entrance, popping out of the realm in their ones, twos and then hundreds. It became organised chaos, but it was working. Elves who were on foot, were taking ropes to the entrance to facilitate the evacuation. The few thousands heading out had become hundreds of thousands. At this rate they might, just might get it done in a day.

It actually took twenty seven hours, but finally Erun minus his sword, which he had been instructed to plunge into the ground near the entrance, was the last to leave. Lelia had left sometime before, protesting vehemently but having understood the need, going anyway.

The plain outside, was a sea of Elves right up to the water's edge, all gazing towards the 'Y' shaped rock , not knowing what to expect. Panri, Johan, Lelia, Sir Cargan and Wispet had taken up an advantageous position on top of a rocky outcrop, where Erun spotted them as soon as he emerged. As soon as he had joined them they too turned their gaze towards the rock.

The first indication that anything was happening, was a low rumbling in the ground and a vibration, indicative of a low grade earth quake. It began to increase in intensity, and virtually everyone dropped to the ground to avoid falling and injuring themselves. Erun and his friends gathered together clinging on to anything they could find.

Land started to appear, rippling out from the sea shore towards the south. Then there was a massive 'Crack' and the 'Y' shaped rock disappeared. The atmosphere started to ripple and blur over a huge area, and the ghostly outline of buildings and roads began to appear, flickering on and off as if unsure of their place in reality. Erun had begun to worry that perhaps the sword did not have enough power, when the ghostly outlines became blindingly bright and solidified. A huge shout went up from the crowd and they started steaming back towards Tor which had been away for five hundred years, but had now, at last, come home.

The crowd split into two as they re-entered their town, each half passing but not touching a steel sword that was gently swaying in the ground at the beginning of a street.

The Diamond Sword of Tor was no more, but as long as the steel one was in Erun's possession he would remember with sadness, an intelligence that had sacrificed itself selflessly for one million Elves and the Kingdom of Cardoney.

Epilogue

Erun and Lelia had returned to the throne of Cardoney armed with a treaty of friendship with the Elves, and with some relief Nordlight and Marta had returned to their home in Vanticor. The fact that it was a governor's mansion made no difference, to them it was now their home; they loved it and were glad to be back. Sir Cargan and Wispet were granted a state wedding before he took up his position as personal guard to the sovereign, and Darlelia moved to the castle to work for the Queen.

Erun had kept his promise and the first piece of legislation that he put before the *Council of the People* for them to polish up into acceptable law, was the 'Rented Rooms Act' which became Royal Decree 7643F. Erun had no idea what the numbers meant, but it kept the *Council* happy so he went along with it. His second law, Royal Decree 7643G, was much closer to his own heart and it bestowed the powers of a Royal law enforcing body upon the Dragon riders. Erun had decided that as a reward for their loyalty and sacrifice in the battle of Tor as it became known, he would expand their powers beyond his original intention. Cardoney had never had a police force, with all of the law enforcing powers residing in the military, and the effect of his law was to relieve them of this responsibility and free them up to concentrate on defending the Kingdom and all of its peoples.

It was almost a month later, when the call came. It had been six months since the last one, and excitement ran rife as suitable children began to be selected. Eggs were about to hatch in the Dragon Hold, and the call had gone out for children, boys and girls, to gather for the selection. The rider was chosen by the Dragon, and within minutes of its hatching it would be looking for a bond mate. The children would stand in a circle around the hatching eggs, in silence, each one wishing desperately that it would be him, or her that was to be chosen. The Dragon, when it was ready, would reach out and feel for the child that fate had decreed would be right for it.

"You had better go," said Jackbert to Falini, "I will wait here for your return."

The mighty brown/green Dragon leapt into

the air and with a single flap of her wings disappeared into the Dragon realm. Only seconds later it seemed, she reappeared over Tor and circled once before landing in the main square.

"**Welknit**," she bellowed, and waited.

In a house a couple of streets away, Welknit's mother turned her head towards the window at the sound of her son's name being called. Between the houses, she could just see the Dragon and immediately recognised its colouring as that of Falini.

"Welknit," she shouted, "Falini is here. See I told you she would keep her promise. Go quickly, don't keep her waiting."

Welknit was out of the door, and running down the street before she had finished speaking, and skidding to a halt in front of Falini he said breathlessly,

"I'm here."

"I can see that young Elf," she said, "The choosing ceremony for Dragon riders is taking place at the Dragon Hold. I wondered whether you would like to go and watch. You will not be there to be chosen, only to watch. Would you like to go? I promised you a ride, so here I am."

"Would I?" said Welknit, leaping for her saddle, "You couldn't hold me back."

Welknit hardly had to time to get any more excited, as they passed through the Dragon Realm and reappeared over the hold in a matter of seconds. Looking down, Falini spotted Jackbert waving as they emerged and settled to the ground as close as she could get without blowing him over. When she had come to a stop and folded her wings, Welknit threw his leg over the saddle and slid down her side.

"Hello young Welknit," said Jackbert, "Come and stand up on this bit of rock here, you'll get a better view. They've started hatching. Two out so far, three more to go

A ring of maybe twenty children stood silently around a dip in the ground that contained two tiny Dragons and three eggs that had already started to crack. The shells on the remainder split apart to reveal the struggling forms of three new Dragons, shrugging aside the bits of shell, and then stretching up into the sunlight.

The five tiny Dragons that were only showing a hint of the colour that they would eventually become slowly walked up the side of the pit to gaze at the circle of children. It looked as if there would be two green, two bronze, and one golden, if the colours they were showing now remained true. The first green gazed around the circle slowly turning its head, until it suddenly stopped facing a young auburn haired girl of about six. Slowly it walked towards her, and when it was almost there, she stepped forward and sat down in front of it whereby it laid its head in her lap,

"*I am Karly,*" the Dragon thought at her, and the first choice had been made.

The process was repeated three more times, with each of the bronze and the remaining green moving forward to claim their rider. But the gold did not move. Its head was moving from side to side as it studied the remaining children in the circle, but it did not move from its position on the lip of the birth pit. Then slowly it began to traverse the pit, its head still moving as if it was searching for something special. It looked as if the rare event of a Dragon not finding its bond mate was about to happen. But then it stopped facing a tall blond haired boy, and started to walk towards him. He looked puzzled but didn't move as it approached. It reached him and he held out his hand towards it expectantly, but it dodged the outstretched hand and walked past him.

A look of complete shock came over Welknit's face, and for a second he looked at Jackbert with a question in his eyes. Then he suddenly got up and slid down from the rock. The Dragon's shuffling steps suddenly turned into a run, and Welknit dropped to his knees with his arms open in welcome,

"*I am Pearlin,*" she thought

"Well I *will* be damned," said Jackbert, as the first ever Elf to be chosen by a Dragon to be its rider stood up with the widest grin on his face that Tor, or Cardoney, had ever seen.

The End

Character List

Amtor----Kingdom to the south of Cardoney--becomes a region of Cardoney.

Arunay----Sovereign King of the Kingdom of Cardoney-- killed in the interstate wars. And succeeded by Erun.

Aspasia----Sovereign Queen of the Kingdom of Amtor-- killed in the interstate wars.

Bardon----Sovereign King of the Kingdom of Partonin-- killed in the interstate wars.

Bethny----Dragon of Solon-- killed in the interstate wars.

Corella----The yellow dragon, bonded with Erun.

D'Arnot, Joshua----Captain and Guard commander. Ultimately discovered to be a wizard of immense power and the villain of our story--defeated by Erun--deceased.

Darthbold----Eldest son of King Arunay--accidentally killed by his brother Nordlight.

Earden----Royal Saddlemaker.

Egmar----A soldier in the Castle guard, and Erun's friend--becomes Captain of the guard.

Erun----Dragon Rider and hero of our story-succeeds Arunay to the throne of Cardoney.

Glenra----Silver Free Dragon and volunteer mount for Lelia. Unexpectedly finds itself bonding to her.

Lelia----Princess of Vanticor and Daughter of King Porden.

Nordlight----youngest son of King Arunay.

Parton----Capitol city of Partonin.

Partonin----Kingdom to the north of Cardoney--becomes a Cardoney Region.

Perquet----A garrison of Vanticor.

Plater, Eloise----An eleven year old girl, who made the historic ride to warn Cardoney of the Amtorian invasion.

Porden----Sovereign King of the Kingdom of Vanticor-- killed in the interstate wars.

Serena of Amtor----Evil witch in the guise of a beautiful refugee--killed by Erun.

Scrivens----King Arunay's Mage--killed in the interstate wars.

Solon----Dragon rider from Pintor-- killed in the interstate wars.

Squerrel----Swordmaster to King Arunay-- killed in

the interstate wars.

Trelon----A garrison of Vanticor.

Vanticor----Largest of the Kingdoms and the name of its capitol city, situated to the east of Cardoney-- becomes a region of Cardoney

Character list from 'The Diamond Sword of Tor'

The Humans

Erun----The hero of our story and the King of Cardoney.

Jackbert----Dragon Rider of the brown/green dragon Falini.

Lelia----Queen of Cardoney and wife of Erun.

Nordlight----Half brother to Erun, Governor of Vanticor and Regent of Cardoney.

Marta----Wife of Nordlight.

Katy----Lelia's maid servant.

Albert----Erun's butler.

Egmar----Captain of the Castle guard, and Erun's friend.

Kaylo----Dragon rider, treacherously tries to kill Erun, but is slain by Cargan.

Panri----Dragon rider joins Erun in his quest.

Johan----Dragon rider, Joins Erun in his Quest.

Cargan----Sir Cargan, knighted by Erun for faithful service, Dragon rider.

The Elves

Farno----Elf charged with looking after the kidnapped queen.

Kirnina----Farno's wife.

Wispet----Kirnina's sister and love of Sir Cargan's life.

Pernol----Older boy in the school where Kirnina teaches.

Darlelia----Daughter of Farno and Kirnina. Serves the queen.

Linten----Elf spy and assassin.

Welknit----The first ever elfin dragon rider.

The Dragons

Corella----The yellow dragon, bonded with Erun.

Glenra----A silver dragon, bonded with Lelia.

Dorna----A green dragon, bonded with Johan.

Clara----A green dragon, bonded with Panri.

Fayna----A golden dragon recently bonded with Sir Cargan.

Jaline----A dragon killed in the battle for Tor that was kind to a young Elf.

Falini----A brown/green dragon bonded with Jackbert.

Pearlin----A recently hatched golden dragon...chooses Welknit.

About the Author

Born in the Royal Military Hospital in Portsmouth, England in 1938, he attended Titchfield (Hampshire, UK) Primary School and Fareham (Hampshire, UK) Secondary Modern Boys School until 1953.

He joined the Royal Air Force as an Apprentice in 1955 and served 14 years, being discharged in 1968. During that period, in 1962, he met and married Kim, and they are still together 55 years later. After a short period as a Prison Officer, he entered the Computer Industry with Golden Wonder Ltd and stayed in that profession with various companies until 1991. He then joined an Inner City Medical Practice in Leicester (Leicestershire UK) as Fundholding Manager and Practice Manager until his retirement in 2003. After spending thirteen years dividing his time between his home in Leicester and Sax, a small town near Alicante in Spain, he has now moved permanently back to the UK and lives in Oadby, Leicestershire.

For more information about Robert and his books, please visit his website at:
http://ravjacobs.wixsite.com/robertavjacobs

www.ingramcontent.com/pod-product-compliance
Lightning Source LLC
Chambersburg PA
CBHW070530260626
47161CB00002B/321